O RUGGED LAND OF GOLD

Helen and Clyde Bolyan, *c. 1918*

MARTHA MARTIN

O RUGGED LAND
OF GOLD

Vanessapress · Fairbanks, Alaska
1989

To
Anna Craig

Cover: Helen Bolyan, 1928

Cover design by Lisa A. Valore, Art • Design

Book design by Lisa Valore and Mary Beth Michaels

Typesetting by Marsha Wendt, Butterfly Publications

Printed by Braun-Brumfield, Inc.

ISBN: 0-940055-007

Foreword

Visualize an Alaskan night too cold to snow and too dark to see much beyond ourselves. Visualize a place where something as intangible as winter air can sting flesh and hold a tear fast to a face. A place where fate and chance still interact freely with integrity and hope. Where friends can gather around a hearth kindled with aspen or birch downed with their own sweat and speak less of fears imagined and more of fears that count. What is your personal challenge, your diablo, one might ask? Shadows of the long, long night? A dog howling in the distance? Hardship clearly tapping at the cabin door? Should we be fortunate enough to find the spirit of Martha Martin in our presence, surely she would answer: all of the above and more.

O Rugged Land of Gold is a book about spirit. Hard to visualize, harder to literalize, we know it when we meet it, do we not? Spirit is less the shadows of the night and more how they are interpreted. The definition of spirit I like best—to blow or to breathe upon —is chilling, and accurate as well. Spirit is who we are when we are alive and what we leave behind when we are not. In life, our strength, courage and hope will live on for generations in the minds and memories of those we have touched. In literature, if we are well-spoken, our spirit is immortalized. Multiplied a thousand times, resurrecting itself again and again, who we are becomes a timeless idiom in a changing world.

Resurrecting Martha Martin has been something of a labor of love. The Vanessapress Editorial Board, like a child unwilling to accept the certainty of the grave, found it impossible to believe that she did not leave behind traces of herself other than her books. And so with photographs and memorabilia graciously loaned to us by her son, we stalked her as best we could. From the photographs we see our author was not unlike many of her Alaskan women contemporaries: sensible, hard-working, adventurous. And like most multifarious women, her face seems to change from setting to setting: comely in her early years, tireless at Cobol mine, cosmopolitan during her European travels, intelligent always. For myself, she was someone I would like to have known well.

In *O Rugged Land of Gold* we are taken by the hand to a world positively honed by the love of God, family, and all living creatures. We are witnesses to pain and sorrow, the birth of a much-wanted child, loneliness, courage, and more. For some, this book will be an affirmation of territory perhaps hard won. For others—those seemingly bound to personal challenges without an infinite vision of hope— please, kindle your aspen or birch, make a place beside your hearth, and read on. There is much spirit here. We at Vanessapress think you will be pleasantly enriched.

Wanda Zimmerman
Fairbanks, 1989

Acknowledgements

The Vanessapress Editorial Board wishes to thank the following people who contributed to the rebirth of this book: Clyde Bolyan for the memories and photographs of his mother, our author, so graciously shared; the Elmer E. Rasmuson Library at the University of Alaska Fairbanks for allowing us the use of a copy of *O Rugged Land of Gold*; Lisa Valore for her time and talent designing the cover; Marsha Wendt for doing our typesetting; LeRoy Zimmerman for reproducing the photographs included in this book.

In addition, we wish to thank Jan O'Dowd and Charla Quinn Ranch whose belief in the importance of our work led them to contribute time and energy towards the fund–raising that made this book possible. We also wish to thank the University Women's Association of the University of Alaska Fairbanks for their generous support in making this project a success.

A special thanks to each and every one.

1

I CAN HARDLY WRITE, BUT I MUST. FOR TWO REASONS. FIRST, I AM afraid I may never live to tell my story, and second, I must do something to keep my sanity.

I must order my mind, make myself think clearly. How can I better do this than by recording all that has happened, and all that may happen until I am released—one way or another?

This strange writing comes from my left hand, and I am having trouble. It is difficult to write with that hand. My right arm is broken, both bones of the forearm broken about three inches above the wrist. My body is battered and bruised. I can't sit down without something hurting me, and I can't lie down without aches and pains, but the ache in my head is the worst of all. I do wish my head would stop hurting. My body is wretched beyond anything I thought I could endure; but I have to endure it, and I will, and I will write, too.

I will do my best to write down everything just as it happened, yet I am sure I won't get it exactly right because my mind is still so confused. Maybe writing about the things I am sure of will help me to reason out the things I don't yet know.

Sam, Don's partner, went away last Friday. Don and I stayed on at the prospect to do odd chores—get more wood, pick up tools, store things away, and close the place up for winter.

When our boy Lloyd left for school in September we promised to send him a fine buck to share with the friends he'd visit till we

1

got back to town, but summer weather lasted much longer than is usual here on this Alaskan coast, and the deer stayed up in the high hills. We kept waiting for snow to drive them down until here it was, the end of the hunting season, and still we hadn't sent our son the promised buck.

So we took a day off, ran with the gasboat to an anchorage below some upland meadows, and hunted there. Don got a buck, but it had only two points and was shot in the shoulder. We couldn't send that to Lloyd. The boy's prestige would suffer far more from a poor shot and a small deer than it would from no deer at all. We needed fresh meat anyway. Lloyd would have to manage without his deer this year, but we felt badly, knowing he would be disappointed. We hung the buck to the boom and ran back to camp.

Next morning we went back to the upper cabin to finish the chores and close it up and to take mine samples. Don thought we ought to have a lot more samples than the few he and Sam had taken.

They have had sharp words about samples on different occasions. Don always wants lots of rock, while Sam is satisfied with so little. Don is fussy and careful about cutting his samples, but Sam says a grab sample is as good as any, and better than most. Don tells him that he might "salt" himself.

"What's wrong with a man thinking his own property is a little better than it might turn out to be, I'd like to know?" is Sam's answer.

Don wants to know exactly what the ore is worth, and so we went into the mine after dependable samples.

What a happy day we had!

Don gets very enthused over ore, rich ore. I do, too. We looked at the walls of the tunnel, at the dike and the gouge, and at our splendid ledge of gold-bearing quartz. We hunted for pieces of rich rock, picture rock, Don calls it; we washed bits of quartz in the tunnel water and watched for the gleam of gold. Don found a beautiful specimen, almost as grand as the prize rock out of the first surface blast. That one fractured into three pieces. Don, Lloyd, and Sam each treasured a bit of it, but there was none for me. Don said I should have this new specimen, and he said, "Don't lose it."

Oh, we had a lovely time in the mine, with lots of chatter and laughter. I held the canvas to catch the bits of rock Don chipped off with a hammer and moil. We cut twenty-eight channel samples. Don gave each one a number and wrote in his notebook where they all came from. I tied them up and stowed them in the packsack, then we started back to the cabin.

Just as we came out of the canyon onto the hill trail, there stood the big buck, chewing away on some brush.

"Today Wednesday?" whispered Don, slipping out of the packsack.

"It sure is," I whispered back.

The mailboat always leaves on Thursday. Lloyd would have a buck.

Don whistled. The buck raised his head, looked toward us, alert, poised to dash away into the brush, and he had as pretty a set of horns as I have ever seen. Don shot him.

What a piece of luck that was! I could just imagine Lloyd's pride when he looked the buck over: Fine head shot, perfect four-point horns, and a big feller, all of which Lloyd would point out to his school pals, implying that *his* father always got the biggest bucks and always made head shots. And I knew just how my boy would strut as he delivered a mess of chops to one friend, a roast to another, and took stew meat to Old Henry who has no teeth.

I took the packsack of samples and Don packed the buck, and we went down the hill. Don left the buck in the skiff, spread it open to let it cool out, then hurried into the pilothouse to look at the tide table.

"Slack tide at 7:42. Cap will come out then. Maybe we ought to run down tonight," Don said, thinking of how all boats must catch slack tide to get through the rapids. "Or we could go in the morning, take the outboard, cross Dry Pass, and save all that run around Jasper Reef. What do you say, Ladybug?"

"I say I don't like the Elto, it's too cranky," I answered. "You go alone, and while you're away I'll go finish at the upper cabin and get my eiderdown and the few things to come from there."

"Why, Martha, that's a good motor. It's run fine since we got the new coil," Don chided me, then added, "But a long trip in an open boat wouldn't be so good for you; besides, the skiff will go faster with only me."

So we decided that I would finish the cabin chores while Don went to meet the mailboat.

"And don't forget to put the tin can over the smokestack," he reminded me.

The barometer was falling. Don scanned the sky for weather signs. Filmy mare's-tails stretched across the heavens.

"I don't like the look of it," he said, looked some more and added, "We'll run behind the island; then if she blows while I'm gone you'll not worry about drifting."

Now, we never had anchored behind the island. Don had suggested it, but Sam complained that it was unhandy—we'd have to walk forty miles across the beach to get to the boat, and there wasn't enough room to swing in that little bight. "Anyway, what's the use?" he said. "This cove is a good-enough harbor."

Don pulled the anchor and we ran behind the island, came around into the little bight and anchored there. Don puttered about the boat, fixing this and that little thing. Then he put out a shore line, and slid the dinghy off the deck. He got the outboard motor and tinkered with it for a while. He stowed the samples away in a locker, then brought out the box of ore specimens.

Don and his rocks got very much in the way of my dinner. Dinner could wait. I shoved the cook pots to the back of the stove, and together we looked (for perhaps the hundredth time) at the chunks of rock spattered with free gold. We used the mineral glass, not because we needed it, but because we liked to make the gold specks look bigger, liked to exclaim over such a lot of gold, thrill at the look of the yellow metal.

"Where's the specimen we found today?" Don asked.

"Oh, Don, I left it in the tunnel. I'll get it tomorrow."

"It'll keep there. No need for you to be tramping the canyon trail after it."

I felt ashamed, and resolved I would get it.

We talked of the mine we would develop and the town that would be built here; even named it—Donsam, it should be called. We felt rich and glad and, oh, so happy.

All evening long we talked of the good things close ahead of us. Of our son gone to town in time for school, of the little one under my heart, of the nice home we would have, of how we would travel to far places, and how the best part of every trip would be coming back to our good home and to the mine which would make all those splendid things possible.

Before we went to bed I hurriedly wrote letters to Lloyd and to my mother, told them about the fine big buck. Said all was well with us and that we would be home for Thanksgiving.

During the night there was some rain and a little wind. I heard Don get up and put a canvas over the big buck in the skiff, and put the smaller one in the hold. And he looked about his lines to see how the boat was riding. All was snug and safe.

I could feel the swing of the boat and hear the weather. My bunk is in the pilothouse, with only a thin planking between me and the elements. I felt so small compared to the great outside, yet I was secure against all harm. I was warm and happy, and I slept well.

Toward morning the rain stopped and the wind died away. At daybreak we had fine weather, but the barometer was still falling.

"I think she'll hold for today," Don said.

I packed a grub box and tied up the bedroll—we don't go across the bay in a skiff at this time of the year without some provision—while Don fixed the outboard motor and filled the gas tank. He said for me not to fret if it should blow up, for he would stay where he could get ashore in mighty short order.

"Bye, Mother," and he kissed me.

The Elto started easy—made a nice purr. I waved to him just before he went around the island and out of sight. He smiled and raised his hand.

I never saw him again. I heard his voice, I do know I heard his voice, but I did not see him. **Oh, Don, don't be dead. Come back to me.**

Whatever am I to do? Maybe I'll die, too, but I don't want to die. I want to live and have my baby. Maybe Don isn't dead after all, for I know he called to me. But where is he? Why doesn't he come? My head hurts. I hurt all over. I can hardly see. My head hurts most of all.

Stop this. Rest.

I have rested and eaten. Now I'll get on with the story.

I stood on the deck listening to the sound of the motor until I could hear it no more, then I washed dishes, pumped the bilge, did all the boat chores, and made ready to go climb the hill.

I felt useful and glad to be doing my part. I thought of how this would be the last trip up the hill until next spring, of how Don and I would now work on the beach cabin for a week—put up shelves, build a little porch, and clear up the building litter—for the beach cabin was new. That done, we would hurry on to Big Sleeve, pick up Sam, and soon be on our way home. Only thirty-one running hours to home and Lloyd. I was impatient to be on the way.

I was in the dinghy when I thought about a gun, so I went back and got Don's gun. I don't know why I took it—maybe because it hangs nearest to the pilothouse door and was easy to reach. Anyway, I did take it, and because the sling is too long for me I had to carry it cater-cornered across my shoulders.

We always carry a gun in the woods. Most everybody in this country does, for there are lots of big brown bears. Our trail up the hill was a bear trail, probably long years before a white man ever came to Alaska. We've killed two bears on that trail. Some people contend these bears are harmless, that if you will let them alone they will let you alone. It's true they usually clear off into the brush when they hear us coming, but sometimes they don't hear us. Even if they do, sometimes they are just contrary and refuse to run. Don says when both men and bear use the same trail, it is advisable to carry a gun to back up an argument over the right of way.

There were cat's-paws on the water when I went across the flat, and by the time I was a little better than halfway up the hill it started to blow hard. At first it came in strong gusts, then quickly the treetops were being whipped about in a full gale, and it rained hard—really poured down. My Dux-bak clothes are supposed to be water-repellent, but that rain, driven by a terrific wind, seemed to go through my coat and pants as if they were nothing more than overalls. In a few minutes I was sopping wet. I hurried, for I know it isn't safe to be in heavy timber in a blow, and I fretted for fear it wasn't good for me to hurry while climbing the steep hill trail. Soon I was near the cabin, in smaller timber with open spaces. There the wind almost blew me over—made me walk like a wobbly calf as I leaned against it.

I was thankful to reach the shelter of the strong, sturdy cabin, and I soon had a roaring fire. I stripped off my wet clothes and put on a suit of Don's woolen underwear. It was heavy and hot, big and itchy, but none of my things had been left in the cabin and I had to have something to wear until my clothes dried.

The storm increased in violence and fury. The cabin creaked in all its joints. I thought of Don on the water. I shivered, and felt ill with fear for him. I wondered where he was, and from the lapse of time I figured out pretty near to where he had to be.

I had puttered around the boat until nearly nine o'clock before I started up the hill, more than three hours after Don had left. It was at least a half an hour later when the first strong wind came. Before that time Don should have met the mailboat, put the deer aboard, handed up the letters, exchanged a few quick words of gossip, and been heading back toward home. At the first wild snort of the storm Don would have gone ashore and pulled the skiff up after him. Oh, Don was safe—he was always careful, never took foolish chances. When the storm was over he would be back and asking how I had made out.

I got on with my job, picked up and righted things in the cabin, put food that would freeze into the cache down under the floor and put dry stuff on the swing shelf. I hung clothing and bedding on the wire line to keep the mice from chewing them up for nests. I left one bunk made and my eiderdown unrolled, for, if the storm kept on, I thought I might have to stay overnight.

There were quite a few dishes and such to wash up, and I needed water. I stuck my head out of the door, saw the porch eave was in the lee of the cabin, and I put the tub out to catch some of the deluge.

I fixed myself a bite to eat, but I wasn't hungry—only nibbled at my food.

I did more chores, and kept turning my clothes about to dry them faster. By midafternoon the rain stopped and the wind had eased up a lot. I went out on the porch and sniffed the air. It smelled fresh and clean. I was sure the storm was over, and I decided to go to the tunnel for my specimen.

My clothes were nice and warm and dry enough. I put them on over Don's heavy woolen underwear, got into my shoepacks and coat, fixed a carbide miner's lamp, swung the gun across my shoulders, and started for the mine.

The landscape bore witness to the wrath of the storm; several windfalls lay helter-skelter around the cabin, one right near to where Sam's tent had stood, but the trail was clear all the way to the canyon.

There is no natural way to get into the canyon. A four-hundred-foot falls shuts it off at the lower end and cliffs box it in at the upper end. At first the men climbed in and out with a rope, let their tools down in a sling, and didn't bother to build a trail until they were sure they had a good-enough showing to make the effort of a trail worth while.

They blasted the trail along the north wall. They had to use quite a bit of powder where the rock was solid. Other places they just used the pick to dig out loose rock and make a shelf-like trail. There is a lot of muck and vegetation between the projecting rock. All manner of moss and ferns grow on the wall. Everywhere the walls are very steep, and in several places they are sheer cliffs. Where the trail comes out of the canyon on to the hill, there is a bit of a slope for a short way and considerable more muck and dirt than in most other places. Alders and other vegetation find enough soil to thrive there.

Most of the way the trail is so narrow that I always got the shivers going over it, especially the places where there is no vegetation below. It is strange how a few worthless weeds, growing on the lower side of the trail, can make such a difference in my feelings when I know very well those weeds couldn't hold the weight of a cat. I know, too, that such places are more dangerous, not being solid, and are apt to give way; yet I can travel there with a minimum amount of quaking, while along the solid rock I quiver and shake from the soles of my feet to the roots of my hair just because I can see clear to the bottom, because no ferns are between me and the bottom.

The trail ended at the portal of the tunnel, which started in the north wall, a few feet above the canyon creek, just high enough to be well clear of the water in wet weather. The tunnel went through country rock until it was deep enough to safely turn and follow the ledge. Even so there is a great deal of water in the mine, which Don says seeps in from the canyon creek through fractures in the ledge.

The canyon trail was fairly littered with small branches, boughs, and such, much of which I kicked off as I carefully went along. In half a dozen places muck had washed down off the wall, and I didn't like those places. I remembered how yesterday—no, not yesterday, but days and days ago, ages ago, in another world —Don had looked up at the walls and said in a most solemn tone of voice, "It's been a mighty dry year."

"It's been a wonderful year. Why so solemn?" I asked.

He didn't answer at first, took a longer breathing than he needed to, then said, "I was thinking how rain for the whole year has been saved up, and now maybe it will be dumped on us all at once."

I didn't say any more and he didn't either. Of course I didn't think anything about it then, but now I think maybe Don thought there might be a slide. He didn't want to tell me what he thought for fear I would be frightened.

The canyon creek was high, almost level with the top of our dump, and rapidly washing the dump away. Above the roar of the rushing water, I could hear rocks bumping against each other as they were being swept away.

I lit my lamp and went into the tunnel, soon found my specimen, and came out quickly. It began to rain again just as I started along the trail.

At the forge I noticed the keg we use for tempering steel had not been emptied. It would freeze in winter and burst the hoops and have to be replaced next summer if it wasn't emptied now. Don always takes such good care of supplies and tools, and I didn't see how he could have missed seeing the tempering keg. Anyway, I was glad I had noticed it. I dumped the water and turned the keg upside down, picked up the lamp and specimen from off the forge where I had laid them while I did the chore, and went on. No more than a minute in time had been lost. Just one little minute.

Oh, God. Don is gone. Now I can't ever see him again. Not ever or ever. I am alone. All alone and so badly hurt. Oh, this terrible wilderness.

I must explain everything and put it all down. The forge was at a tiny draw where a small spruce tree grew. The trail was wide enough for the forge to be set up close by the tree. In fact, it was the only place for it, because everywhere else the canyon walls were almost straight up and down. I had passed the forge ten or twelve steps. No more than that. Suddenly I heard a sharp crack, the sound of breaking and tearing, and almost at the very same instant the terrified voice of my husband shouted a warning to me.

Don's voice is the most confusing and distressing of all my troubles. I know Don was not there. I could not have heard his voice. Still, I know that I did hear him, and I reckon I ought to know the sound of my own husband's voice.

I must try to reason this out. I am so unsure of many things. Maybe this writing will help me to get things straight.

At Don's warning cry, I instinctively jumped ahead.

The cracking and breaking and tearing instantly became a mighty rumble, a roar, a great booming, the blast of cannon, all the claps of thunder rolled together to make one great solid sound, echoed, magnified, and reechoed by the canyon walls. The air was full of noise and flying debris. The noise seemed to have physical strength, to be not only a great sound, but also a great wind.

It was a noise with body, solid like a wall. A sound with strength and force and power. The giant thundering became a wind, and the wind created a violent hurricane. The sound and the force of the sound were one, great and mighty, filling all the earth and all the space between heaven and earth, a monstrous convulsion of the universe, chaos.

The noise and the vicious beast that was the noise jerked me off my feet, snatched me up, cuffed and beat me, scourged and lashed me, lifted me high into the air, whirled me about in a caldron filled with violent hurling parts of disintegrated earth.

I can't remember anything hitting me, but I know that many things did hit me. I was turned about in every direction. I can't remember stopping. I felt no pain, but I was hurt and hurt bad. Maybe I was too frightened to have any feelings. Soon I just stopped knowing anything.

It was the gun that saved me. I want so much to stay alive. I do want to live. I wish Don would come. My head aches terribly. I am so tired.

If Don were alive he would come to me. He does not come, and he is dead. No, I don't believe that. Deep in my soul I know Don is alive. Maybe he is hurt and needing me. Please, dear God, let me get strong enough to go find Don.

2

I AWOKE TO A SILENT WORLD, A STILL NIGHT WITH STARS OVERHEAD. Battered and broken, sore and bleeding, I was held fast in the alder brush, the scrawny alder which grew in rock crevices near the top of the canyon wall. The gun I wore across my shoulders had wedged among the branches and held my body suspended over a sheer drop to the bottom of the canyon.

It took time to realize where I was, to understand my predicament. I was resting on my left side across a tangle of alders, my feet dangled in space, and my head was pointed obliquely up toward the end of the canyon trail. The gun was wedged above me, and the sling passed down under my left hip, across my stomach, and pinned my right elbow to my right ribs. Small branches were in my face. I still wore my gloves, but my hat was gone.

When I finally grasped where I was and how dangerous it was, I clamped my left hand tight onto a branch and cried out. I shouted and screamed for help until I could call no more. My nose bled and there was the taste of blood in my mouth. My head hurt awful bad. I either slept for a while or became unconscious. When I awoke again, the stars were still overhead. I had no idea whether it was the same night or the next. All was still. There was no sound of wind and there was no roar from the swollen canyon creek. The last thing I remembered was the mighty noise and movement. When I awoke all was silent.

The gun sling held me tight and I kept quiet, not daring to

move, unable to think. I turned my head a little and looked at the stars. I wondered about them, and as I was wondering they all went away. Why had they gone? Suddenly they came again. I knew then I had closed my eyes when they went away. I moved a little, and I began to have feeling in my body.

My right arm was of no use at all, and it hurt with every movement. I tried to put my hand inside my shirt to keep it warm, but I was fuddled and couldn't seem to get anything done. From the knee down my right leg was numb. It felt asleep. My clothing was wet and sticky. Every moment I was afraid of suddenly coming loose and falling down into the canyon. My head was cut and bleeding, blood was sticky on my face and it was even in my ear. I felt awful lonesome and helpless, and I got panicky.

I called to Don for help. I cried and screamed and begged him to come. Then, out of the silent night, from far above the canyon, I heard Don's voice. From far away, soft as the whisper of an angel, yet clear and distinct, the voice of my husband came to me again and again.

His voice had been the last sound I had heard before the mighty thundering of chaos—now it was the first sound to come to me in the stillness. The voice of my beloved husband, calling to me from above, guiding me up out of the canyon.

I know I didn't really hear him. I know he wasn't there, yet I did hear his voice. I believed he was calling me, and believing that, I did not feel hurt or helpless any more. I felt strong enough to try to go to him. The will to make that supreme effort was far greater than courage.

I began to struggle and grasp, to pull and hold on, never looking below, for below me was utter destruction, while above me was life and the solid earth. When I rested and stopped for breath, I could hear Don calling, then I would try again. Somehow I freed myself from the gun sling, stretched out of it, clawing, clinging, grasping, holding to twigs with my teeth. With only one good arm and one good foot to help me, I moved upward.

I struggled and strained in the darkness, felt about for another alder limb, gripped it, and stretched a little farther. Inch by inch

I climbed, and all the time my husband kept calling to me, guiding me.

Slowly, slowly, I worked up and onto the trail. I lay there and slept, and Don's voice awakened me. He urged me on, begged me to crawl along the rock shelf that was the canyon trail, and I followed the call of his voice. I inched my way, kept moving until I was out of the canyon and onto the hill. Then the sound of Don's voice came to me no more, and I did not know that it came no more. I did not know that it had ever been. I lay still and slept.

When I woke up I was so thirsty. I had to have water. It seemed I would die of thirst. I found a little puddle in the hill trail and I drank. Then I knew I must go to the cabin. I did not try to walk. I crawled. Crawled, not the way a baby crawls, but as a worm crawls. When I came to puddles of water, I would drink from them, for I was terribly thirsty all the time.

Crawling and resting, sliding and pulling myself along through the trail mud, over roots and humps, around trees and across grassy spots, drinking from all the puddles, down the steep hillside to the cabin I made my way and at last was within the cabin door.

It was day and the sun was shining.

I looked at my arm. It looked awful. I thought it was broken in two places, but now I think it was broken in one place only and just dislocated at the wrist. I couldn't think about anything else. I had to fix it. I knew I must make my arm straight and whole again. My entire being was centered on it. I did not even think of my other hurts.

I stretched out on the cabin floor and held my broken arm to my breast. Then I saw a coil of fuse on a low shelf. Nearby was kindling wood. I needed no more. Reaching the fuse, I pulled a long lot of it free and passed it around the post which holds one end of the shelves. I made a slip loop from the double strand and gathered some kindling wood to me. I edged myself backward alongside the cabin wall and braced my foot against the shelf post. I unfastened my belt and put it over my hurt arm at the elbow, then I fastened it again and made it as tight as I could. I was so tired that I had to lean against the wall and rest.

After a while I inched forward and placed my hurt hand in the slip loop, pulled with all my strength, and braced my good foot against the shelf post. With my sound hand I held the broken place, twisted and worked it until I could feel the bones fit together straight and right. Then I poked kindling wood up my sleeve and along my arm. I bound it there with the free end of the fuse, and when I took off the slip loop my arm stayed straight. I put lots more kindling wood up my coat sleeve, all around my arm, and wrapped more and more fuse around it.

My head hurt something awful and my nose was bleeding again. I was very tired, so I just leaned against the cabin wall and went to sleep.

Some time in the night I awoke. My arm was hurting bad. I fumbled in the darkness, unwrapped the fuse, and took away the sticks. My arm was swollen enormously, my hand felt puffed, and I could feel dents in the flesh where the sticks of kindling had been. But it was straight. I was so glad. I opened my shirt, unbuttoned my underwear, and very gently lifted my arm and placed it under my clothes, my bloated right hand on my left shoulder; protectingly I held it there, tenderly stroking it as I leaned against the wall. Then I went to sleep again.

I am thankful I had the gun across my back and that it kept me from falling to the very bottom of the canyon and being buried alive under tons and tons of muck and rock. I guess I wouldn't have known anything about it. I don't know too much about it as it is.

The gun is still there. It's Don's new gun. He was so proud of it. Lloyd and I gave it to him for his birthday. Don said it was the best shooting gun he ever had. Why in this world did I have to take Don's new gun? Why couldn't I have taken my own gun? I wish I could get Don's gun and clean it and oil it and take care of it. It was such a good gun and Don liked it so much. Oh, I do wish I could get it.

Oh, Don, I can't even take care of your gun. How then am I to take care of your children—our son and this tiny mite under my heart?

3

I AM IMPROVING. MY RIGHT ARM IS STRAIGHT AGAIN. OH, I'M thankful to see my hand fitting onto my arm as a hand should fit. I'll take very good care of my arm and keep it straight. My nose has not run bloody water for several days, but my head still aches. I do feel much better. My brain seems to be working better, too. I am thinking clearly and remembering straight. I pray God to let me stay alive. Maybe He will let me live for the sake of my baby.

I think about myself and about the little one who has nestled under my heart for nearly six months, remembering that she can keep on living only if I live, and that I must take care of myself for her sake. I think awhile and pray awhile, consider what I can do for myself, then get busy and try to do something.

Now back to my story: The second day in the cabin I made a fire, which was no trouble, since we always leave shavings at hand. I put water on to heat and found a thin board, the side of an old powder box, and I split it to make splints for my arm.

I got my coat off, though it was an awful task. I thought I never would manage it. Without the use of my right hand the left sleeve was hard to get out of, but the rest was easy. I didn't try to take off any more of my clothes; it was too much trouble. I rolled up my shirt sleeve and I was going to wash my hurt arm in hot water, but I was getting too tired, so I only tied it up with the board splints and the towel and the dishrag. I drank lots of

16

water and went to sleep again. I didn't try to get in the bunk; I just sat and leaned against the cabin wall and slept.

In the night I awoke and was thirsty. I got a drink, then slept again. Soon it was day, and I knew I was much better. I was hungry. I made another fire and fixed tea with lots of sugar in it. I ate raw oatmeal and raisins and drank my hot tea, and I felt good enough to see how dirty I was. I wanted to be clean. A shirt of Sam's big underwear was hanging on the line just above my head. I pulled it down and planned to wear it. I put water in the basin on the floor and got a washrag. I took my hair down, and lots of it came off in my hand. One of the big hairpins was broken in two. I think the rock that hit my head must have cut my hair and broken that hairpin. My hair was matted with dried blood and I couldn't do anything about it. I washed my face and my neck. Then I reached into the can where we keep bacon grease, got out a good lot, and rubbed it all over my head and on my chin.

My right hand hurt too much for a real wash, so I only washed it a little bit, and that very gently. With the butcher knife I slit the right sleeve of Don's union suit, and got out of the top part, stripped down to the waist. Then I did manage to get Sam's clean undershirt on, but only barely managed. My head began to hurt much worse and I got awful dizzy, so I stopped trying to do anything. I sat on the floor, leaned against the wall, and slept.

I was there an awful long time. Sometimes I knew things and sometimes I didn't know much. All my body had a strange, prickly feeling, and the cabin seemed to be swaying like treetops in a breeze. My head ached and roared and seemed much bigger than it should be. Sometimes I opened my eyes and it was day, then it would be night again. I never could remember which it was the last time. I thought I should try to keep track of the days, and I fretted a bit because I couldn't remember.

I woke up. Wide awake. It was dark, and I knew something had awakened me. At once I knew where I was, but I didn't know what had awakened me. Then suddenly I realized the mice were eating me. Not me, but the dried blood and bacon grease in my hair. I shooed them away. They came again and licked grease off my chin. A mouse's tongue is rough. I was afraid of their sharp white teeth, and I kept trying to shoo them away, but every time they would come back.

Then it was day and the mice went home.

I moved about. I was thirsty and hungry, and I found food and drink. I felt much better. I was not dizzy any more, and after a little I found I could move easier. I felt pretty good. I had soiled and wet myself, and I was filthy. I couldn't stand to live in that condition. I needed lots more water, and the pail was nearly empty. I was upset until I remembered the tub out under the eave—plenty of water there.

The men's work clothes had all been left in the cabin, but none of my things were there. I wouldn't have wanted my things anyway, for I couldn't bear the thought of anything tight. I decided to wear Sam's things. He is the biggest and he gets things about four sizes too large for him. He wears suspenders, and the tops of his pants are so wide that chips and bark and muck and all sorts of things get into his pants. He just shakes a little and things come falling out the bottom like going through a funnel. He stags his pants off at the bottom. He looks funny and we laugh at him.

Getting the clothes down off the line was an enormous lot of work, but I got all that I would need, and I found soap and towels and clean dishcloths to make a better bandage for my arm. I rested lots of times. I could go on my right knee, but I couldn't stand on my right foot. I was worried about that leg; it hurt a lot, hurt bad.

I made another fire and brought in a little water. My right shoe-pack had a hard knot, and I couldn't get it undone. I didn't try very much; and I think maybe I didn't want to get it off, didn't want to see my leg, for I knew it would look awful. The leg part of my shoepack was as tight as tight could be, and I knew my leg was badly swollen to make it so tight. I took the butcher knife and cut my pants leg and the underwear, and pulled them off over the shoepack. The left one I got off without trouble.

I took a pretty fair sponge bath, I went to the toilet properly, and I put on clean clothes. I put a fresh bandage on my arm, and

I was happy to find the swelling going down and the arm still straight.

I ate raw dried apples and peanut butter, made more tea, and drank it scalding hot and very sweet. I shook some kerosene out of the lamp and rubbed it all in my hair to discourage the mice.

I got to the bunk and my good eiderdown. By that time I was all worn out and it was getting on toward night. I went to bed, lay down for the first time since I had been hurt, and I slept well.

Some time during the night I woke up, and I still felt good. My hurts were itching. I rubbed them—scratched them gently, and they hurt nicely, not like pain. My leg was itchy, and I wished the shoepack was off so I could scratch it. I lay there a long time rubbing my hurts and being glad and so thankful the pain was gone. As I lay there just being lazy, a faint fluttering came in my abdomen. It came again and again, and each time it seemed to be stronger. It was my baby stirring within my womb, the first time since I was hurt that I had felt the child move. And it was the first time that I had thought of the little one; I had never once remembered, always and forever I had been thinking of myself. What an utterly selfish creature I was! Suddenly I was frightened. Then I was joyful. All my hurts might have killed the child. But the child lived and was strong. How glad I was!

We have waited twelve years for a second child. I must let nothing harm this little one. I must take gentle care of myself. I will rest and do no more work than is necessary to keep the fire and cook a little food. Every day I will write, and that will make the days go fast. I thought of Don and wished that he could know that our child lived, that soon I would be well, soon all would be well.

4

I THINK LOTS AND LOTS ABOUT DON, AND REMEMBER MANY THINGS.
I have a wealth of good memories. Oh, but I am rich in memories.
I know now that memory is the best of all life's blessings. Certainly it is my present great blessing. I can think back over things
that happened years ago, and it seems as if I were living them
again.

I remember the first time I ever saw Don. It was at a Christmas party in Baltimore, at my uncle's house. Uncle Ben was a pro-
fessor of Latin at Johns Hopkins University. Don wasn't in his
classes—he was studying math and science—but Uncle Ben had
met him and thought he was a fine young man, and he invited
him to the Christmas party to meet his daughters and nieces.

Don and I always loved each other. We didn't know it at first,
but we came to know it. We were quite impressed with each
other at Uncle's Christmas party, and I danced more with him
than with anyone else. Next day we went horseback riding together. I can remember the ride as if I were taking it right now.
We went down to the old Shot Tower and we were late getting
home. Aunt Nancy gave me a cross look, but Uncle Ben was
sweet and he gave Don a drink of brandy. Uncle didn't give his
brandy to everybody, not even at Christmas time.

Two years and four months later we were married. It was a
beautiful church wedding, but Tommy Saunders almost spoiled
it. The person who was to pump the organ couldn't be found,
and Mrs. Saunders grabbed her twelve-year-old son and put him

behind the organ to do the pumping. Tommy couldn't see the
bride, and the only reason he had come to the wedding was to
see the bride, so he felt he was being cheated out of his rights.
His mother let him out while the minister was saying his say, but
she pushed the child back before the say was finished and gave
him instructions to pump good and hard so that there would be
plenty of air for a grand peal of music when Don and I marched
down the aisle together.

The poor child was weeping, and about halfway through "God
the Father, God the Son, God the Holy Ghost, bless, preserve,
and keep you; the Lord mercifully with His favour look upon
you," came a most miserable sob. It could be heard all over the
church. Don thought it was my mother weeping, and I guess
other people thought the same. I don't remember what I thought,
but I do remember hearing, ". . . and fill boo-hoo you with boo-
hoo all spiritual benediction and grace; that boo-hoo ye may so
live together boo-hoo . . ."

I remember how proud we were of this prospect. It was sure to
make a mine, and a dandy one. Both Don and Sam said so. That
means lots of money for all of us, money and all the things money
can buy. It means more than just that to us, too—it means that
all the years of prospecting and trudging over rugged hills, all
the leg aches and the back aches, all the hard climbs, the wind and
rain and cold, the hunger of soul and body, discouragement and
disappointment, all that and more have not been wasted effort.
It wasn't all for nothing. The men did find a mine, the kind they
wanted to find—low cost for development and lots of high-grade
free-milling gold ore. Now Don and Sam are rewarded for their
perseverance and determination, and I for my waiting.

The men prospected in dozens of places before they came here,
maybe even a hundred other places. Sometimes they thought they
had found a mine, but always it turned out not to be a mine.
This ledge was hard to find. They knew a ledge was somewhere
on this hillside, but it was difficult to find the ore in place.

Don first found float on the beach, half a mile away from
where it should have been. It was a fine piece of quartz, literally

peppered with free gold, and they kept on looking and looking for the ledge that piece of float came from. When they did find it, after two long years of searching, they still couldn't figure how the piece of float got so far away. In fact we never did figure it out; old Mother Nature took a hand and showed us. The float had come down the canyon in a big snow slide, had been embedded in ice, had floated down the creek to the salt water, where the tide had come along with an easterly wind, and the gold-bearing piece of quartz, still locked tight in the ice, had drifted for more than half a mile along the beach, then dropped where Don had found it.

The next summer they widened out their hunting grounds to take in the canyon creek, and there they found lots more float and knew for sure the ledge was up that creek. But the creek ran through this very bad canyon, which they could not get into without a rope. They had none and it was late in the season, so the third summer they came prepared, climbed down into the canyon, and there at last they found the ore in place.

Now we are called lucky by people who can never know of the hard work behind our luck. Still, we call ourselves lucky, too, because we could have missed this ledge so easily. We are lucky, or we were until the raging storm took my Don away and the slide buggered me all up. Why couldn't one of us stay well and unhurt? Why can't Don take care of me? or I take care of Don? Why must harm come to both of us at the same time?

I hate this mine. I want Don. I know something terrible has happened to him. I have thought of many things, but I still don't know what has happened to him. At first I wouldn't let myself believe that he is dead. Even now I refuse to believe it.

Maybe the motor balked before Don got halfway there, and he cranked and tinkered with it until he knew it was too late to contact the mailboat, then turned back and reached our boat by the beginning of the storm. He would have waited out the storm on the boat, then hurried up the hill; not finding me in the cabin he would have gone on to the mine. He might have been nearby when the slide came; he would know the meaning of the first sounds, and call a warning to me. That could be true, very true. Then where is Don? On the hill trail? and I haven't gone to look for him? Oh, I couldn't go.

Is this sane reasoning? Surely I am not out of my mind.

If only Sam would come. Why doesn't Sam come? When in the world will he come? Sam is good, but I never liked him much. He's a restless, impatient man, and every so often he just has to get drunk. He's not at all like Don. I can imagine how he's fretting and fussing right now, and cussing because we haven't come to pick him up.

Sam should have stayed here until the work was done. This mine is as much his as it is ours. It's all Mat Logan's fault. That bewhiskered old plug with his jug of moonshine hooch coaxed Sam to go with him. Of course, Sam doesn't require much coaxing; still if it hadn't been for Mat, Sam would have stayed.

Sam is a good man; his heart is kind even when he is drunk. I'm sorry I didn't like him. I like him now and want him here. Sam would go find Don and bring him to the cabin—and when he comes he'll take care of us both. I must wait, wait, wait until Sam comes.

What would Don want me to do while I am waiting?

Don was so tender and kind to me. He loved me always. His first thought was for my well-being—his last words for me.

This was such a good summer, and we all had a happy time. We worked hard and for long hours, all of us, even Lloyd and I. Don said we helped lots, said we were as good as two more hands. All our days were busy and filled with achievement and gladness. Now comes this sorrow and disaster.

If Sam never comes, I will die a worse death than being buried at the bottom of the canyon. No. I will not die. I will live and have my baby. It is going to be the girl-child we have wanted so long. I will help myself all I can, and please, dear God, help me some, too.

I think so often of Don. If he is dead, I want to find his body and bury it before the bears or the ravens find it. I lie in bed and fret because I have made no effort to show my devotion to my husband. I remember how his voice guided me. If Don is in the canyon, I must find him, I must.

I feel very much better. I am plenty strong enough now to go and find where he is. I'll go tomorrow.

5

I AM WEARY TODAY, AND BONE-TIRED. I DID GO UP THE HILL YESTER-day, but first I fixed my sore leg. It had been bothering me, and I felt I just had to get the shoepack off. I knew my leg was not broken, for it was perfectly straight; but I thought maybe it had been cracked the way a cup can be cracked, and I was afraid that by pulling at the shoepack to get it off it would be completely broken, so I cut the bottom from my shoepack, and cut the bottom off my sock, too. I rubbed my foot and worked my toes, and right away my leg felt better.

I rested from my efforts, then started up the hill.

I did not turn off at the canyon trail, but kept on the hill trail to where the station for the rope had been. It was a hard climb. I had to rest most of the time. My foot was bare, sticking out from what was left of my shoepack, and when I rested I rubbed it and worked my toes. It felt good. I kept my hurt arm inside my shirt, but I used that elbow often. It was very helpful. I don't think I could have made it without the use of my elbow. After a long time I reached the slide. A great chunk of the mountain has broken away and gone tumbling down into the canyon.

The slide is as big as its thundering roar had proclaimed. The rimrock is now several feet behind where the hill trail used to be. All sorts of debris, even whole trees, has gone down, nearly filling the canyon. The slide is quite long. It goes way past where our tunnel was, and it makes a dam across the canyon creek; more than a dam, a ridge. The water has backed up behind the

25

ridge and made a lake. No wonder I didn't hear the roar of the creek the night I hung in the alder brush: there was no creek. I could see no sign of the forge or the tree that stood beside it—everything is covered with rock and muck. The portal of our tunnel is buried so deep that no one will ever dig it out. Our good mine is gone.

I sat a long time near the rim of the canyon and looked down at the scene of destruction below me, and across at the opposite wall. Over there things were in their same old places, and it seemed strange, but I was glad to find familiar things to look at. The whitened snag where the downy woodpeckers made their home looked just as it did last summer when I turned the forge blower and heated steel for Don to sharpen. I liked helping to sharpen steel, and Don said I did real well, but at first I burned a few pieces, got them so hot sparks crackled and Don had to cut the burned part off. He said he couldn't ever temper steel that had been burned. I learned to watch the steel instead of the woodpeckers flying about, gathering food for their young up in the old white snag, high, high on the wall of the canyon.

I went up the hill meaning to search until I found Don, but when I got there I was too tired to move and I forgot why I had come. For a long time I leaned against a little tree, just sat there and looked. After a while I did begin to think about Don and to wonder where he could be, but I didn't think of hunting for him. Not physically, that is, but I hunted in my mind, looking at this place and that and saying, "He is not there."

Then I saw a great stone in the middle of the slide—rather the ridge made by the slide—and I said, "Don is there."

The stone is a large square rock and it looks as if it had fallen last, or toward the last, for there is no muck over it. It doesn't look as if it had tumbled down, but as if it had been placed there on top of the first part of the slide. It has the look of a monument, and is square with the canyon. I wanted to believe Don was buried beneath that stone. I thought it a worthy resting place for a good and honorable man.

Then something happened to me. I wanted to be dead and under that stone with Don. I wanted to throw myself into the

canyon and stay forever beside my husband. I needed to crawl
only the length of my body, no farther, to go over the edge of
the rimrock, and I know I would have done so if I had had the
strength to move. I was overcome by a feeling of weakness and
utter helplessness. I was too weary to move, too exhausted to
make any little effort, too helpless to even end my helplessness.
My brain was weary too, and I even stopped thinking, just leaned
against the little tree.

After a while my hand picked up things. I hardly knew what
my hand was doing. I watched it as if it didn't belong to me,
and I became interested in what was there to be picked up and
dropped. I forgot all about wanting to be dead. I looked around
for things, and moved to get those beyond my reach. It seemed
very important to pick up litter and drop it. I must have been
out of my mind, but I remember what I did. Maybe for a long
time, maybe not so long, I crawled about picking up things and
dropping them. It was such a senseless thing to do, yet I did it.

Then I found Don's glove. It was an old, old glove and had
lain there on the ground for months. I know it was Don's glove,
because he had the only pair with red tops.

Was the glove a token to me that Don lived? A pledge that
he would come back? My heart said, "Yes, yes." My brain
couldn't think. I couldn't answer questions. I could only know
I had Don's glove. I held it tight to my breast. Then I cried for a
long time. I lay on the ground and just gave myself up to crying.
It seemed I would go on crying forever. I had not cried before; I
had shed no tears; now a flood of tears came.

After the crying was over, I lay for a time resting, maybe
sleeping. Then I felt cleansed. I no longer wanted to be dead, and
when I remembered that I had thought of such a thing, I was
contrite. I felt hot with shame, and I made a vow, calling God to
be my witness:

"I will not again think of suicide, no matter how hard my life
may become, or how great pain wracks my body, or how lonely
I may be, or what bitter sufferings I must endure. I will not give
up. I will use my intelligence to the uttermost and I will work
with all my strength to help my condition, to give birth to our

child, and to keep my husband's home in readiness for his return. God be my witness to this, my vow."

I said it over several times, and it brought a feeling of peace to me. Peace and gladness, glad to be alive, glad to believe Don's glove was his promise that he would return.

6

I WAS SICK AFTER MY TRIP UP THE HILL, NOT HURT BUT SICK. I HAD a fever, and I lay in the bunk two days and did not make a fire. When the fever left me, I made good progress toward recovery. My hurts are healing and my mind is no longer tormented with confusing thoughts.

I've cut my hair. The hurts on my head had been neglected, and they bothered me a bit. I thought it would help to have short hair. The scissors up here were never very good—they've been used to cut tin and every such thing—and then left-hand cutting isn't satisfactory, but I managed to get most of it off. I cut it as short as I could.

It still rains and my tub overflows, which, with the spring at a distance, is a blessing I am not unmindful of. I brought in water and heated a big potful. I sat on the floor and washed my head, soaped it thoroughly and soaked the scabs loose. It took a long time and made me tired, but I did get my head well washed and rinsed.

And I examined my cuts in the shaving mirror. The big one is over two inches long, and with the scab soaked off it looked awful. The scalp has pulled away and the cut is wide. A very sharp rock must have made it. I don't see how it missed knocking my brains out. No wonder I had such bad headaches. The inside of my head hurt so much I didn't think about the cuts on the outside. There are two more big enough to count, and some others too small to be mentioned at all. I'll have a bad scar from the

29

biggest one. A doctor could sew it up so it wouldn't look so big. But why should I mind a few scars? I'm alive!

I am sure that I have been here alone for more than two weeks, probably three weeks, and well past the time we were to have picked Sam up and gone home. Both Sam and Lloyd will wonder what has become of us, and soon Sam will do something about it. Soon he will come; surely in only a few more days he will be here.

By this time he should be over his drunk. He is probably getting very impatient. Sam doesn't wait gracefully. He will fuss and fume and swear, then he will get someone to bring him up here to learn what has kept us from coming for him at the promised time. The boat is in the bight behind the island, and cannot be seen from the beach cabin, but Sam is a great one for walking around and looking everywhere. I know he will go along the beach and see the boat. He will find the dinghy ashore and think we went up to the mine. He'd know there is no other place to go. As soon as he finds the dinghy, he will figure it all out, then he will start up the hill. Sam is quick and nervous, and he will waste no time wondering about anything, but hurry to find out what has happened. After he starts up the hill, he'll be here in only forty-five minutes. That's all the time it takes to make it, if you aren't packing a big load.

Sam is a born detective. He sees every little thing and figures out all the whys. Every blessed time Lloyd or I did something we didn't want him to know about, he caught up with us, figured out exactly what we had done, and told Lloyd off. He would never say anything to me, but he would bawl Lloyd out for what he knew perfectly well I had done, and he always did his talking where he was sure I would hear every word he said and be properly impressed.

I will never forget the first time Sam told us off. The occasion was on our first prospecting trip with the men. Lloyd was only six years old then. We stayed a little over two weeks, and I do believe Sam did all in his power to make our time as miserable as he could and still appear to welcome us in their camp. Sam didn't want us anywhere nearer than Washington, D.C.

The men had established their camp near a big river and they were prospecting in some close-by hills. Lloyd and I had no firsthand knowledge about camp life in the wilderness, so we slowed up proceedings considerably. It was toward the end of the season, and the men wanted to look the country over before they left to be sure they hadn't passed up anything big. They had planned a trip around a mountain early in the summer, but at first bad weather kept them from going, then we came and hindered them further. They had to keep to terrain that we were capable of managing without breaking our necks.

Don made Lloyd a water wheel and helped him set it up in the little stream where we got cook water, and I decided to build a fireplace. We stayed in camp, alone, one day, puttering at our projects. That gave Sam an idea—we could stay alone while the men took their trip around the mountain. He pushed his idea for all it was worth. He brought rocks for my fireplace and scattered them about where I could find them, but where I would have to work to get them where I wanted them, and he talked to Lloyd about stamp mills and a cam shaft and showed him how to make improvements for the water wheel. The planned trip would keep the men out overnight. Don didn't much like leaving us alone, but I urged him to go and he knew I am never afraid.

So, early one morning, the men took their packs and left. Now, there was no reason at all why Lloyd and I shouldn't have continued with what we had been working on, but somehow neither of us had any interest in our projects any more. We developed a desire to go fishing. We had brought new fishing line and it had never been wet. That day we decided to christen it and catch some fish. We would push the boat out into the river and fish from it.

We cut some poles and fixed our lines and hooks, got a chunk of lean ham for bait, then got into the river boat and started the fishing expedition. There were no ripples on the water at our landing and the river didn't look swift, or maybe we didn't know what a swift river should look like. Anyway, we pushed the boat out and made ready to fish.

We didn't fish long. Soon we were just racing downstream.

I barely knew how to row; I should say, rather, that I had had oars in my hands maybe half a dozen times in my life, and my six-year-old son couldn't be expected to know anything about rivers and river boats. Quickly we lost all desire for fish and developed instead a desire to be on solid land.

I managed somehow to get us to the bank, and it happened to be the same side of the river the camp was on. That will always be a wonder to me, because the boat turned around so many times we became doubtful which way camp was. Once we got out of the boat and onto the river bank we stayed there. We had had all the boat ride we wanted for one day. We headed toward camp pulling the boat upstream. The boat was contrary and we had lots of trouble, but we did manage to get it back and tied up exactly as it had been—so we thought. We agreed never to mention the fishing expedition, remembering too late how we had been told to stay away from that river!

It was late afternoon when we returned to camp. The men were to be gone for two days, so there was no reason for us to hurry around and do anything.

Then we heard them coming. We ran to meet them, and I never knew I could be so glad to see anyone. Don had been uneasy about us and had turned back. Sam had followed along, grumbling.

Lloyd and I were as good as people with guilty consciences always are. We hurried around and helped cook. We were very happy and agreeable. When Don asked what we had done all day, I answered:

"Oh, different things. Now tell us about your trip."

Sam never said anything, just looked around camp. The men were tired, and they rested. Lloyd and I washed up with a right good will.

When we were nearly finished, Sam said: "I'd like to know who you think you are, young feller. The Pope of Rome? You've been a-fishing on that river. You can't fool me. You tied that boat up with a rope, and you know danged well beavers gnaw boat ropes. They do it every time. What d'ye think we got a quarter-inch cable for anyhow? What kind of a school ye been going to?

'Ain't ye learned yet ropes are for pulling boats, and cables are for tying them up? And just look at this camp. Don't even look like white folks lived here. Never done a tap of work. You been gone all day."

He told us of all we had done and how we did it. You would have thought he had been there watching us. He made poor little Lloyd seem like a terribly bad boy, and it wasn't the child's fault at all. I should get the blame; besides, if Sam had been willing for us to go with them we wouldn't have gone on the river.

I told him, "You should have taken us with you."

"Now let me tell you something, young man," Sam said, not even looking toward me. He kept right on talking to Lloyd. "Nobody can find a mine dragging a family around the hills. Prospecting ain't for a family. Kids should stay home where they belong."

He classified me as a kid along with my six-year-old son. I said no more.

That night Don told me what a foolish thing I had done, as if I didn't know that already. He made me promise never to do such a thing again.

Sam will be here soon—maybe tomorrow. He'll help me down the hill and onto a boat and we will go fast to find Don. And while I wait for Sam I'll tend my injuries, bathe and rub them, make myself seem nearly well—when he comes.

7

I THINK TODAY IS DECEMBER 1ST. I MARK THE DAYS WITH A CROSS and the nights with a circle. That way I should be able to keep track of time, but I did not start at the beginning and I have to guess how many days passed before I invented my system. At times, after I was hurt, my mind was so confused I only knew dark from light. I didn't know whether I had awakened twice in the same night or slept through the whole day. In two places I have circles together and I have three crosses in line. I don't know why I have them down like that. Anyway, I'm calling today December 1st.

I am getting well fast, and I feel better all the time. I am very pleased with my leg. The discolored flesh still looks a ghastly yellowish-purplish-greenish, and there is some swelling but not much—more after I have been hobbling around for a while than when I first get up in the morning.

My hurt arm is so much better. I can do things with my right hand now, and I keep trying to use it, rubbing it and working the fingers and making a fist. It is not nearly so stiff as it was, and I can pick up things, lift a light weight.

I am thankful to have a body that heals quickly. My head still aches at times, but not all the time, and not bad like it used to. Right now my leg is the most troublesome. I cannot put my weight on it, and it does ache at times, but it is so much better than it was that I could shout for joy. To know I am getting well is a very wonderful feeling.

34

I have been checking over supplies. There is plenty of grub. The men had planned to start working early next spring, before the snow was gone, and so we laid in extra things last summer. We never came up the hill without packing a load. Now there are enough supplies to last two or three workingmen about two months. Don made a cache under the floor on the upper side of the cabin, boxed in a place with puncheon, packed moss around it, and banked it well with dirt. It's frost-proof and chuck-full of canned goods.

The swing shelf is loaded with flour and cereals. There are four twenty-five-pound boxes, each better than half full of dried fruit—raisins, apples, prunes, and peaches. Plenty of milk and sugar, coffee and tea, beans and rice, vinegar and shortening are here. There are cans of butter and bacon, dried eggs and cocoa. I could stay here all winter and never want for food. I would run out of fuel long before the grub was used up—still, there is right much wood on hand. Like grub, we also got wood up ahead, but not nearly enough for a whole winter.

There was so much work to do last summer, and the mine always came first. Lloyd and I helped with the chores and the wood. We helped with everything, whenever the men would let us. The corner behind the stove, under the grub shelves, is filled with split yellow-cedar kindling. Lloyd split it, brought it in, and stacked it up. I didn't think then that I would be here to use it. It has been a splendid thing for me to have; makes getting a fire easy. Stovewood is handy too, and stacked high on the porch. There is a cord of wood blocks in the yard, so I need not worry about fuel for the short time I'll be here.

There aren't many matches, less than a quarter of a box. Plenty of carbide is here, and two lamps—the best lamp was lost, for it was the one I took to the mine. I looked at the lamps, and the flints seem to be all right, but I didn't try them. It takes two hands to light a carbide lamp. A miner's lamp is a wonderful thing to carry in the wilderness. One flip of the flint and you have a light—one that it takes a strong wind to blow out. If you have no matches, you can get a fire going quickly with a carbide lamp. Don and Sam always carry them, and they usually start their campfires from the carbide flame. Carbide flames are so hot that a fire can be started with wet wood and in the rain.

Lloyd and the Smiths will be getting anxious. It takes a lot to worry Lloyd, but when he does start to worry he really works at it. Poor child, his schoolwork will suffer, and he wasn't exactly an A1 student to begin with. I do hope I can get to town before worry about us interrupts his studies.

I know what he is doing now, every day after school: he will rush down to the harbor to see if we have come. He will go aboard all the newly arriving boats and ask for word of us; and, being a friendly lad, he will make many new friends among the fishing fleet, gather a wealth of information about hooks and lines and bait, and for a little while forget that we are over-due.

Lloyd is a big boy now, almost a man in this country; he doesn't need a mother to tag along and look after him. The Tom Smiths are old friends, a splendid family. Mary Smith disciplines her own children, and Lloyd will surely be properly bossed. Lloyd and Joe are such pals, in the same grade, and they have many common interests. Lloyd may worry, but he will have the comfort of kind friends. He shouldn't be too worried yet.

It would be grand if Don did meet the mailboat before the storm, and Lloyd got the big buck. But then, if Don is stranded on one of the islands with a stove-up skiff it would be a lot grander for him to have the buck. With the content of the grub box plus the deer and plenty of clams Don can make out for a long time. Either way, I like to think of that big fine buck.

Perhaps no one, except Sam, will be very concerned about us yet, for the weather has been stormy. Along this rugged coast, people out in small boats are often given up for lost, when suddenly they come chugging into harbor. Lloyd will certainly think we are just waiting out the weather, and he will remember the time it took us twenty-six days to get over here from town. He was along on that trip, and he will think of it now. He will also remember the trip we made in twenty-six hours—the luckiest trip we ever made with this boat—tides and winds with us every-where, and we just sailed along. Don figures thirty-one running hours to get home; winds and tides can shave a little off that or add much to it, and they usually add—sometimes several days.

Lloyd must have had a premonition of evil, must have felt a shadow of foreboding ill. He begged so hard for me to go with him. Dear boy. He couldn't think up any good arguments why I should go. All he did was to ask me to go, ask again and again, and keep right on asking after the decision had been made. He sounded babyish, and Don was ashamed of him. Sam called him a sissy and said he needed a nursing bottle. I thought he was acting spoilt.

Usually he doesn't care whether I'm with him or not, often doesn't even know if I am along or not, for he is interested in things and likes to talk with people. He has taken trips alone before. When he was only seven years old, he traveled from Seattle to Washington, all alone, and had the time of his life.

With all my heart I do wish I had listened to my son and gone to town with him. This summer went so fast; it seemed we were here only a little while until it was time for school. I knew I couldn't come next summer, not with a tiny baby, and I do so love being here with Don. Somehow it did seem right for me to stay. But we would all be together now, and safe, if I had gone with Lloyd. Sam would have stayed with Don, and postponed his drunk until he got to town.

Sam would have waited anyway if it hadn't been for old Mat Logan and his jug of whisky. Mat stopped by here to see how we were doing. He gave Sam a few nips from his jug, and Sam developed a thirst for lots more. Mat was in his fishing boat and on his way to Big Sleeve, where a number of Sam's old cronies work and where liquor flows often and freely. Sam saw his chance to get drunk and no reason why he shouldn't take it. Of course, that's not the excuse he offered us for going off a week ahead of schedule. Sam never does say he's going to get drunk. Goodness, no! There is always some other very important business he has to attend to right away—something which just can't wait. This time our hand steel was too short. We needed longer drills to make deeper holes, so we could blast bigger rounds and get the job done faster. Well, we did need longer steel, but since we were in the process of closing up for the winter there was no great rush about getting it. But Sam was in a rush to get to Big Sleeve, and nobody was fooled about what he was rushing for.

I am always mad at Sam when he gets drunk. I can't help being mad, but I do manage to keep my mouth shut. Don doesn't like it either, but he thinks so well of Sam, otherwise, he tolerates his failing and says nothing about it. I think poor Sam never had much raising. He couldn't have, for he ran away from his home on a farm in Ohio when he was twelve years old, made his way clear to California, and he was working underground in a mine when he was only thirteen years old. He has lived in bunkhouses and camps ever since.

Sam is a good man; he is fair and honest and dependable and everything else that is desirable in a prospecting partner. Don said Sam was the best partner any man could ever have, and Don should know, for they've been partners twenty years this last summer. Don said Sam knew more than he could ever hope to learn about all the tricks of mining and prospecting, hunting and camping, building cabins and mills, logging and working in big timber. Sam is one to do his share always, and usually a little bit more than his share.

He is fifteen years older than Don, and he looks old enough to be Don's father. Years before I came into the picture, they got together in California, where Don was straw boss on the construction of a tramway. Sam drifted along and asked for a job. Don hired him and soon raised his wages. He said Sam was the best workman he had ever seen. And Sam said Don Martin was the best boss he ever heard tell of, said Don had sense enough to let a man alone after he told him once what he wanted done. With such mutual admiration, they were certain to become friends.

Before Don met Sam, he had already been bitten by the gold bug, had done a little prospecting, and hankered to do more. Sam's whole life was prospecting, and he only took a job now and then in order to get enough money to go prospecting again. Sam worked for Don until the tramway was finished. Then he said, "Let's go prospecting."

"Nothing I would like better," Don answered, and that's how they became partners. They've been together every summer since.

Sam never did have much use for women; considers them a nuisance and a needless expense. He didn't want Don to get married, told him all women ever do is spend a man's money. He wanted Don to keep me in Washington, D. C., told him that he would see more than enough of a wife during the winter months when they couldn't be prospecting.

It was never Don's intention to take me into the partnership. He was going to find a mine which would be worth not a cent less than a million dollars. Then we'd have a lovely home, travel the wide world over, appear at the mine now and then, and stay just long enough to pick up the gold. Things didn't work out that way, but they almost did the first season they were in Alaska.

They were placer mining up in the Yukon country, and out of the first hold they sunk they took $11,000 and a little over. They put down five more holes and didn't get enough gold to buy their grub. Along came a sucker and asked them if they wanted to sell. Sure, they wanted to sell. Did he have $50,000 to pay for the claim? Well, now, how about $25,000? Split the difference. Make it $36,000 and the sale is on. Sold. Just like that the deal was closed.

"And here's where fools meet," Sam told the buyer. "We're fools for practically giving you the mine, and you're a fool to pay such a God-awful price for nothing but a hole in the ground." Sam and Don took the $36,000 and laughed up their sleeves. They didn't laugh long. That sucker took $1,120,000 out of the claim they had sold him. No matter, there was lots more gold in the ground. Next time they wouldn't fool themselves. Don bought our Washington home with part of his money. I don't know what happened to Sam's share, but I do know he was soon broke.

For a few years I didn't mind being left alone from April to October, or even later. At first I lived with my parents, then Don bought our home and I enjoyed being mistress of my own house. Lloyd was small, my relatives were nearby, and always I knew this would be the last summer; this summer they would surely hit it.

I must say our winters were grand. Don is a good storyteller, and he had so much to tell. We went to parties and we entertained and we danced. We went to church and to the theater. We heard good music and read good books. There were new clothes and dinner parties and company and visits, talk and laughter. Life was nice when Don was home.

Then I got tired of being a widow all summer, and I asked Don to take us with him. He was horrified. I pestered him all winter and extracted a half-promise.

"Just as soon as there is a proper place for you to live, I'll take you," Don said. He didn't mention that a mine had to be found first.

About the end of May I met Minnie Lewis and her mother. They had just come from their home in North Carolina and were visiting some relatives in Washington before going on to Alaska, where they planned to make their future home with son and brother, Tom Lewis. They were leaving on June 8th, and since Don was in Alaska they asked me to go along and surprise him. Why not? I went along and surprised everybody—even myself.

I wrote Don a letter telling him what I was doing and said we would be visiting at the home of Tom Lewis in Nome, Alaska, until he could come for us.

It was a wonderful trip. Lloyd and I enjoyed every hour. Lloyd kept right on having a wonderful time after we arrived in Nome, but I was rather taken aback. When I told a friendly Nomite where my husband was, he brought out a map and showed me that I was at least two thousand miles away from him. The kind Nomite also gave me some information about transportation in Alaska, and predicted I might have to return to Washington without seeing my husband.

Well, it didn't turn out quite that bad. My letter was a month old when Don received it. Through a streak of luck, a tramp steamer just happened along bound for Nome. Don reached us two weeks later. During all that time I studied Alaska geography and picked up a little education in other ways, too.

Don was good about our coming. He didn't say any of the things that he had every right to say. He acted as if everything had been done according to plan. He wanted us to like Alaska and Sam—whitewashed the rascal scandalously—and hoped we would have a happy time. He did all he could possibly do to show us how glad he was that we had come. I loved Don so much it seemed my whole being overflowed with love for him.

Don said he would take us back with him to where he and Sam were prospecting. But no boats run from Nome to southeastern Alaska. We had to go all the way to Seattle, then take another steamer to get to Wrangell, and from there we had to take a river boat to get to the camp up on the Stikine River.

Sam met us at the steamer, cold sober. Don was overjoyed, for he so much wanted Sam and me to be favorably impressed with each other. Sam was very pleasant and seemed to welcome us, but his heart was full of meanness and he did every blessed thing he could think of to discourage us from ever coming again. He carried it a bit too far, and I got on to him. I became determined to beat him at his own game. I wouldn't have complained for anything.

The camp was primitive, the weather was bad, and life was pretty rugged. It wasn't easy, but I loved being with Don and I believed I could learn to live happily in the wilderness.

The next spring Lloyd and I persuaded Don to take us along again. Sam met us in Seattle and spoke his piece.

"Send them kids back to Washin'ton where they belong!" he said.

I was stubborn and so was Sam. Then Sam gave Don his choice —either send us back or he would quit the partnership. We compromised and sent Lloyd back to Mother. I went with the men and was most agreeable and obedient. Since then Lloyd and I have been with Don at least a part of every summer. When this property was found to be good, we sold our Washington home, bought a place in Alaska, and we have all worked together fairly well ever since.

It took a long time for Lloyd and me to learn the ways of the wilderness. Often we grieved and distressed Don, I know, and we aggravated and vexed Sam. Yet we finally did learn some things. Don was a patient teacher, slow to censor and quick to praise. I know we have rewarded him by conducting ourselves so as to make him proud of us.

Sam still pretends to dislike our being here. He has been kind, especially to Lloyd, whom he truly adores in a sort of left-handed way, but he wouldn't give me a word of praise to save his life.

He will say things like this: "Sure, the bread is good—good enough. A man can eat it. I've ate better. Burned half a cord of wood baking it. Man can't do a thing round this place but cut firewood."

This can hardly be called high praise, but I'm on to Sam. I know he thinks well of me, because Mrs. Linton, in Big Sleeve, told me one of her boys asked him what I was like.

"Don Martin's got a right fine woman," was Sam's answer.

I am sure Sam likes Lloyd a lot; he likes me some, and respects me a great deal, but he loves Don as his other self. Sam would die for Don. Soon Sam will come searching for Don and me.

Perhaps he will come today.

8

MORE RAIN HERE, SNOW ON THE TOPS OF THE HILLS, NO WIND. IT would be good weather for a boat trip. I have cleaned up the cabin a bit, and I have a feeling company may come.

Today is my best yet. I feel fine.

I am amazed at the fast healing of my hurts. I really am doing very well. My leg is much better and can bear my weight. I use it for very little more than a balance stick, but even that is a great help, a big improvement over crawling around. I bathe it and rub it every day, and I take hot rocks to bed at night to keep it warm and drive away the ache.

And my arm is nearly well. I am writing with my right hand; doing fine, too. I won't use it much, though, because I don't want to tire that poor hurt hand. It is so wonderful to know that I shall have the use of my good right hand again. I have been singing all morning, songs of gladness.

I will keep the splints on my arm, however, until my leg becomes so strong I need have no fear of its giving away and making me fall. I can't take any chances of hurting myself all over again.

My head is doing well, too, both inside and out. I still have headaches, but they become less and less severe, and pretty soon now I expect them to fade completely away; then I'll forget I ever had them—I hope. The scabs are scaling off the edges of the cuts, and the soreness is going away. I am very well pleased with the way I am getting on.

The child seems to be all right, too. I feel quite a bit of movement, especially after I go to bed. Apparently she waits to take her exercise until I have finished mine. Poor little one has had pretty rough treatment, and it is a wonder she could live.

I haven't made a thing for the baby. I had planned to do sewing and knitting as soon as I got home. There is still nearly two months, and plenty of time to get together a layette. My people will send gifts; there will be lots of them. Mother is probably sewing right now. I wrote her and my youngest sister about the baby, and of course Lloyd knew.

The rain is gone and this is one fine day.

I woke at dawn, made a fire, and didn't go back to bed as I usually do. I stayed by the window and watched the first pink of morning grow to bright flame and touch the snowy peaks with color, reflected in the waters of the bay. I love the view from this cabin. I have always thought this a delightful spot. For that matter I have always liked the whole of our ocean shore, that little world which lies between here and Big Sleeve, with myriads of islands and reefs, numerous waterways, fiords, and tide flats, with dark timber bordering the shores and reaching up the steep hillsides, and great snowy peaks.

I like the tides which never forget to come and go. They are so dependable that often we have told the time from them. And I have learned the ways of the winds—which bring rain, which bring sunshine, which will bluster about and only make a fuss and a flutter, and which will blow into a mighty rage.

Best of all, I like our wild creatures, especially our nice little deer. This morning a doe and her fawn browsed across the open spot below the cabin. The young feller looked nearly as big as his mother. Fawns have such long legs, and their funny little faces are black and round. Their coats are long and woolly, and give their bodies a round, chubby look.

Two ravens flew over this morning to see how I am doing, and said, "*Caw—clok*," by way of making polite conversation, turning themselves half over in the air as they said the "*caw*."

Ravens are wise birds; they will follow a hunter half a day

to get the waste from his kill. Some folks say they will tell the hunter where a deer is, but I doubt that. I think it is more likely they will tell the deer where the hunter is.

Ravens will kill very young fawns. Once Don and Sam saw a raven flopping up and down and went to see what it was doing. They found a poor infant fawn all scrunched down with its head poked in a hole under a root. Just its ears stuck up, or rather what was left of its ears, for the raven had pecked most of them off. The little fawn had its head far enough under the root to keep the raven from getting at its eyes and killing it. It was nearly smothered, and of course the poor thing was terribly frightened. The men freed it and carried it into the woods, thinking the mother would come soon.

When they started away, the fawn jumped up and followed them. Don picked it up and carried it back. Again it followed them, and again they carried it back to the woods. This time Sam took out his pocket knife and cut a lot of brush. They made a nest for the fawn, covering it lightly with the brush so that only its nose stuck out. That time it stayed.

It is more than a month since the storm and the slide, and still no one comes to look for us. Something is very wrong, and the situation will become worse. It is now well into December, and long past time for winter to set in.

Some years winter is late; some years there is little or no snow before Christmas. Last year was a fine open winter, and the men stayed here longer than usual and worked in the mine. They drove 108 feet of tunnel last winter. Don was home for Christmas, then came back, saying they would work until the snow drove them out. They stayed until the 12th of February, came off the hill in a snowstorm, and it kept right on snowing until the fourth day of May. No two years have exactly the same kind of weather, and this good weather might keep up for another month; it might snow two feet deep tomorrow, too. I can't afford to be caught here by snow, and I've decided to go to the beach.

Yes, definitely I am going to the beach. I will go tomorrow.

9

I AM IN THE BEACH CABIN NOW. . . .

I am weary—weary. My hope is gone.

The skiff is not here. Don never came back to camp.

I must have help. There is none. No one will come to this wilderness place in the wintertime. I am all alone and it is raining—cold rain, half snow.

If Don was shipwrecked, he might beachcomb materials to repair his skiff, and then he would come. Don will come as soon as he can. His troubles are surely greater than mine. He, too, must wait for rescue or death, and he doesn't even have a cabin to wait in.

The Indians might come, but not for a while, not until toward spring. They begin to trap near home, and move their camp from cove to cove, catching all the mink and otter in one place before going on to the next. It's more than twenty-five miles to the Indian village, and it is not likely they will be here for a month or more. They weren't here when Don left the mine last year. He said he saw them coming the very day he went away, and that was in February.

My child will be born in February. I need help now. I cannot wait until February. No one will come to me in time to save my child. I would help myself if I only knew what to do. Where is my intelligence? Why don't I know what to do? Why doesn't God tell me what to do?

God in heaven, let me know what to do, and I will work to do it; so long as I have an ounce of strength, I will work.

But what? What shall I do?

My leg hurts and my head hurts. I am sick and unhappy.

I have poked the can off the smokestack and built a fire and made tea. I have my hurt leg close to the fire, and the warmth is good. I am feeling much better, yet I'm afraid my mind is confused. If I think through yesterday, then perhaps I can go on to make some workable plans.

The night before my trip I cleaned the upper cabin and stowed things away. I slept well and got up at daybreak and made shavings. I didn't make a fire because I had enough cooked food for breakfast and lunch.

After breakfast I washed the cook pot and dressed warm. I'd ruined my right shoepack cutting it off my foot, so I had to wear one of Don's minepacks. It's much too big for me, but it just had to do. The sky was clouded over and a misty drizzle was falling. The world was enveloped in a soft grayness. I felt fine, excited, maybe, but filled with purpose and hope.

The elevation of the upper cabin is 1,004 feet, and the trail down to the corner of the beach cabin is 2,511 feet by the survey chain. That isn't far. Of course, the trail zigzags and the survey chain went straight, but even if the trail is twice as long as the survey measure, which it isn't, it still is no great journey. It's all downhill except for the last five or six hundred feet across the flats. I thought it would be no trouble at all for me to go down. I had planned to sit on my bombosity and slide down the steep places. I carried a prospecting pick to hold me back should I start sliding too fast.

The trip was hard, and it took longer than I expected it to take. There are five windfalls across the trail, two of them very difficult to get around. I slid as much as I could, and that was most of the way, but once, a little better than halfway down, I slid too fast, lost control, and banged into a tree and bumped my sore leg. It hurt so much that tears came and I felt sick at my stomach. The injury is right in the same place as the first one. I could hardly bear to touch it. I didn't walk or slide an inch more. All the rest of the way I crawled.

As soon as I came out of the timber, I looked along the beach for Don's skiff. Nothing was on the beach. Then I looked at the cabin and I saw a can over the smokestack. I knew Sam had put it there. Don never would have fooled with any old smokestack; he would have rushed up the hill to me. No one but Sam would have bothered to put a can on our smokestack and lean a forked pole against the cabin roof to take it off again easily. It had to be Sam.

Hoping I was wrong, sick and distressed in mind and body, I crawled to the cabin door.

Sam had closed the door!

I thought I would die. I could hardly breathe, and I felt inert.

The door is fastened with a leather shoestring which goes through a hole and wraps around a peg in the log. Sam always jerks the string under and yanks it tight and makes it hard to undo. Nobody else fastens the door like Sam does, and we can always tell when he's been the last one out of the cabin.

Shaking and fumbling, I unfastened the shoestring and pushed the door open. Cigarette butts were all over the place—Sam's cigarette butts. He smokes Prince Albert tobacco and rolls his cigarettes in wheat-straw papers, and he is messy. When he is worried, he smokes lots and throws butts every which way. He had been in the cabin a long time, and he had smoked and smoked. I picked up the butts and counted them. There were fifty-eight brown-paper butts and three white-paper butts. Someone was here with Sam—somebody who used white papers and who doesn't smoke very much, or maybe he didn't stay all the time with Sam in the cabin. Don doesn't smoke. The other man couldn't be Don.

Two men were here, and neither one of them walked the few steps along the beach to where he could see the boat. The stupid, lazy things! Even a foolish person will look around a little. Why didn't they look? If Lloyd and I had hid the boat, Sam would have found it.

I tried to fool myself for a while. I went out and looked at the can on the smokestack, looked at the door, and stared at the cigarette butts. It's absolutely ridiculous the things my mind did. Instead of feeling sorry Sam had been here and gone, I suddenly experienced terrible pain in my leg. It hurt worse than it did when I bumped the tree; then my knees hurt and I trembled all over, and I just couldn't breathe. I know now that my hurts were no worse, but it sure seemed as if they did hurt a lot worse.

Now that I am certain Don never came back and that Sam has come and gone, I must keep writing or I will lose my wind entirely. I must do something, and not just sit here staring. Let me see what I learned in school.

"*Gallia est omnis divisa in partis tris.*" Maybe I am, too; but instead of *Belgae, Aquitani, et Celtae* I am divided into life before Don, with Don, and after Don.

Jamestown was settled in 1607 and it was the first permanent English settlement in America.

Patrick Henry said, "Give me liberty or give me death."

"In a little old cabin down by the sea someone is waiting." And it's me!

"Honor thy father and thy mother," is the fifth commandment.

My brain is working all right, but my body is lazy. I do nothing. I'll go stark raving mad unless I do something.

What can I do?

Where can I go?

"Go to the ant, thou sluggard. Consider her ways and be wise."

Hmp, an ant!

I can go back to the upper cabin, but God deliver me from the climb up that hill with this aching leg. Still, I can go up the hill on my hands and knees. No, the hill is out—it's too hard.

There comes heavy rain, pounding on this shake roof. Don't I have troubles enough without more rain?

I can stay in this beach cabin. It's a good well built cabin. There's no bedding, only a few old canvas squares we used to cover cargo. Very little wood, but there is an ax. Only enough grub to keep a stranded traveler from starving for a couple of weeks or so, and then he'd have to dig clams to eke out the meager supplies.

And I could go on the boat. There is plenty of everything on the boat. I would soon use up the fresh water, but it rains lots. The coal and wood would not last too long, yet if I made small fires, and only for cooking, the fuel would last much longer. Of course, there is plenty of wood on shore and I might be able to gather some. Climbing from the dinghy to the deck with wood would be pretty much of a chore shortly before the baby comes. The boat is cold and damp, and my hurts ache so when they get cold. I could stay in the bunk and keep covered up when the fire is out.

I would get mighty tired of lying abed for hours and days on end. There is so little room on the boat, but it is easy to keep a small place warm. I could live on the boat, but how would I manage if my child were born there? How will I manage anywhere if I am alone. I must not be alone when the child is born. Absolutely, I must not be alone then.

Oh, Don, how I need you.

Don said the wilderness was good, said God had put here all things necessary to men, that the hills and forests and sea would provide shelter and food and clothing for all who have the understanding to make use of the bountiful supply. He taught Lloyd and me how to build campfires even in the rain, taught us to hunt and to fish, to find roots and leaves and berries for food. And he taught us the ways of the sea: how to steer the boat, to quarter with the wind and waves, to read the chart and be guided by the compass.

I can run that boat. I can! I can! I know I can run that boat. That's what I'll do. I'll run that boat home. My prayer has been answered. Now I know what to do.

I'll go at once and make ready to run our boat home.

10

I CAME ABOARD LATE YESTERDAY, JUST AT TWILIGHT, AND I HAVE had a fire going ever since. The boat was so damp, and all the bedding and everything so clammy, that I had to keep a fire going all night to drive the chill away.

I'm glad to be on the boat. I am joyful with the thought of going home. I sing and hum, and the fire and kettle and the rain keep time to the music in my heart.

After I found Sam had been here and gone away, I think I wasn't right in my mind. I didn't trust my thinking, but now I know I'm all right. I am glad to be going home—serenely confident.

I wrote on the cabin door with a piece of charcoal that I was going home in the boat. I left the writing I've done in the cabin, so if Don should come he will know what has happened.

Oh, I didn't put the can back on the smokestack. How could I forget to do that? The stove will be ruined and it's a new one. We just got it last summer. I won't go back. I'm on the boat, and I will stay here until I get home.

The dinghy was full of rain water. I pulled the plug and all the water ran out. The dinghy was well up on the beach, and I had considerable trouble getting it into the water. The tide was going out and night was coming on. I couldn't wait for the next high tide. Anyway, it wouldn't have been high enough to come to the dinghy. I crawled around and found some driftwood for skids, and managed to work the boat down across the beach. And

51

all the time I was doing it I was thinking how lucky it was that the dinghy was so little and light. I never in all the world could have gotten our skiff into the water. The dinghy was troublesome enough, and I was so glad when I could get into it and row the short way to the boat.

I pumped the bilge—108 strokes. Not all at once, and not all last night. That's right much water, but then it hasn't been pumped for more than a month. The water was up to the floor boards, but not above them, so I guess 108 strokes wasn't too much water after all.

I just had a good meal of eggs and potatoes.

I opened the engine valves to take the compression off and I turned the engine over. I'll turn it many more times and keep a good fire and get the boat well dried out and the engine warm. I will do everything right and proper, then I'll start the engine and go home by myself.

I never did start the engine. In all my life I never started any engine, not even the outboard motor. I have watched Don start it and I have watched Lloyd, too. I heard Don tell Lloyd all the things to do, and why. I know how to start it all right.

This is a big engine—twenty horsepower, heavy-duty. It's name is "Enterprise." It is very dependable. Don said if properly taken care of, it would always get us to where we were going.

It is very hard to start. It always has been, and I may have to try several times before I get it going. I know ahead of time that it will be difficult, so I'll expect nothing else. I will keep on trying, and not ask the Lord to make it easy to start, although, of course, I would be most thankful if it did start easily for just this one time.

I do ask the Lord to give me the strength to keep turning over that big flywheel again and again, until the engine makes up its mind to turn the heavy thing itself. Once I get it going, I need never let it stop until I get home. I won't practice starting it. I'll start it and go. While I wait for the dampness to dry out and all that engine iron to get a little bit warm, I'll do other things.

My leg still aches, and it's swollen up like a stuffed pup. I cannot put my weight on it, but I don't have to do much walking any more, or even stand on it. I'll sit on the stool to steer and prop my leg on the bunk. I'll wrap it up and keep it warm. It is so good to be going home. How thankful I am for this boat and for the charts to show me the way.

First off, I am going to make a cast for my arm. Don always kept a tightly covered can of cement on board, said we might hit a rock some time and knock a hole in the hull. Cement would make a good quick patch. I'll make a cast out of Don's patching cement.

I have no sand to mix with the cement, and it is too much trouble to go ashore for some. There isn't much sand here anyway. This beach is made of rocks and gravel. But I have figured out how to use something else. I have six samples made up, and I will use the one which turns out to be the best. In two samples I have flour; cornmeal in two; and oatmeal in the other two. I have twice as much cement in one lot as I have in the other, and I measured carefully with a teaspoon and marked down the proportions.

I will make a good cast to protect my arm from a bump. That bump I got on my sore leg coming down the hill bothers me a lot. I know a bump on my arm would be much worse, because the arm was broken, while the leg was only bruised—or maybe just cracked a little. I can't have my arm broken again.

The cement cast is on now, and I am just sitting here waiting for the concrete to harden. I used the cornmeal mixture; the flour didn't get hard and the oatmeal was crumbly. The cornmeal was just right. The wetness came through the sample sack and made the skin smart. It frightened me for a little while. Thinking cement is somewhat like lye and might take the skin off, I put the cast aside and washed my arm well. I looked about for something to put between the skin and the cast, something which water would not easily go through. Don's marine charts seemed suitable, so I tore a piece the proper size from the corner of one of his charts. Don wouldn't like to have his charts torn, but then he wanted me to have anything in this whole wide world. He wouldn't mind now; he'd be glad.

To make my cast, I put the cement mixture in a sample sack, put the bottom splint on the table, laid my arm on it with a piece of towel on my arm, next put the chart paper over the towel, then the sample sack with the wet cement in it. I hurried, because I thought the concrete might set before I was ready for it, but I think now I needn't have rushed. I worked the cement in place, shaped it well around my arm, and smoothed out the wrinkles. Now I must be still and wait for the cast to get hard. While I'm waiting, I can rest and do my writing.

I am glad I like to write, for I do think writing is good for me now, when I have no one to talk with. It seems to help me think straight. Sometimes I still get confused and doubt if my mind is clear. It always has been, but then I have never before been under such a strain, nor seriously hurt, nor really sick.

My worst trouble is in knowing a thing and being stubbornly determined to believe something different. When I came in sight of the beach cabin, I knew Sam had been there, but I would not allow myself to believe it. I hurried on toward it, crawling along on hands and knees, but I wouldn't look at the cabin again. All I told myself was that my leg hurt awful bad.

Well, Sam has been at the beach cabin and he has gone away. He didn't find us, and now they will say we were lost in the storm. They'll go down to the open ocean and cruise along the shore looking for wreckage from our boat. They might find Don!

They'll find Don's skiff. I know they'll find it. It has to be there somewhere. It couldn't sink. It wouldn't have drifted out to sea because the storm was an onshore wind—every single windfall points inland. I know they'll find the skiff, then they'll look around and see the smoke from Don's fire. Don had matches —in his safety matchbox—not very many. He could get a fire from a gun shell—I think he had shells in his pocket—left from hunting the day before. He had gasoline for the Elto. He could short the battery and get fire. Don will have fire.

Maybe I'll meet them coming with him. Meet them halfway down the Arm. Oh, glorious! Don will hop aboard and we'll go home together.

Poor Sam. I am sorry for him. He will feel so badly. He will be all broken up, for he loved Don. He'll get awful drunk. I have my baby and Lloyd to think of, but Sam has no one. I must tell him all that has happened, and try to be of some comfort to him. I will call him "Uncle" and tell him he is like Don's brother to me, which he truly is. Don never had a brother, but if he had had one he couldn't have thought more of him than he did of Sam.

Sam may hang around the islands all winter. There are more than a thousand islands, islets, and reefs down by the open ocean. It is a nice place to go beachcombing in good weather. There is wreckage from all over. We find glass balls from Japanese fish nets, bamboo, too, and hardwood from the tropics.

Don is sure to be stranded on one of the islands. If he had been on the mainland, he would have walked here before this time. Maybe Sam has already found him and taken him to a hospital, because he must have been badly hurt.

Perhaps I should go to Big Sleeve and tell them there to go help search for Don. No, I could never manage to get through Devil's Tail Pass. I could if I got slack tide—at least I might, but I know full well I could never make it when the rapids were running, which is almost all the time. They run one way when the tide is coming in and the other way when the tide is going out. Several boats have wrecked there. Don never liked that pass, and he always waited for slack tide. Devil's Tail Pass is like a spillway through which several hundred square miles of tide-water go in or out four times every day. There are huge swirling eddies in it, and a sharp turn about halfway through. If you don't swing the wheel hard over quick, you will pile up on the rocks, and if you swing too quickly you will pile up on some other rocks.

I won't try to make Big Sleeve. I had better keep going toward home. There are no very narrow passes between here and home, and I suspect I need plenty of room for my kind of navigation.

11

It took the cast a long time to set. I didn't want to risk breaking it or getting it out of shape. I hardly moved after I fixed it; I got pretty tired of just sitting in Don's bunk, my leg cushioned with pillows and covered with blankets. It kept warm, but it ached.

The fire went down, and I couldn't reach either the stove or the fuel, but I did manage to reach the waste concrete. It was set and pretty hard. A firm pinch didn't dent it, so very gingerly I crawled out of the cast and left it to finish drying without my arm in it.

I saw two deer out on the beach, a doe and a fawn. Such pretty creatures. I like to watch the deer, and I hope these come back again so that I can see more of them.

I called a doe and her fawn to me once. We were out on a prospecting trip, high up in the hills. It was a lovely summer day. The men and Lloyd had found a ledge in a gulch to scratch at, and I wandered away, knowing Don would call when they were ready to go on. I found a nice little hump to be lazy on, and I stretched out to sun myself. Soon, a doe and her baby came up the hill to see me. I called and called to them in a singsong voice:

"Oh, you pretty things, come here, come, come, come here. Oh, you little dearie, dearie, dearie deer. Come on up here. Come, come, come to me. I won't hurt you. I wouldn't hurt you for all the world. Oh, you pretty little dearie deer," and much more of the same.

56

They kept right on coming. I sat perfectly still, just kept calling to them; and they came on, slowly, a few steps at a time, the mother perking her ears and sniffing, the fawn a step away, at her side and not alarmed about anything. The doe was sleek and plump and round. The fawn still had his spots. He was woolly and furry, too small for his skin, so very cunning. His little head was short and dark and round, and his legs were long and skinny. I liked them so much and I wanted to keep them near me, but I just couldn't go on forever singing singsongy.

When I stopped for want of breath, the doe looked troubled, nudged the fawn with her nose, and put up her tail. Quickly, she turned about and trotted away into the brush, out of sight.

I have lots of good memories, memories of places and things, of animals and of people. I think I like most to remember the stories I have been told of my ancestors. I like to think of their spunk and determination, of their failures and their successes. Since I have been prospecting with Don, I have often thought of my people and their struggles in the early days when all America was mostly wilderness.

Many times I have admired the things a great-grandmother did, and I have sometimes hoped I might be a credit to her. It looks now as if I may have the chance. That little woman had hard times, too, just as I am having—maybe worse. Her name was Martha, like mine, and I was named for her. She was a daughter of the South, and wasn't raised to do a tap of work. Her home was a big plantation with dozens of slaves, not far from Richmond, Virginia. Slaves waited on her hand and foot. She didn't learn how to comb her own hair until after she was married and had left her father's house. Martha certainly lived a life of ease and luxury until a young Irishman came along and carried her away to a wilderness home.

My Irish great-grandfather was new in America. He was fresh out of Trinity College, Dublin, and he was looking for a job. He wasn't exactly a beggar, for he brought with him three dozen ruffled shirts of fine Irish linen, all handmade with the tiniest little stitches. Mother has one of them. It's yellow with age, yet still treasured.

Well, Martha's father hired the young Irishman to teach his children. Martha was sixteen and the oldest girl; she had three older brothers.

Now, this young Irishman had quarreled with his father before he left Ireland. In fact, he had left home because his father had told him to get out and never darken his door again. They had quarreled over religion. The young man had changed his religion while away at school and came home dedicated to converting his brothers and sisters. The old father was in a mighty wrath when he realized the success his educated son was having. He drove all the converts from his house. Five of his nine children all left at once, left forever and for America. Three of them died on the way and were buried in the Atlantic Ocean.

A brother stayed in New York, but this young radical went south and got himself a job teaching school. He hadn't changed one bit. He didn't believe in slavery and he didn't keep his opinions to himself. He taught Martha slavery was wrong and, because Martha was in love with him, she believed what he said.

Her father seems not to have paid much attention to what sort of things this Irishman was teaching, and it went on for nearly a year before he learned about it. Suddenly the teacher was without a job. Martha wept and wept and refused to be comforted. Some of the folks began to whisper that "Old John" was too hard on the young people.

John Kritridge was a proud man and would not have such things said about him. He sent for the Irish schoolteacher and asked him if his intentions were honorable. When he received an affirmative answer, he asked his daughter if she wanted to marry the scalawag. She answered that in all the world she wanted nothing more. So they were married, but the father wasn't through yet. Neither were the young folks.

John Kritridge believed that the only people who were against slavery were those who had no slaves. He meant to prove his point by giving the young folks slaves as a wedding gift. So that it wouldn't be too obvious, he offered his daughter a choice between several slaves worth a great deal and a much smaller amount of gold money. He received a surprise when Martha answered:

"I'll take the gold, thank you, Father. Thomas and I are going to Indiana Territory."

She got the money, all right, and saddle horses, and as much finery as could be carried on pack horses. She rode away without her father's blessing—rode away to the west.

First, they stopped at Washington, where my great-grandfather traded a part of Martha's gold money for government land at $1.25 an acre and got a sheepskin deed to it.

They kept riding west until they came to what is now the central part of southern Indiana. They made a home in the wilderness, and Martha learned to work. She had to learn, for she had no slaves to help her. Nine years they lived there before a child, my grandfather, was born to them. From the stories that have come down to me, all those years were radiant with happiness.

When my grandfather was six weeks old, his father died—died of some kind of fever. With her own hands Martha buried her husband. She covered his grave with rocks so that wild animals might not desecrate it. The land is still in the family; a second cousin lives there today. The grave is still marked by a pile of rocks, often added to. I have seen it and have added my share of rocks to the monument of my Irish great-grandfather.

Martha took her infant in her arms and rode back to her father's house. That spunky little woman traveled all alone through wilderness and sparsely settled country, through dark forests where hostile Indians still roamed. She rode more than seven hundred miles, and much of the way was little better than a blazed trail.

May the courage and strength of that lone woman reach down through the years to me. May the spirit of my great-grandmother descend on me in my aloneness, in my time of trial and distress. God grant that I may be worthy of my heritage.

12

ANOTHER DAY ON THE BOAT. THE WEATHER IS COLDER, BUT STILL the rain continues. There is snow up near the timber line. I can see it creeping down the mountainside. I hope I do not have to travel through snow. To steer a boat, one must see well, and it could be most awkward if thick snow were falling when I was trying to negotiate some bad spot. I will watch the compass and write down the bearings, which may be of some help. I pray this rain will stay rain, not turn to snow just yet, not for a few days.

I have eaten generously, mostly onions. I ate them raw like apples, and they were good. I have done my chores and tended my injuries.

The cast is drying nicely, but more slowly than I expected. It fits snugly and comfortably. I am so glad I made it. Now I have protection for my arm. The cast is not bulky, and I can slip it on and off easily.

I have oiled the engine and drained the gas trap, polished up the ignition points, and gone over every part just as I have seen Don do. I have turned the flywheel dozens of times, and it turns easily enough with the compression off. I haven't tried to turn it against compression yet. Time enough to do that when I'm set to leave.

Thirty-one hours is a long watch. I will be very tired and sleepy by the end of that time. I am resting all I can today, trying to "sleep up ahead," as the fishermen say. I will have no time to cook, either, while I'm running the boat, so I am also cooking things ahead.

I have cleared up the decks, made everything fast and ready to go into open ocean. Don always pulls the dinghy on board, but I can't do that, so I will have to drag it behind. I have made it fast with a long line, then pulled the line in short to keep the slack from getting into the propeller. I tied the line with a loop to the rigging right beside the pilothouse door. One handy pull, after I get well under way, the loop will come undone and the dinghy will swing far out behind where it belongs.

The weather seems to be clearing and it is getting colder, but not down to freezing. It looks as though I will have good weather. If all goes well, I'll be on my way soon after daylight tomorrow.

Right now I shall try to store up a little more sleep.

This is tomorrow, gray dawn of tomorrow. The weather is holding. The barometer is rising and the sky is clearing. There is a faint offshore breeze, fine weather for traveling this coast. The tide is going out; it is about half-tide now. I hope and pray I may go out with the last of the tide, get well down toward the ocean before the tide turns. Then I will be far enough along to get back inside, get into the straits on high slack tide, and if the Lord blesses me with a good voyage I will come around into Innian Pass at low slack tide, or very soon thereafter, before it is too dark.

From Innian Pass on I will have lights to guide me, and I'll need them, for it may be pitch-dark by the time I get there. Once through the pass I will have plenty of room to navigate in, for Icy Strait is wide and I need not bother thinking about icebergs at this time of the year.

I have my charts at hand and Don's log book with his running time from point to point all marked down for every trip he has ever taken in this boat. The compass bearings are also written down. I am thrice blessed with the chart and compass and log to guide me on my way. My blessings will be fourfold once the engine starts.

The old moon is about half over to the westward. Strange,

how the moon and tides cooperate; the tide comes in until the moon is in the south, then the tide goes out until the moon is in the west, then again comes in until the moon is in the south on the other side of the world, goes out until the moon is east, then starts over again.

It is getting lighter. I'll start the engine now, and by the time it has warmed up for half an hour I will be able to see clearly enough to get out of this little bight. I have checked and re-checked the engine. I know I have done all the things that needed to be done, and I believe there is nothing left undone. I have the can of priming gas setting in a pot of hot water.

No luck with the engine. It didn't start. That engine pulls hard against compression. I bandaged my leg and put a splint on it, and I tried again and again, and still it didn't start. Without two legs to stand on, I couldn't brace myself to yank hard enough, and the compression slipped out because I came over too slowly with the flywheel.

Again I tried, but the engine wouldn't start. I brought the stool to brace my knee against so that I could yank hard enough to flip the flywheel over against compression, but no luck. I am so tired. I must rest a bit longer.

I plan to untie the shore line and just drop it over the side. That will be the last thing I do after I get the anchor up. I won't need that rope, but I must take the anchor, for I might need it. It isn't very big. Don said it wasn't big enough and that we'd have to get a bigger one. I'm glad he didn't get a bigger one.

Finally the engine made a poof. I am trembling and have to rest again. I'm feeling confident it will surely start next time.

Not even a poof on the seventh try, so I set the pot of water on the stove, with the can of priming gas in it. I took off the compression and turned the flywheel to blow out the excess gas. Then I primed it with gas that was plenty hot.

It started! "*Ca-poof, ca-poof!*" it says to me.

Oh, I am glad. "*Ca-poof, ca-poof,*" my engine keeps on saying.

It didn't take so long, really, not even an hour, but it seemed like it was taking a year. The clutch works, both forward and reverse. I tried it easy, just enough to be sure. And the engine speeds up and slows down exactly as it should, and as it always has done. I slowed it down and it's idling now. I know I have to go out of this bight slowly, with just enough speed for steerage way.

It's still early—plenty early. The tide will be going out for more than an hour yet, and the old moon hasn't gone home either; he's still looking at me.

I am so eager to be going, going fast, but I'll wait until the engine has had plenty of time to warm up. Then I'll hoist the anchor, untie the shore line and drop it over the side, shove in the clutch and be on my way.

The anchor is a bother to me. I do wish I dared leave it, but I dare not. I might need it badly. Besides, whoever heard of a boat without an anchor? I know that I must take it with me, and I can pull it all right, too. I practiced yesterday, and I did lift it off the bottom with my one hand, pulled it up quite a long ways. I could have gotten it all the way up if I had wanted to.

"*Ca-poof, ca-poof*"—I do like the sound of my engine. I'll keep it going until I get home, or until all the gas is used up. There are two gas tanks, and they each hold 125 gallons of gas. They are nearly full.

Soon I'll be going home.

13

AGAIN MY HOPE IS GONE. I WILL HAVE TO STAY HERE. I CAN'T GO home now. I can't tell anyone to go find Don, either. My child will be born here, and I'll be all alone with no one to help me. It is too hard to bear, too hard.

That anchor was too much for me. I had it up and my hand on the cross rod, then I slipped, and both the anchor and I went into the bay. The anchor chain goes off the boat through the chock way up at the very bow of the boat. No guard rail is there, only a two-by-four strip. I had my back to the bow, pulled with my left hand, brought the chain tight across the strip, and held it there until my hurt hand pulled away the slack. Then I put my knee on the chain and made another pull. It was a good system, and it would have worked if my knee hadn't slipped and if I hadn't been so tired out from starting the engine.

When I had the anchor up far enough to take hold of the cross rod, I fell overboard. My knee was hurting from pressing on the chain, and I think I must have shifted it a bit. Anyway, my knee slipped, the anchor went down fast, and I went with it. Why I didn't let go of the cross rod is more than I will ever understand. The anchor was on the island side of the boat, and if I had floundered ashore on the island I would have been stranded there and the eagles and ravens would have picked my bones.

Well, I stayed with the anchor, but I didn't stay with it to the bottom—at least I don't remember any bottom. I went under the boat, came up on the other side, and saw land. I didn't see the

64

boat until after I had reached the shore. I didn't think what I was doing. Instinctively, I swam toward land.

I didn't have my coat or my shoepacks on; we don't wear shoepacks on the boat because they are too hot. We wear slippers, and I had on mine. They came off in the water and are lost. I had a hat on because I always cover my sore head outdoors.

Back East I used to swim a lot every summer, and I swim fairly well, but I have never tried to swim in Alaskan waters. Nobody can stand this cold water for very long. I was so cold I could hardly move, and the boat wasn't over a hundred feet from shore. I'm glad the tide was out. High tide would have made my swim nearly twice as far. I think I would never have made it. I was not afraid while I was in the water, but on the beach I was terrified. Maybe terror kept me from flopping on the beach and just staying there until I was too cold and stiff to ever move again.

Now I am back in the beach cabin. I am warm and partly rested. My clothes are dry and I have them on again.

It is the custom in this country always to leave shavings and matches and a little food in all the cabins. I didn't make more shavings when I left to go aboard the boat because Sam had made enough to last a month. I'm sure he and his friend sat here and smoked and whittled. I am most thankful for all the shavings they left, thankful, too, for the shelter and warmth of this beach cabin. I know it saved my life today. Not today—yesterday. It was cold last night and there was ice. I couldn't have lived through the night without shelter and fire. I would have died from exposure, and my baby would have died within me. I am distressed about the child. While I was in the icy water I felt her move strong and jerky. She moved again when I was on the beach, but she hasn't moved since. I hope she is only resting as I have been.

The boat engine is still running. It ran all night, and it will keep on until all the gas is burned up. The valve isn't half open, and the engine is going slowly, just idling. I doubt that it will burn more than one gallon an hour. When it is wide open it only burns two gallons an hour. My engine will run for maybe two hundred hours. That is over eight days, more than a week.

All the time I can hear it go *"Ca-poof, ca-poof, ca-poof."*

I stayed beside the fire all the rest of yesterday and drank lots of good hot sweet tea. I kept poking wood into the stove to get my clothes dry. Warm dry woolen underwear is most wonderful. There are no proper clothes here—an old overall jacket and a dirty pair of pants. I put them on when I got out of my wet clothes. The crawl over the rocky beach to the cabin was an ordeal, and I got so tired. I was afraid to stop and rest too often, or for nearly long enough, afraid to stop moving, afraid I might become too cold to move. It was a grand feeling to get inside the cabin. I was grateful for the strength to make a fire. No earthly perfume could smell sweeter than the first whiff of that cedar smoke.

This bunk is not much good. The boughs are old and the needles are dropping off. There's no bedding here, not one old sugan, but there's a lot of canvas. Before we built the cabin, we had two tents here. When we no longer needed them, we tore them up for canvas tarps to cover cargo. Canvas in lieu of blankets is no good at all. It's as cold as sheetiron. Gunny sacks are much better. I have three gunnies.

My hurts are none the worse for my ducking. My arm is fine, and the cast stayed in place. To protect my leg while I was trying to start the engine, I made a quick bandage from a dish towel with two files and four case knives for splints. I bound them pretty tight, too tight, and they hurt. As soon as the engine was going, I took the bandage off, and that was a blessing. The extra weight might have added to my troubles. I think my leg is better. I keep it in the oven much of the time, and the warmness is good.

I will have to go back to the upper cabin. I dread the climb up that hill. Give me strength, O God, to make the climb.

14

A GREAT FLOCK OF SWANS WENT OVER THIS MORNING, WINGING their way to the land of summertime and song. This is very late for them to be going south, but then the weather has been mild; only a few freezing nights, not really cold at all.

I am getting ready to go back up the hill. I think I shall go tomorrow. I'll see how I feel when tomorrow comes. Right now I feel pretty good, and that after a lot of exercise and work.

I made myself a crutch out of the broom. It was an old broom and not much good, but it made a fine crutch. I had to burn the handle off a little to get it short enough. It is quite a good crutch. I am surprised to find it such a help in getting about.

This morning I went over to the garden and harvested that part of the crop which we left in the field—a lot of small carrots, some soft cabbages, and maybe half a bushel of marble-sized potatoes. Some were a little bigger; some were as big as my fist. My treasures nearly filled a gunny sack, and I was pleased to drag home so much food. I had thought to take a part of it with me to the upper cabin, but now I think I'll do well if I get myself there. So I am eating my garden truck as fast as I can. It's a pleasant addition to a diet of cereal, prunes, and tea.

Eleven geese came into this cove. They are on the beach now, up at the high-tide line, working away at pulling grass roots. The watchman, standing tall, making his neck long, is on guard for possible danger. Geese are wise birds, but they can be fooled.

Once Lloyd and I fooled a smart old gander. It was funny to

see his confusion. We were prospecting in Marion Bay; the men had found a little ledge to dig on, and Lloyd and I puttered around, sometimes at camp chores, sometimes with the men, but more often exploring along the beach and through the lower timber. That day we were walking along a deer trail, back a couple of hundred yards from the beach. We came to a little draw with a steep hill beyond it, and since we didn't want to climb the hill we went down the draw. A pair of wild geese were nesting in the draw, but we didn't know about it until we came right up to the goose on her nest.

She lit out of there shouting to high heaven. The old gander was out front watching the beach. He hadn't expected any disturbance from the woods, and was no end surprised. He made an awful racket and looked everywhere for something to fight. He saw a poor little deer, much too far away to have been able to do any harm to the nesting goose, but since there was nothing else he could see to fight he flew at the deer and beat it with his wings. He beat it and thumped it, scolded it and cussed it. The startled deer tried to get away from his tormentor, but the gander stayed with him until the deer got into the woods. Then the gander came back to the goose and they held a noisy conversation. No doubt he told her what a brave gander he was. We backtracked out of there when they came toward the nest.

It is still fine weather. Scum ice formed during the night, but the morning breeze soon took it away. Horny peaks are glorious in the rays of the low sun—flame and gold, purple and pink— vibrant brilliancy shining through from heaven. Nothing is so lovely as my snowy mountain peaks. No matter how unhappy my condition here may become, I will still have the full beauty of sunsets. The hills shut off the sunrise. I see only the lights on the summits.

The baby has moved again, and I know all is well with her. Poor little one, she has had a bad time and I have often been afraid for her. Babies must be less delicate than most folks say they are. According to all my information, I've had enough bumps and straining to lose this child a dozen times over; still, she lives and seems well.

It will be a hard trip tomorrow, and I must make most of it on my knees, which still show the marks of my crawl back from the fall in the bay. The hill trail is largely muck and moss, and it will not be so painful as the rocks of the beach. Another day or so more for healing and storing up extra energy might be a good idea, yet I hate to waste this good weather. Snow would make my way too impossible. Somehow I feel assured there will be no snow until I am safe in the upper cabin.

With a hot wire I have burned a hole in the handle of the prospecting pick and put a string through it. I will tie the pick to me, for my life may depend on it. I cannot take the chance of dropping it and have it go tumbling two or three hundred feet down the hill.

I have made a very satisfactory splint for my leg out of yellow cedar twigs. First, I bound the hurt with a canvas strip, loosely, then poked thirty-one small straight twigs down between the folds of canvas. I used frazzlings to weave in and out, over and under the ends of the twigs in basket-weave style to hold them in place. The twigs are pliable, yet they do give support and some protection. My leg troubles me. It was badly bruised by the canyon fall, then hurt again in the very same place on my way down the hill. I dare not have anything else happen to it.

My broom crutch is a splendid help. It is especially good on the beach when the tide is out, and I can get over the hard gravel real fast. But it isn't much good in soft muck; it sinks in too far; still, it helps even there. I couldn't get around without it, not unless I crawled or hopped.

I have no shoes, and that is my big problem at present. These old shoepack bottoms aren't much good. They leak, but that isn't the whole trouble: they don't stay on, and so far I have found no way to keep them on. By shuffling along and never lifting my foot, I do well enough; but I am forever forgetting, and there is my slipper shoepack left behind.

I found five empty bottles, and I sent them forth on high tide with a call for help. I went nearly to the point and threw them into the water soon after the tide had turned. I waited a few minutes between tosses so they wouldn't all be in a bunch. I wish I had thought of sending bottles out sooner. I wish I had found the bottles sooner, I mean. They gave me the idea. I had no corks for them, so I made stoppers with little sticks and strips of canvas. A few pebbles went into each bottle to hold it upright and keep water from seeping in and sinking them. I made the message brief, stuck one into each bottle, and forced the stoppers in tight. One bottle landed upside down and stayed that way; all the others were upright with the white stopper flags sticking out of the water. Anyone who sees them will wonder how come and investigate.

Maybe one bottle will float to Don. Oh, I wish one would! It would make him so happy to have a note from me.

It gave me a happy feeling to see my squadron sailing forth all in line—four battleships and one gunboat—very like the queen's navy. No queen ever pinned more hope on her navy than I do on my bottles.

I pulled up the puncheon and buried my potatoes and carrots under the floor. They are such scrawny things, yet they are food and there is no sense in leaving them to freeze. Besides, I thought maybe Don might come and be so hungry. I wrote a note telling him where they are buried and put it on the wall right above them.

The engine has stopped! I can't hear it any more. It shouldn't stop yet, but it has. All is silent. Why did the engine stop so soon? There was enough gas to keep it going much longer—at least a week. No matter. It can't make any difference to me now; there is no possible way for me to get back on the boat unless I swim, and I've had enough of swimming; yet I do wonder about it.

The geese are still here, and if I had a gun I could eat roast goose to celebrate the launching of my navy. My Krag is on the boat, and so is the twenty-two. They might as well be in China for all the good they are to me now. Anyway, it's a lot of trouble to get all the feathers off a goose, and besides they are often fishy. Sometimes they're so old and tough that after being cooked for two days you can't stick a fork in the gravy.

Well, I've finally fixed my slippers so they will stay on. I burned holes in the rubber, put strips of canvas through them, and bound them on my feet like ballet slippers. I think they'll do.

Tomorrow I'll go up the hill.

15

I AM HERE! SAFE. GOOD, GOOD FRIENDLY CABIN.

Two Steller's jays welcomed me back with a flit and a hop and an extraordinary lot of chatter, half scolding me for deserting them, half telling me they were glad to see me and to hurry up and give them some scraps. Jays make such a discordant noise. They are sneaky, too, and mean to other birds. I never used to like jays, but I do like these. They seem so friendly.

I have been here two days, and it took me two days to get here, so this is the fourth day since I left the beach. And it's a good thing I didn't fool around at the beach any longer, because it started to snow before I got here and has been snowing ever since—light, mist-like snow at first, but heavy snow today.

I have eaten lots, bathed and changed my clothing. I am still tired, but not with a heavy tiredness. I don't have that exhausted feeling any more: it's just nice lazy tiredness.

I left the beach early in the morning and I felt fine. The snowy peaks were aflame with the rising sun, but the sky flaunted mares' tails, threatening a change in weather. There was no scum ice and the breeze was southerly, but it was still good weather.

I ate, packed myself a lunch, and put the can over the smokestack. The prospecting pick was tied to my belt and my crutch was at hand.

The way up was pretty bad. Still, I might have made it in one day if it hadn't been for the mallard. Being a good Samaritan to a mallard in distress used up considerable energy.

71

Soon after I left the beach cabin, and just before I got to the point where the trail turns into the woods, a bunch of mallards flew up from where they had been feeding down at the mouth of the canyon creek. I stopped for a minute to watch them fly and to listen to the "*quack-quack*" which mallards always make as they take off. I was just starting to go on when I heard more quacking. I saw a lone mallard, on the beach, trying to fly and making an awful fuss about it. Wanting to learn what all the commotion was about, I hobbled over to him. A big cockle clam was fast to his foot.

It was a beautiful drake with a pretty green neck, orange-colored feet, and a little curl in his tail. I couldn't leave him to such a miserable fate, but perhaps I might have if I had known what an effort it would be to rescue him. Mr. Drake had no more liking for me than he had for the cockle clam. He couldn't fly and he didn't go near the water, so I suppose he knew he couldn't swim either. He certainly managed to keep out of my reach, though, and kept on escaping me until I was disgusted with him. He flopped back and forth across the creek until both my legs were wet to the knees. He'd be still until I reached out to get him, then "*quack-quack*" and flop-flop, and he'd be ten feet away. But I did catch him and, once I had him in my hands, he didn't seem to have such strong objections to me. He hardly struggled at all, but he eyed me sideways with a suspicious gleam which served notice that I had best keep a tight hold on him.

The cockle was a big one and was closed tight over the middle toe, up past the first joint and over the next toe to a little past the toenail joint—claw, I suppose it would be called on a duck. I couldn't get the clam open. I just couldn't hold the duck and, at the same time, hit the clam with the prospecting pick hard enough to break the shell. I sat on the beach and rested, holding the duck between my thighs while I thought up what to do.

The bone of the middle toe was already broken, and the web on either side of it was bleeding. I decided to break the bone in the next toe, put my knee on the cockle clam, pull hard, and hope the web would cut off clean. It took a bit of maneuvering to get myself, the drake, and the cockle in place for the operation.

The drake did some complaining all right. I told him to stop his quacking and hold still; that he would drown when the tide came in (if an eagle didn't eat him first); that I would eat him if I had time to get his feathers off; told him he wasn't the only thing in the world with hurts, I had a few myself.

After a try or two, I got my right hand and arm around his body, my left hand on his foot and leg, and my left knee firmly on the cockle. I gave a good quick yank. The duck foot came away clean, not bleeding much, no ragged edge. I'm sure it will heal, and the drake will hardly miss the little bit of two toes the clam will have for breakfast. Before I let him go I pulled out one of his green neck feathers to pay me for all the bother he had been. Then I thought about Don. I told the drake to fly down to the islands, find a poor hungry man there, light nearby, and get himself caught by another clam.

"*Quack-quack*," he said as he flew away, and he did go down the Arm, which is toward the islands.

The mallard looked so happy flying away that it made my heart glad. I didn't grudge either the time or the energy it took to save his life. I am pleased even now to know that somewhere he is with his fellows, living a nice quacking life.

My progress, even across the flat, was painfully slow. Parts of the hill trail were glaciered over from water which continually oozes out of the ground and freezes with the first cold snap. I picked the ice in some places to make it rough: went around it in other places. I rested often and tried to conserve my strength, but I gradually got tireder and tireder, until at the steepest place (the Golden Stairs, Lloyd named it) I gave out altogether. I tried and tried—hands and knees, worm crawling—to find a way around on one side, then on the other side. It was no use, and I simply had to give up, but not until day was done.

In the twilight I crawled to the foot of a fair-sized spruce tree, scratched around it, gathered the moss and debris, and made myself a nest in a good spot with a big root on the lower side. The root gave me assurance that I would not roll back down the hill if I went to sleep. With the prospecting pick I raked more moss and needles. When I had a goodly lot, I spread my canvas, sat on it, and wrapped my game leg well with the gunny sack. I snugged much of the litter close to me, drew the canvas up over and around it, and settled into my nest.

Dark came down, and all the forest was pitch-black. Through the spruce boughs I watched the stars of night slowly saunter into eternity. The Three Wise Men marched across the sky, dim and misty as they faded away. They can be seen from practically every part of the earth. An old sea captain told me that, and he should know because he has been many times around the world. Behind the stars trailed a pale and sickly old moon, and he brought mist with him, which later thickened into clouds and oozed a drizzle soon after daylight.

I dozed a bit, maybe slept a little. I thought about lots of things. I recited poetry to myself, out loud, and said some of the nicest psalms. Sometimes I sang. Often I was cold, and I wiggled about to get warm.

An old bear came and sniffed me. He really did. It was in the first gray of dawn. I had dozed, and the sound of him coming roused me. I kept perfectly still, hardly breathing, and strained my ears and eyes to learn what and where the sound was. Then I smelled him and knew for certain it was a bear. All the primitive instincts of fear within me were aroused. My heart pounded in my throat, and I could feel my flesh creep. I drew myself up and made myself little and tight. I kept still as death.

The bear walked completely around my tree, not close, but a little bit away. Then he came straight at me, and there he was— a great big black thing right by my side. I covered my child with my hands and waited breathlessly for what he would do next. He stood there for what seemed a long, long time, but it probably was no more than a few seconds, then he sniffed loud, and growled low in his throat. He raised his hair like a dog does, and he grew bigger and bigger right there before my eyes. He made another growl, lower this time, went backward two or three steps, then turned and departed with great dignity.

I was exhausted, weak, limp as an old sock, and without enough awareness to feel glad or thankful, or afraid, or anything else. My mind was blank. I relaxed. My nest was good, and I was content to stay in it. I lay curled up there until long after full daylight.

By and by I got aches in my bones and stiffness in my joints. I sat up and rubbed my hurts, then got up and tried to move about. I went around my tree just as the old bear had done. My nose remembered the most—that bear stunk! His breath was foul, rank, filthy.

I ate some of my lunch, dawdled over eating. My body felt light and somewhat indefinite. My movements were slow, but I didn't care. I had no ambition. I didn't seem to think I had to hurry. There was a ringing in my ears, at first like faraway bees, which seemed to keep time with my heartbeats. I started humming, and it all made most pleasing music.

I just fooled around until it began to drizzle, then I gathered up the canvas and the gunny sack and started to climb the Golden Stairs.

I made it up those Golden Stairs, made it on the first try. As I climbed I wondered how I failed to find the holds and steps the day before. Perhaps I'd been too tired to see well. From there on to the cabin I had no serious trouble, but I did have to rest often. Every time I rested, I wrapped the canvas around me Indian fashion, to keep some of my warmth in and keep out some of the cold drizzle which turned to snow before I got to the cabin.

16

SOME TIME DURING THE NIGHT THE SNOW TURNED TO RAIN, AND it's still raining. My tub overflows. I needed the water and I'll make good use of it.

I have made a new crutch. It's a dandy, much better than the old broom, and very helpful to me. I made it from the board side of Lloyd's bunk. He found a one-by-six piece of fir floating in the bay, fished it out, and brought it home. Don told him he had done well and as a reward he might use it for himself. So, he made his bunk more comfortable with part of it. I don't know what he did with the rest. It was quite long—eighteen or twenty feet, and all nicely planed.

Carefully, I burned one end in the center and scraped away the char to make it slightly concave and a right fit for under my arm. Then I burned off the other end to the right length. I made notches at the level of my hand, to hold the leather shoelace which I bound on there and tied tight with a reefer. Then I took the wooden handle off the saw file, heated the sharp end of the file red hot, and with it burned holes in both ends of the handle. I brought the ends of the leather lace through the holes in the file handle and tied them back, making a fine hand hold. I padded it under the arm, and now I have a dandy, comfortable crutch. I threw the old broom away on the Golden Stairs. Crutches are no help for very steep hill climbing.

Two deer visited me today—a big four-point buck and a little spike. The little feller was just tagging along, and the big one

76

didn't seem to make him very welcome. When the young one came close, I saw the big buck shake his head and stamp his hoof. When he stamped, he laid his ears back like a horse. If I had a gun, I certainly would be having deer liver for dinner tonight, and I'd have the finest sort of fresh meat most of the winter. But not from the big feller. Already he has lost weight, but the little feller is still in fine shape.

The deer stayed where I could see them from the window for about half an hour, then sauntered away. They're back now, but I am sure they will go down the hill before dark.

I think the weather is going to turn cold or be stormy. Deer are wonderful weather prophets. They always get down into the shelter of timber when blizzards come. I'm sure those bucks smell bad weather coming.

I will look to my outside chores and bring in lots more wood.

I think that old bear was going to his den for his long winter sleep, and goodness knows it was time for him to be denned up. It really is awful late for bears to be still out, but then the weather has been mild. Don says the male bear stays out as long as the weather is mild. One year Don killed two bears on the 26th of November. That was ten years ago. He killed them with the two prettiest shots he ever made in his life, so he says.

I forget where he was or where he was going, and why Sam wasn't with him. Anyway, he was alone except for a little dog some fisherman had wished on him; the dog got seasick and the man was going to kill it. It was a nice undersized Irish terrier. Don liked it, took it to save its life, and later brought it home to Lloyd. Its name was Micky. Well, this little dog was with Don and they were traveling a bear trail, facing into the wind. Don had a heavy pack on his back. The little dog trotted along a few steps ahead.

The trail curved around a rock projection, and the dog went out of sight for half a minute. Then he flew back to Don and got right between his legs. Don didn't wait to learn why the dog behaved so scared; he unlimbered his gun, barely had time to snap the safety off and raise, when a huge bear came tearing after the dog. Don blazed away and rammed another shell in the chamber, intending to give the bear a second shot. We always do, just on general principles. But before Don could pull the trigger, a second bear appeared, and Don let him have that shot. The second bear fell right on top of the first one. In both, the shot had gone through the throat and hit the backbone. Don stepped the distance off, and it was just nine paces to those bears.

Don had his camera along and took a picture of them, lying one on top of the other. I had an enlargement made and framed, and gave it to Lloyd one Christmas. Lloyd keeps it hanging beside his bed at home.

I don't like bears. In fact, none of us like bears, but we all respect them. We never hunt bears because we made a treaty with them. Of course, we don't expect the bear to understand about our treaty, yet some of them behave as if they did understand.

Bears are the road builders of the wilderness. Year after year, generation after generation, bears travel the same trails up and down the mountainsides and across the flats, their great paws making the way clear for man to travel. As a sort of toll for the use of their roads, we have given them our solemn promise we will never hunt them. That is our part of the treaty. The bears' part in the deal is that they must keep out of our way and never come within gunshot of us. We have emphatically told them that we will shoot to kill whenever and wherever one dares to come within range. We seldom go far from camp without a gun on our shoulder, with a bear shell in the chamber to back up our words. It is our policy to shoot first and ask later about honorable intentions. Don and Sam have helped to bring out two men who either trusted the bear or didn't shoot straight. What is left after a bear finishes mauling a man isn't a pretty sight.

All bears aren't bad. They need understanding, within limits, of course. Bears are as afraid of man as man is afraid of them— maybe more afraid. Usually, they will get out of the way quick enough, if given fair warning. Don told Lloyd and me always to talk loud and make a lot of noise through the woods, then we need never see a bear. That's quite true, for most of the time and most of the bears. But a hungry bear will not leave his food, a female will not leave her young, an old male will brook no disturbance to his love-making, and any bear, when surprised, startled, or cornered, will turn and defend his rights. Don said so, and he knows lots about bears. He has killed twenty-six and let dozens and dozens more go on living when he could have killed them.

He and Sam have both had arguments with bears, and some close calls, but I never had any trouble with them. They have all been very polite to me; even the old bear on the trail did not wish to disturb me. I do respect bears, and I think they are far more honorable than lions and tigers, yet I still don't like them.

I have washed my clothes and now everything is nice and clean. I also washed myself, soaked and scrubbed my head and got the scabs off. I looked at my scars in the shaving mirror. They are pinkish and itch, and they are not nearly so big as I thought they were going to be. I rubbed them well with kerosene-flavored bacon grease. Apparently the mice are not partial to kerosene smells, for they haven't bothered me since I first used it.

Those horrid mice gnawing on my head! All the rest of my life, I will have no mercy for a mouse. I'll kill every one that dares to give me a chance.

I washed my hair, too, that is, the hair I cut off. I made three small locks, tied them well in several places, washed them and rinsed them thoroughly. I will always keep them to remember what nice hair I once had. Of course, my hair will grow again, but it will take a long time for it to reach even to my shoulders.

Don admired my hair and called the curls "laughing hair." He said there was sunshine in it. There are gold glints in it, and I get them from my redheaded Irish grandfather. He was a doctor, and a very good one, but he would never take much credit for curing people. He always said, "Nature effects the cure; the doctor merely amuses the patient."

I would have enjoyed some amusing from a doctor these last couple of months, yet I do seem to be getting along well enough with Nature.

My child is doing well. Mostly she sleeps peacefully all through the day and takes her exercise at night, soon after I lie down. Sometimes she romps around considerably. I do believe she is a strong child, but certainly not very big.

I must eat more often. At mealtime I eat all I can hold, but my stomach seems unable to hold enough, as I am starved before the next meal. Habit can be ridiculous. Here I am, often hungry and with plenty of food on hand, yet I only eat three meals a day because I never had the habit of eating between meals when I am in the house. Out on a trip across the hills, we always carry raisins, or some such thing, in our pockets. We munch as we go along. From now on I am going to eat as often as a chicken does. I am determined to put some fat on my bones. My face looks haggard, and my arms are like long skinny match stems.

I am living here just like a minor queen in her castle, with everything so nice and handy. I have made myself a toilet on the porch, which is very comfortable and extremely satisfactory. I have a powder box to catch the waste. Our proper toilet is a ways off, as it should be, and an uncomfortable journey for me to make.

I went to the spring today and brought a little pot of water to drink. We have a dandy spring; the water comes out of a rock fissure. The spring is not far, the water tastes so much better than the rain I catch in the tub, and I do like to drink spring water. I brought only a little this time, and the trip wasn't a bit troublesome. The two jays followed me all the way, commenting extravagantly on the news and gossip of the country. I liked the open air exercise, the smell of the out-of-doors, and the surrounding view.

I probably won't go to the spring many times more, for the snow is now about a foot deep, and may soon be much deeper. Besides, with all the rain that's come it is not necessary for me to fetch water, and my sense of rightness says that I shouldn't use strength and energy for unneeded chores at this time. The Lord has sent great plenty of water down from the skies. I have all the pots and pans and every possible receptacle filled against future needs. When this storage supply is gone, there will be snow to melt. But this has been queer weather; snow that turns to rain, then rain that turns to snow, and one or the other continuously coming down.

There isn't very much material here to make suitable clothing for my child. I made a list of things needed for a baby, the absolute minimum requirement, and looked about for materials. I haven't started sewing yet, just checked up on what is here. There's plenty of fine thread and enough needles—my thimble, too, and lots of coarse patching thread, which I'll not need. The materials on hand are several flour and sugar sacks, some of which have been used for dishtowels and bread cloths, lots of both well worn and nearly new woolen underwear, two wool shirts, and several hickory shirts. How much I would like to have nainsook, sheer batiste, fine flannel, bird's-eye, Saxony wool, lace, and embroidery thread. Still, our Savior was wrapped in swaddling clothes, and who is my child that she should need more? The materials here are sufficient. I will make them do.

I have plenty of time; at least two months. It might be a week either way, because my time is not exact. The child will be born near the end of February, for it was the last of May that Don gave the little one to my keeping. It was when he came to town for supplies and to bring Lloyd and me here.

Don will keep the vision of me before him, always be thinking of me—breaking his dear heart because he cannot be with me now. Often I feel as if he were near—here in the cabin. I am alert to every unusual sound or movement; constantly I expect him to come. Surely our love seeks out each other. Surely our love reaches across space to comfort the beloved.

17

QUITE A PATCH OF SEA CAN BE SEEN FROM HERE. BUT NOT THE beach on this side, only about half the Arm and most of the beach on the far side of the bay. I keep looking at it, thinking my bottles have had time to float a long ways. Surely one of them will be picked up somewhere. Often I get the feeling that someone is coming, and I have to stop whatever I am doing, go look and listen. I listen for the *chug, chug* of a boat.

I should have heard Sam when he came. I wonder why I didn't hear the boat that brought him? Of course, visitors have come several times without us hearing their boat; we didn't know a soul was near until in they walked. More often, though, we heard the boat as it came round the point.

Some boats sound louder than others, and the weather has a lot to do with it. In windy or rainy weather the sound might not carry up here. It certainly wouldn't if the wind was in the wrong direction.

I had such an awful headache and such a roaring in my head, those first days after the slide, I wouldn't have known if it was a boat I was hearing or not. Perhaps Sam came early, right after the storm, much sooner than I figured he would come. I wonder what I would have done if I had heard his boat.

I am having grouse for dinner. An owl caught it for me, but he had no intention of doing me a favor. He figured he would have grouse for his own dinner, then I came along and took it away from him.

Rather late yesterday afternoon, I needed fresh air and had an

82

urge to go farther than the porch to get it, so I took the little
cook pot and went to the spring again for drinking water. A bit
off the trail to the right and near the spring, an owl flew up, lit
on the limb of a nearby tree, and didn't go away as he should have
done. I wondered why he was hanging around and went to investigate. I found a grouse with its head eaten off. The rest of it
hadn't been touched. It was still warm and bleeding. I could see
the marks in the snow where the owl had swooped down and
caught it.

"Thank you, Mr. Owl," I said. "I need this more than you do;
and besides, you can catch yourself another one."

I picked up the grouse and came back to the cabin, forgetting
all about drinking water and even forgetting the pot. I left it
beside the trail, and now it is covered with snow. I won't find
it until next summer.

It started to snow about daylight—fine sugary flakes from
the northeast. At first there wasn't much, but now it is coming
thick and fast, and it's getting colder by the hour. This is the
beginning of a real blizzard—winter in earnest.

I am well supplied with everything I need. I am the minor
queen in her castle. Let the wild blizzard rage!

I plucked the grouse yesterday, but darkness came before I
got it well cleaned. I finished the job this morning, cut it up,
and now it is boiling, giving off the best good smells. It's an
old hen grouse, and nicely fat. It had been living off blueberries,
and the lining of its gizzard was stained purple from grinding
great quantities of the berries.

There's some blueberry jam here—if I could get it. It's on the
high shelf way up nearly to the cabin peak. I made quite a lot
of jam between times last summer. We didn't eat it all up. What
was left Don put on the top shelf.

"We'll save this good stuff," he said as he put it up high.

I'll have some of that jam for my dinner, if I can figure a way
to get it without breaking my neck.

I got the jam!
To get it I unloaded the table, worked it to the wall, put

two powder boxes on it, climbed up and stood on the boxes, balanced there with the help of my crutch. While I was up there I moved all the jam down to a lower shelf, within easy reach for next time.

I had such a good meal. The grouse was cooked until the meat came off the bones. I drank a cup of hot broth an hour before dinner, and cooked dried peaches for my dessert. I liked my dinner very much and I hope the owl didn't have to go hungry; I hope he caught himself a dozen mice to eat.

Don always praised my cooking most generously. Often we were short of items of food a woman finds necessary to make a good meal, and I would have to rack my brains to think of something pleasing to make out of what was on hand. When I had luck, and we ate lots and wished for more, Don would say to Lloyd:

"Son, we have a wonderful little mother. Why, she can take a pail of water and a bundle of sticks and make a good dinner."

If my cooking failed to turn out as expected, we ate it anyway and never mentioned the matter.

Don and Sam always got breakfasts. I stayed in the bunk until the meal was ready. Don cooked one morning and Sam the next, and they never forgot whose turn it was or missed making the meal. Don would get up quietly, so as not to awaken me, but Sam tried to see how much noise he could make. He banged things around, dropped pots and pans, slammed the door, stirred the hotcakes as though he was beating the bass drum for the Salvation Army, and talked to himself like a tribe of monkeys. I always heard him coming.

Sam wouldn't sleep in the cabin when I was here. He'd set up his eight-by-ten tent a ways off, but he ate with us and took turns at making breakfast.

Breakfast is a big meal with stewed fruit, sourdough hotcakes, mush, potatoes, ham or bacon and eggs (if there are any). When Don got breakfast ready, he called folks to come and eat. Sam never called anybody, but he had ways of getting information across. If Lloyd didn't get up right away, he'd sing out, "Old

Lloyd Martin laid in the bed and laid in the bed and laid in the bed and he died in the bed." That meant breakfast was ready.

Some mornings Sam got up so early that even Don would be provoked at him. Don preferred to wait for daylight in a horizontal position, but not Sam! Sam wanted to greet the coming day with bass drums and cymbals. Sometimes he would have cooked breakfast and eaten his share long before daylight. He'd sit and drink an extra cup of coffee and smoke and never let up talking about all the lazy people he had known in his life and what happened to them. Some died in the bed after getting bed sores. Lazy people never did amount to anything, he'd say, always wanting to borrow money because they were too lazy to earn their own. He'd say the fire was going out and he wasn't going to build it up again.

"Can't be cutting forty cords of wood round this place just to keep a passel of lazy hulks a-sweating in the bed," he'd shout.

We'd get the giggles and nearly pop giggling. Sam pretended he didn't hear us.

Sam used all sorts of tricks to get us out of bed, and never repeated himself; he didn't have to, for he had a whole bag of tricks. When we did get up promptly, Sam's day was ruined. He never did want us to get up without persuasion from him, and because it was fun to have him persuade us we usually waited for it.

Once he pulled this trick on us:

"I won't stay round such a place," he shouted loudly one morning after he had gone through his usual songs and talk of lazy bums. He got up, walked noisily to the door, and opened it with a jerk. Then quickly and softly he closed the door again, tiptoed to Don's gun, grabbed it, snapped the safety off with a click, and like a flash he was outside the door.

Such behavior could only mean a bear in camp. We three Martins bounced out of bed, scrambled for guns, and rushed to be in at the kill.

When Don opened the door, Sam was standing there grinning.

"Thought that'd fetch you," he said.

But we got even with him for that one, or rather Lloyd did. Lloyd stole Sam's false teeth and blamed it on a raven.

Sam will take his teeth out and lay them any place that happens to be handy to where he is working, then he forgets all about them until he starts to eat his next meal. That same day he left his teeth on a stump where he and Don had been cutting some mine timbers. Lloyd found them and put them in his pocket. Sam sat down to dinner and took a gulp of tea before he missed his teeth. He remembered right where he had left them and went bounding after them, grumbling and cussing. He was soon back.

"You kids seen my teeth?" he asked.

"I saw a raven fly over with something pink in its beak," angelically answered my son.

"Them blankity-blank black birds. Steal a man blind. *How'm I gonna eat?*" and he looked pitiful.

"We have a meat grinder. I'll fix something you can eat," I offered.

"Martha will fix you up in a jiffy," Don said, then added, "Sit down and drink your tea while she gets it ready."

Sam picked up his tea mug. I thought he would pop. His teeth were in it, but neither Don nor I had seen Lloyd put them there.

"Think you're the Pope of Rome. You whistle punk," Sam roared, instantly spotting Lloyd for the criminal.

"Scare a little boy to death, then fool him. I'll get even with you," brazenly said Lloyd.

"You might amount to something yet," Sam chuckled as he fished his teeth out of the tea.

This really is a blizzard—the grandfather of all blizzards. When I look out the window, I get the feeling of being suspended in space with clouds flying past me. Sometimes I can't see the nearest trees for the swirling of the snow, and when I do get a glimpse of them it's as if they were hurrying past me. I don't know how cold it is, but I do know it is pretty cold. Some of my water supply froze last night. I was smart to save that water, and I'm going to keep on saving it. No more baths for a while. It's too cold anyway. I'll just wash the front of my face until the weather moderates.

I put on extra clothing and stay close beside the stove. A small fire must serve all my needs. The time to save on fuel is when you still have plenty. That time is right now.

I have started sewing and made a little shirt from Don's old underwear. The material is all wool and it will be warm. It has been washed many times and is nice and soft. The shirt looks pretty small, but then my baby will be small.

She seems to be doing well, and for that I am glad and thankful. I, too, am doing fine. Don't have an ache or pain worth mentioning, except for my leg, which does hurt now and then when it gets cold. I keep warm wrappings lashed around it and often sit with it next to the fire, and sometimes I can forget I own such a complaining leg.

18

THE BLIZZARD BLEW ITSELF AWAY YESTERDAY MORNING. THE sky has cleared, and all my world is glittering with a bright sun on the new snow. On the upper side of the cabin, the drift is clear to the eave. There is not a sound or sign of life, not a breath of air is stirring. Even the jays have gone home. Since the wind died away the cabin seems much warmer, but I think it is actually as cold as ever—maybe colder. It only seems warmer because there is no wind to suck all the heat out through the smokestack and drive the cold in at every crack.

I have been on the porch for a breath of fresh air, pushed some of the snow away with the broom, cleared out from around my toilet, and brought in more wood. This cold weather is hard on my wood pile, and I am as stingy and miserly as any person could possibly be and still not suffer.

I now have a wider variety of food, for I can open cans without much trouble. It does take two hands to open a can, and since I am able to accomplish that feat I'll just call my broken arm healed, but favor it as a weaker appendage. I'm going to stop pampering it so much. It is straight and shaped exactly like my other arm. I'm proud of my bone-setting job. There is a little lump on each of the bones, but I believe it is normal for small lumps to grow where there has been a break. Anyway, the lumps are small and don't show at all. I wouldn't know they were there if I didn't work my fingers along to find them. I'll be thankful and not complain.

The northern lights were out last night in all their radiant splendor. They stretched across the sky in a never ending line, twinkling and dancing, forever changing their places and shapes, and blending their colors. I wrapped myself in an old sugan and sat by the window a long time, watching the heavens declare the glory of God.

I was raised in a religious home, but I had to live in the wilderness to experience the meaning of faith. In the States I accepted what my people believed, conformed to what was prescribed, and bothered my head no further. Here the slate is wiped clean of all creeds and doctrines; faith is stripped down to the fundamentals; and it becomes clear that all religion is no more and no less than the human soul reaching out to the Creator; that the individual, alone, of his own free will and accord, must do the reaching. For me contact with God comes through his creation; the forests and the hills, the winds and the tides, the birds of the air, the creeping things upon the earth and the fishes in the sea, the starry heavens, the loyalty of a friend, love and devotion, faith and work, honor and awe.

I worship my God humbly before his manifestations, which go far beyond the ritual of any Church. From deep within me my worship surges forth. I am thankful and humble. A divine force— a spiritual guidance surrounds and envelopes me. This I know, not how or why: I only know that I do know, and it cannot be different.

As your needs are great, you will pray. This I ought to know from experience. I have said prayers since I could talk—mumblings and say-words—yet I have never prayed truly until there was nothing else possible for me to do. These last few weeks I have prayed more than in all my life before.

My prayers will be answered only if I pray with all my heart and humbly accept the answers to my prayers. To receive help I must do my part ungrudgingly, no matter how hard it will be.

I must work with all my might and intelligence and pray as I work. Then all will be well with me and my child. Yes, I do sometimes doubt and question—much less now than at first. After all, I am only a mortal being, and I have been sorely tried.

I keep asking myself how I failed to hear the boat which brought Sam and his friend. There is no answer, so now I must keep a close watch on the bay to make sure such a thing never happens again; strain my eyes for a darker speck on the gray water, tune my ears for any unusual sound, for if a strange boat did come in our cove there would be no reason for anyone to land and find my writings in the cabin. A stranger might come in, cruising for timber, maybe, and go out again without knowing I am up here.

I have been thinking and wondering what to do to prevent this. I believe I have the solution. I'm going to send off a signal with blasting powder. Three shots are a call. Anyone hearing them is morally obligated to investigate. Three blasts from what appears to be a deserted cove will certainly demand attention.

I have never set off a dynamite blast, never even lighted a fuse, and I have been thoroughly and properly impressed with the danger of it, but I have seen the men fix the fuse, load the drill holes, and light the primers. I know I can do it without blowing myself to kingdom come.

I am going to set off three sticks of blasting powder if I hear a boat or see one coming.

Blasting caps and fuse must be kept dry, so they are right here in the cabin, and the cap crimpers, too. The men made up their primers here. I have cut three lengths of fuse—two foot, three foot, and four foot long. I have crimped the blasting caps in place and hung my primers on a nail where I can reach them quickly. All that is set and ready, but I don't have the powder yet. It is in the toilet, and I can't possibly get it until this snow settles a little. It will be a day or two before I can flounder out after the powder.

It seems nice to have things all planned out and to know what I am going to do. If a boat should happen to come before I can get the powder, I will set off the caps by themselves. They won't make much noise, but I'll hope and pray they will make enough.

19

I CUT UP UNDERWEAR TODAY TO MAKE DIAPER SQUARES. SOME OF them came out pretty small; still, they seem plenty big for a tiny infant. By the time she grows, surely I'll have something to replace them—bigger and better ones.

I carry the child quite high and I hardly look pregnant. My abdomen should be much bigger. It seems that my stomach has drawn up and gotten smaller, or perhaps the child is crowding it; but I feel quite well and she does seem to be all right.

The days go so fast. Time does not drag. It is nearly Christmas, and if I were home I would be very busy making gifts, sending off packages to my people, baking fruitcake and cookies, and all the silver would be out ready to shine up. Lloyd likes to polish silver, and he would do most of that chore. He is as much help at Christmas time as a daughter would be. He loves preparing feasts.

I think I'll make a Christmas feast for baby and me. It will be something to plan for, and I'll like doing it. I can make a fine Christmas dinner from the supplies on hand and have everything but the turkey. It would be nice if the owl would supply me with another fowl. Anyway, I will have something and name it turkey. I'll be naming the day, too, because I'm not at all sure about the exact date. That won't make any difference, though, as long as I have a Christmas feast, the songs, the tree, and a Christmas spirit.

I am cooking salt meat today, and for no reason at all it reminds me of the moose we packed out of Jimson Creek. That was

91

the last summer before we came over here to prospect along this west coast. We were in British Columbia in a region of glaciers, rugged mountains, broad valleys, and swift streams.

Our camp was right on the bank of a big river, but the prospect the men had found to dig on was about a mile away on a mountainside. We had a good campsite, got enough river breeze to blow away some of the mosquitoes, and the weather was fine—bright and sunny all summer long. The country was grandly beautiful. We had two good poling boats and a splendid camp outfit, two tents and all sorts of gadgets. But we were not without our troubles.

The mosquitoes were so thick we could measure them by the cubic mile, and the contrary moose and mountain goats nearly starved us to death. We had figured to get our meat on the hoof, for the country was known to be teeming with game. As a consequence, we took in only the supplementary supplies. If we didn't get meat, we knew we wouldn't have nearly enough grub.

We had no luck hunting all that summer. The goats put out sentinels, and when we went after one they all headed for the very tops of the mountains, always keeping ahead of us, just out of gunshot. We only got three goats the whole summer, and we never did kill a moose. Finally, we got so meat-hungry we were reduced to eating porcupine. Porcupine isn't bad eating.

One day I stayed alone in camp to bake bread. I had my loaves all shaped and set to raise, and was stoking the outdoor oven, when an old feller stopped at our landing.

He asked if we wanted some moose meat. We certainly did—any kind of meat! He offered me three-quarters of a moose and all we had to do was to go after it ourselves. It wouldn't be much trouble, he said, because we could go all but a very short ways in our boat. Splendid!

I fired three shots to call the men, waited a minute, and fired another to let them know (as agreed) I wasn't in serious danger and only wanted them on business matters. They didn't have to hurry back to camp.

The old man told me he had been prospecting up Jimson Creek, found nothing there, and had decided to pull out, when at the last minute in walked a young cow moose. Like us, he had been unlucky with hunting all summer and was meat-hungry. Even though he already had his tent down and his boat loaded, he shot the moose. One-quarter was all he dared to put onto his already well loaded boat, and it was all the meat he could use anyway; but, like all men of the hills, he did hate to see the rest of that cow moose go to waste.

He drew a map, wrote a few words for Don, drank a cup of coffee, and took off down the river before the men got to camp.

Everybody was happy at the thought of fresh meat. The men said they had to hurry up and get it before an old bear found it, or the flies blowed it, or the birds ate it up. All was hustle and bustle around our camp. Lloyd and I put in to go along. Even before the men returned to camp, I'd been scheming to go with them. I pulled my oven fire and slammed the bread in. I didn't care if it was the right heat or not, or if the bread was raised enough, either. I just couldn't be left behind because of a little old bread dough. My efforts were not in vain, for we managed to overrule all objections to our tagging along. I don't know how we did it because we had not yet proved our worth.

We hurried through lunch, grabbed packsacks, jumped into the boat, and were off in record time. Lloyd and I were very excited and happy.

The place turned out to be much farther than Don and Sam had figured. Worse yet, our boat was a lot bigger then the old man's boat, and of a different shape, and it drew too much water to get very far up Jimson Creek. We had to leave the boat and finish the trip on foot. The men were sure it couldn't be much farther. It was much, much farther.

The whole valley was of glacier flow. Loose gravel and round rocks skidded about underfoot to make walking real drudgery. The birch and cottonwood brush grew thick and was overpopulated with mosquitoes, moose flies, no-see-ums, and other menacing things with wings. Don watched Lloyd and me for signs of exhaustion, and fretted and stewed for fear the trip was beyond our endurance. Lloyd and I strained to keep up and keep smiling. We pretended we were having a wonderful time, and knew better than to complain. We did do all right, and didn't mind the going half so much as Don minded it for us.

By and by we got to the man's trail and soon found the moose. It seemed awful big to me, being the first one I had even seen close to. It was nearly black, with a mulish head, and much longer legs than a milk cow has, nearly as long as a horse's.

First thing, Sam made a fire and cut forked sticks. Don cut a pile of small steaks. Lloyd was told off to help with the moose, and the men kept him busy.

"Here, young feller, grab hold of this!" Sam would call.

"Give me a hand, son," Don would say.

My job was to broil the steaks and be generally useful. I managed not to ruin all of them completely and still hop around the moose and see all that was going on.

We took time out to eat broiled steaks, and Sam had remembered to bring salt. Honestly, I don't know when food tasted so good.

Our packsacks were filled, shaken down, and a little more put in, and still not half of the moose was gone. We did hate to waste all that fine meat, so we cooked some more steaks and ate them.

While Sam's back was turned, Don hefted his packsack and said: "Sam thinks he's still a young feller. He wants to make a pack mule of himself," and Don took out some of Sam's meat and put it into his own packsack.

Then Don took about half the meat out of my packsack and threw it on the skin. He said to leave it because I couldn't carry so much.

Pretty soon Sam came and hefted Don's packsack and said: "Thinks he's the Pope of Rome. Muscled like a jaybird, he is. Has to wear two pair of pants to cast a shadow, he does," and he took meat from Don's packsack and put it into his own.

About that time I managed to get my hands on a big chunk of meat and shoved it into my packsack. All the while, Lloyd and I were laughing. Lloyd thought it was the funniest thing in the world the way Don and Sam stole from each other and tried to make the other feller's pack lighter than his own.

The way back to the creek was easy enough, but from there on it was awful. The weight of that meat made a big difference in walking over the loose gravel. Sam soon got fed up with the hard going, headed straight for the creek, and took off down the middle of it. We followed. That creek came right out from under a glacier, and the water was only a few degrees warmer than ice. We soon got used to the cold, or, what is more likely, our feet became so numb we didn't feel it any more. The way wasn't all wading; there were lots of bars where the going was easy. We had other troubles, though. The water was opaque with glacier flour and silt. It was difficult to know whether the next step would be only four inches deep or four feet deep. Sam misjudged a few steps, then went to the bank and cut himself a pole with which to test the depth at every step.

We were getting along fine and were two-thirds of the way to the boat when Sam's knee went on the bum. He hurt his knee logging in the big timber years and years ago, and ever since it takes spells when it refuses to function as a knee. There seems to be nothing he can do about it except rest. We stopped right there. It was time to stop anyway—nearly ten o'clock. Sam said it was time all honest people were in bed. It was still broad daylight, for in this fair northland it is day most all night during the summer.

We waded to the bank and made three fires, hoping to discourage the mosquitoes by lots of smoke. We fixed up a pretty good siwash camp. Our packs were lightened a bit when we ate more steaks. I hid my packsack for fear Don would learn I had put back the meat he took out. The other packs were opened and shaken to air the meat.

We all settled down in our leaning places and were soon asleep. We were so tired we couldn't have kept awake if we tried.

While we were sleeping an old bear came and stole our meat— stole all of it but mine. That bear dragged those packsacks two or three hundred feet away. He ripped them to pieces and ate our good meat. Just looking at the remains of the packsacks gave me a terrible feeling. What if our clothes lay scattered about in such shreds and we were in the bear's maw? How glad I was for the bear's choice of meat!

We all did a lot of talking about that old bear and a lot of looking at where he had come from and which way he had gone.

"He came from over that way," Don said, studying the ground. "See here—pigeon-toed. Look here. See that claw mark? Grizzly!"

Then Lloyd happened to look toward the creek. He started hollering. It had raised more than a foot during the night. Again we could hardly believe our eyes; but glacier streams are like that, and will rise or drop suddenly with no apparent reason.

"We're going to eat meat," Sam said, "bear or no bear. Go get the boat, Don."

Don rushed off through the brush, Lloyd tagging along, going with all his might to keep up. Before too long they returned with the boat. We went back to the moose, and the bear hadn't found it yet; it was just as we had left it. We brought away everything but the head, the hide, and the biggest bones.

That was a fine moose.

CANADA

British Columbia

Skagway

Haines

Glacier Bay

Juneau

Chichagof Island

Cobol

Admiralty Island

Sitka

Petersburg

Wrangell

Gulf of Alaska

Prince of Wales Island

Ketchikan

Pacific Ocean

Southeast Alaska, showing the location of Cobol

Helen Bolyan at Cobol

O Rugged Land of Gold
THE PROSPECT

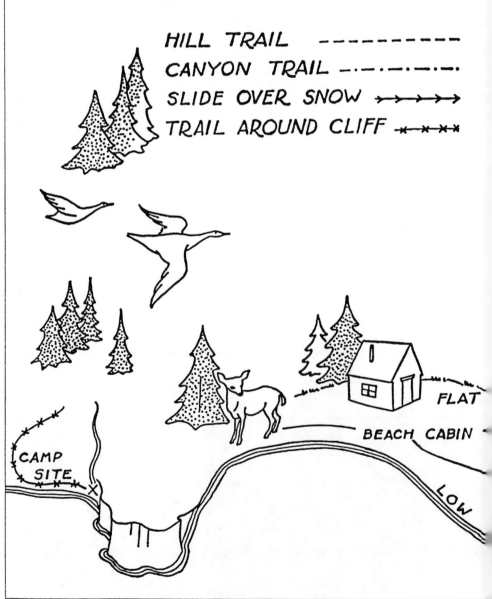

HILL TRAIL   ----------

CANYON TRAIL   -.-.--.-.

SLIDE OVER SNOW   >->->->

TRAIL AROUND CLIFF   -x-x-x-

CAMP SITE

FLAT

BEACH CABIN

LOW

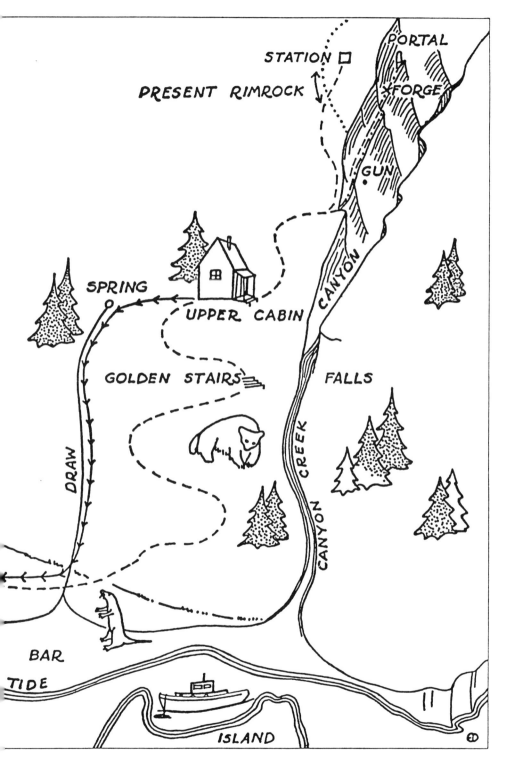

Map of Cobol mine, as it appeared in the 1953 edition

Helen and George
Bolyan at
Wasilla Lake,
1928

Helen and
George
at Cobol,
c. 1940

Dace, George, and Helen Bolyan at Cobol, c. 1940

Helen at
Cobol, in front
of the house
she built

Helen Bolyan on
her trip around
the world, location
unknown, 1954

20

THE WEATHER IS CHANGING. IT'S WARMER AND THE SKY IS CLOUDING over. The days are so short at this time of the year that I don't have enough daylight to do my work, and the nights are so long I cannot sleep them through. With clear weather I seldom light a lamp, because I like the twilight, but in cloudy weather I have to make a light.

I am always awake before dawn. I get up with the coming of the first gray light, make my fire, put the kettle on, crawl back into the bunk, and watch the flickering firelight come and go, get a whiff of wood smoke, listen to the cheerful crackling of the fire, and wait for the song of the kettle.

All my wood is yellow cedar. It pops and crackles as it burns, and gives off the nicest spicy, perfume-like smells—a clean smell, and it leaves white ashes.

When the kettle sings I get up, put more wood on the fire, stand close by the stove (barefooted on a deerskin), and put on my clothes. I try to stay up until darkness comes, then I go to bed and try to stay there until it is day again.

I've made a snowshoe for my crutch, and I am proud of my inventive ability. I put an enamel saucer in a gallon tin can, mashed the top flat, poked my crutch inside and all the way down to the saucer on the bottom. Then I nailed the can tight. The nails didn't split the wood, and I can get them out if I want to. The saucer evens the pressure and keeps the end of the crutch from making a hole in the can. It is a very satisfactory arrangement. I tried it out by going for the powder. I just couldn't stand waiting any longer. If a boat does come, I want to be all ready.

I got the powder, all right, and tied the sticks to pieces of kindling wood, but I didn't make the holes to put the primers in, for the powder is frozen as hard as darnicks. I handled the powder very gingerly; still, I managed to get myself a headache from it. Don never wanted me to touch powder, and said it was so easy to get a "powder headache." He often got one from loading the drill holes.

I was going to do some sewing, but think I had best not be near my baby's things for a day or so. I don't want her little clothes to become contaminated by the blasting powder. It's funny how I always say "her," but I do feel sure the newcomer will be a daughter.

In hopes of driving away my headache I went to the spring. It was a nice outing. The snow is deep and the drifts are deeper; but knowing I really didn't have to get anywhere, and could always turn back and follow the broken trail to the cabin, I kept going easy-like, a step and a push through the snow, a look around at my world.

I enjoyed the trip, but I didn't get any water. I forgot to take along a pot. But now that a trail is broken, and since my crutch snowshoe is so serviceable, I will go often to the spring. Fresh air will do me good. I like the trip and I do like spring water.

Five little ptarmigan have come. Now I have friends and am alone no more. They are darling birds about the size of a banty hen I had when I was a child. All day they have been picking at the brush or sitting in the snow below my window. I have seen ptarmigan many times in summer, whole huge flocks of them, but always at a distance and in movement. This is the first time I ever had the opportunity of seeing them close to and watching them for hours on end. In the fall ptarmigan shed their mottled clothes and put on snowy winter garments. They are so like the snow that, once I take my eyes off one for a minute, I cannot see it again quickly. Often I have to follow the tracks to find the bird.

They are eating the buds from the brush, very busy eating, eating. They stay in one place until all the buds within reach are gone, look about for another branch, move quickly to it, and remain still with only the head moving until all those buds are eaten. When they stretch up to get at higher buds, they look tall, but when they move they look rather dumpy, with their bodies snugged close to the ground and their heads put well forward.

Ptarmigan have shiny black eyes, black beaks, a black feather on either side of the tail, and I believe the outside wing feathers are black, but I can't be sure about that. Their legs are short, and their shanks and feet are covered with feathers.

There is no better-tasting food than fried young ptarmigan. We have eaten them lots of time, but we never killed any in camp. We would have to be in great need to kill any game in camp. If a wild creature trusts us enough to stay nearby, we want to be worthy of the trust. We have had pet deer, squirrels, and families of grouse.

I split a block of wood. Didn't need to because there is still lots of stove size, but I thought I would see if I could manage. I did very well. From now on I shall split one block every day, then I will always have stovewood ahead. I use wood sparingly, and am very stingy with it.

I made bread and ate some of it hot from the oven, doused in butter and well spread with blueberry jam. My hands feel so nice and soft from working the dough, and they look so clean. They make me think of Sharkey, an old Finn, said to be the dirtiest man in Alaska, which is quite a distinction considering the looks of some prospectors and fishermen.

If Sharkey ever took a bath, washed his hands, or changed his clothes, it was before our time. He is a kindly soul, and doesn't seem to know he is dirty. His dilapidated old boat is as unkempt as its owner. Sharkey is friendly, and will ask the men to come aboard for coffee; but the men manage to duck the invitations by saying they have just finished eating, don't have time, are off their feed—any excuse to keep from eating with him. To avoid asking him to eat on our boat, the men give him food: a chunk of meat, bread, spuds, anything for him to take to his own boat and eat by himself. They don't dislike him, but they just can't stand dirt.

One day Sharkey's hands were clean. It was so unusual we couldn't help noticing. Don kidded him.

"So you're going to get married," Don said to him.

"Me? Get married? I ain't going to get married," Sharkey answered in all seriousness.

"Not going to get married? How come you're so spruced up?"

"I'm not spruced up. Why you say so?"

"Now, don't tell me you don't have your eye on a squaw. Look at your hands."

Sharkey looked at his hands, turned them over and looked at both sides of them. He seemed puzzled for a minute, then he brightened up.

"I ain't been a-washing my hands," he said. "I made bread today."

I have another friend. Rather, I am a friend to another creature, but one that isn't a friend to anything within my knowledge. A weasel has come into the cabin and is catching the mice. Bless him. He's welcome to all he can catch. I think he's been around for several days, but I didn't happen to see him until this morning. I have heard commotions and squeakings, more noise than mice usually make. Now I know it was Mr. Weasel after them.

The end of his nose is pink and his eyes are jet black. The tip of his tail is black and all the rest of him is snowy white. He humps up his back as he walks. He swore at me when I moved toward him, then went home through a hole in the floor.

Later today my little ptarmigan returned. There were six of them this time. I heard their soft "*qu, qu, qu,*" and looked and looked before I could see them. Ptarmigan go in flocks, and very likely these are part of a large flock. They didn't stay long; I wish they had. I hope the weasel doesn't develop a ptarmigan appetite. I hope he likes mice much better.

This cold hangs on. It is clear again, and a strong northeast wind is blowing. North, northeast, and east winds do not hit the cabin directly, but the backlashes and whirlies do come here. West wind hits hard, and the southeast comes with an awful bang.

The mountains across the bay are smoking—great plumes of snow smoke. I wouldn't like to be out on the water today. How good this cabin is!

Oh, Don, Don! Are you out in this cold? With all my heart I hope you have shelter and warmth today. The islands are littered with driftwood and wreckage; it's been more than a month, and surely you have built a hovel by this time. God be merciful to Don.

I wonder what has become of my bottle messengers. Will they go a thousand miles or more before anyone picks them up? I didn't mention what part of America I'm in, only gave our name, thinking they would be picked up by someone with local knowledge. How puzzling my message would be to someone in California! But those bottles just couldn't go all the way to California.

How I wish someone nearby would find one.

21

THERE HAS BEEN A QUICK CHANGE IN THE WEATHER. SNOW IS falling, and the wind drives from the southeast. I think it is getting warmer, and soon the snow will turn to rain. I have put the tub out. I need to replenish my water supply. I also hope for a bath and water to do some laundry. I would like to be clean at Christmas time, and the Day is almost here.

My hair has grown at least an inch. Funny thing: I kept thinking of myself with short hair forever. Stupid of me to think that. My hair will keep right on growing, and be as long as it ever was. The scars are drawing up and getting smaller. I wish they would draw up to nothing at all, but I know they won't. I'll have them to the end of my time. Who was it said, "A saber cut—a dirty livid white."? I think it was Stevenson. Sure, it was Stevenson in *Treasure Island*. My scars are pink, but in time they probably will turn whitish. I hope they won't have a dirty livid look. I hope I will always be able to hide them with my hair.

I have been giving my leg some extra attention. Since I went down the hill, it has been my most troublesome ailment. Right now it is the only one I need concern myself about. I believe it was originally hurt more than I realized. I could see how crooked my arm was and could look at the cuts on my head in the shaving mirror. My head ached so very much I scarcely noticed anything else. Now I've decided the bone of my leg was cracked, first by the slide, then again when I bumped against the tree going down the hill. I've concluded this from observing deer bones.

102

Yesterday I prepared some salt deer meat. It had been butchered with an ax and chopped into mess-size chunks. One chunk was the upper part of a ham, which I cut in three pieces. I soaked out the salt, then cut it again into serving-size chunks. I trimmed the meat off the leg bone which had been chopped in two. I didn't examine it for cracks, just threw the lot into the pot and cooked it. When the meat was done, the bone came apart and was in four pieces. It had appeared whole and solid when I put it into the pot, but I am sure I would have found little crack lines in it if I had examined it closely.

I think the bone in my leg is somewhat like that deer bone. I think it had cracks, or maybe one crack, but was held together by the connective tissue around it. It was almost broken on both occasions. I can now learn something of the state of the bone by feeling it, and I find a long lump there. I do know the bone was not completely broken, because my leg is straight and shaped as it should be.

I never did take as good care of my leg as I did of my arm, but from now on I am going to pamper it plenty.

The snow has turned to rain, and it drives in almost horizontally. A southeast gale is blowing. Soon I will have a great wealth of water to use for bathing and washing clothes.

Three deer came up the hill today to tell me there is to be a spell of mild weather. They were all bucks, and one of them had lost a horn. He looked so unbalanced. He must have just lost it, maybe not more than an hour before he came visiting me, for a little red spot, a few drops of fresh blood, marked where it had been.

One of the others, a small two-pointer, had been in a fight and had a scar about six inches long on his throat. It showed plainly as Mr. Buck kindly turned his head properly to give me a good look at it. That little buck was just too frisky around his big brothers and got himself tossed on a horn, or it might have been made by a hoof. Deer have very sharp hoofs, and they use them in fighting. The scar was an old one, quite healed.

I didn't make shavings last night, and this morning I had to suffer the consequences. The first law of this land is: Make shavings! The old-timers are pretty scornful of anyone who disregards it. Like Pete, for example.

Poor Pete. I wonder where he can be now.

Pete came one day when I was staying in camp washing clothes. That was in my early Alaska days, back in the time when I thought muck was dirt and when I had an ambition to keep my family looking clean. I did a lot of laundry under most primitive conditions in those days, before I got around to believing the men when they told me, "What sticks on from God's out-of-doors can't rightly be called dirt."

That day my laundry was interrupted by a fine tenor voice singing, "Faith of our fathers living still . . ." I looked up to see a cracker-box sort of craft coming toward me. It was Pete. He tied up at our landing and came to camp. He was sweet, looked so young, and had the nicest smile. His manners might have been learned in the king's palace. He took off his hat when he talked to me. He introduced himself as William Peter Malcom.

"That's three-fourths of my name," he said. "If you please, madam, I had rather you did not ask me the other one-fourth lest it bring embarrassment to the bishop, my father."

Pete said he was looking for a position. Prospectors don't hire help, and I might have passed the information on to him; but he interested me, and I wanted to keep him around for a while, so I told him he would have to ask Don. Said I would take him to where the men were working.

He was a merry, friendly sort, and rather child-like. We talked as I finished my work. I liked him. Soon I was through, and we started for the workings. I noticed Pete carried a cane, and asked him about it.

"This, madam," he said, holding it up for me to see, "is a shillelagh."

He wore tennis shoes and used a necktie to hold up his pants.

Sam was visibly and volubly displeased with Pete. If Don was pleased, it was neither visible nor voluble. Lloyd took to him at once, and mentioned a ledge from where he had been watching a cow moose and her calf. Pete was interested, and followed

Lloyd. I stayed with the men, trying to make myself useful by cleaning up their lunch things.

Soon Pete burst forth in song and the mountainside rang with *Te Deum Laudamus*. I was astonished. So was Don, and he stopped work to listen. Clear, sweet were the words in a high tenor:

"We praise thee, O God; we acknowledge thee to be the Lord. . . .
"Holy, holy, holy, Lord God of Sabaoth. . . .
"The glorious company of the Apostles praise thee. . . .
"Thou art the King of Glory, O Christ. . . .
"Thou sittest at the right hand of God, in the glory of the Father."

And on to: "We therefore pray thee, help thy servants, whom Thou hast redeemed with thy precious blood."

Sam listened but he didn't stop working. He had to listen because he couldn't help but hear the song. However, he showed no appreciation. It wasn't his style of music, Sam would have preferred "Old Dan Tucker," "The Gumboots in Mrs. Murphy's Chowder," or "Owned the Pennsylvania Railroad and Had Hetty Green for a Wife."

Sam kept right on shoveling muck and talking to the atmosphere in general: "Singing jackass. I can size a man up. Slipper shoes on in the hills! Humpf! Won't work. Offer him a job and he'll run from you." And more of the same.

Back in camp, Pete remained standing until I was seated, and in other ways showed his fine manners. He complimented the dinner, thanked us handsomely, said he was embarrassed at his appetite, naïvely remarked that he was famished, and told what his last meal had been, when, and where.

Don gave me a most accusing look. I had broken the law of the land by failing to offer a guest food. I hadn't even given him a cup of coffee. I was still new to the country, and back in Washington we didn't feed everybody who passed our way. I had shamed and disgraced my husband.

Pete got a job then and there to make amends for my sins. In recognition of the newly acquired position, Pete lifted up his voice in "Those in Peril on the Sea." That was just a starter.

He went through "O Worship the King, All Glorious Above," "The Lord Our God Is Clothed with Might, the Winds Obey His Will." He swung to "Sweet Afton" and "Annie Laurie." Lloyd, Don, and I joined in, and it was nice.

Sam just sat while we sang a dozen songs; then Pete gave forth with, "At the Cross, at the Cross Where I First Saw the Light and the Burden of My Heart Rolled Away." Sam began to mumble, then joined in the chorus. His deep bass came in, and it made a low rumble as he repeated "rolled away." We laughed; we couldn't stop laughing. Now we knew Sam had somewhere and at some time been to church, and that was a hard thing to imagine. He looked ashamed, turned his eyes up until we saw only the whites, got up and stomped off to bed.

Don had hired Pete without inquiring about the kind of work he wanted. Now it seemed in order to ask what he could do. Pete said he was trained to translate Greek, Latin, and Hebrew, interpret French, German, and Italian, play the pipe organ and direct a choir. He said he was capable of doing many other things and had never refused any employment. His last position was assistant to the Atlin Indians, procuring and preserving fish for dog food. He had held that position eleven days. For remuneration he had been given a share of the product and the boat.

"It's a little beauty, now isn't it?" he beamed.

It was the most ungodly craft that ever rode a river, but seaworthy, Don said. Pete didn't wait for praise of his boat, didn't seem to realize none was coming, but hurried to get some of his smoked fish, proclaiming it a great delicacy. He offered it generously, not even knowing people aren't supposed to relish dog food. Surprisingly, it was king salmon, and very good. We ate a lot of it.

"The Indians are a kindly people," he told us. "So generous. Think of them giving me that splendid boat."

"Good idea to give *you* some means of transportation," Sam observed sarcastically. (He couldn't stay in bed—might miss something). Pete didn't notice.

"I quite agree with you, sir," he replied seriously, "and a horse is also a fine means. Back in central Canada a farmer gave me a horse. It was a very good horse, blind in only one eye, and that horse carried me all the way to Fort Connelly."

As nearly as we could piece things together, Pete was from England, the son of an Anglican bishop. The first twenty years of his life had been spent with special tutors. Two years ago he walked away from all that education and never looked back. He worked his way across the Atlantic and Canada, doing all sorts of things, even spending some time as assistant to a Salvation Army captain. He wanted to see the world, and hoped to be in India when winter came.

Don gave due consideration to employment for Pete, and decided it would be best for him to stay in camp and help Lloyd get the wood, which was a promotion for the boy, since he'd never before been responsible for the wood. Lloyd was delighted. Don said I could go with him and Sam to their diggings, which meant he wanted the boys to have some uninterrupted enjoyment.

At the end of the day the two boys had bucksawed a dozen or so blocks of wood, small stuff, and both ends of every block were decorated with charcoal drawings. Pete could draw well; he had made recognizable pictures of every one of us. Lloyd drew boats. The blocks were lined up like paintings in an art exhibit.

Sam grabbed his picture, split it to pieces, threw it on the fire, and said to Don: "We might run short of powder. The Frenchman went past here the other day with a whole box of powder."

"You're right, Sam," Don said. "We have only a little better than half a box left. Yes, we might run short before summer is over. Maybe you better go see if you can't bum a few sticks off Frenchy."

"I'll go first thing in the morning. Be back in a couple of days," answered Sam, pleased at Don's cooperation, then added: "Ought to have some meat. Ain't had a goat all summer. One man can't do much digging."

All of which meant he was clearing out until we got rid of the greenhorn; but we should show him a good time before we sent him away.

Sam took the boat and had gone before I was awake next morning. Don said the rest of us would go up and get a goat. Pete politely begged to be excused from hunting. He did not want to see God's creatures killed; besides, he had taken a position and felt morally obligated to render service. Don said that was fine, but he didn't look like he thought so.

"Do you want to stay and work with Pete while Mother and I get a goat?" he asked Lloyd.

Lloyd hesitated. Pete was a grand new friend, yet it would be wonderful to stand high on the mountain and look out over the world, see his father as a mighty hunter getting the game. Lloyd decided on hunting.

Don said Pete was to come with us as far as the diggings, and do a bit of trail work from there toward camp.

Don showed Pete how to level off some rough spots in the trail, told him not to work too hard, told him to go back to camp when he was tired, and said we probably would be down early.

It was a beautiful day, and the climb was easy enough and stimulating. The views were inspiring, and we three were very happy. We saw several nannies and their kids, and were quite close to one with twins. This old nanny didn't like us at all, and she worked hard to get her babies away. She had one on each side; they were very young, no more than two or three days old, Don said. She had short black horns growing straight up and curving back a little. Her coat was snowy white, long and shaggy to the knees. From the knees down the hair was short and tight, and she had the rear look of a fat banker dressed in golf pants. The two little ones were wobbly. She took a step or two, then turned back to push a baby ahead with her nose, turned to the other side to bring up the other baby, eyed us, stamped her hoof, and repeated the performance. We watched for a few minutes, then hurried on so as not to worry her.

The mountain was full of goats, herds of them, with thirty or forty in every herd. They all kept well out of rifle range, except the nannies and the kids. Don was determined to get a goat, and began to hunt in earnest as we came up near the snow line.

Often he left Lloyd and me in a safe spot while he tried to sneak up on a herd, but always the goats outmaneuvered him.

Finally he suggested we stay in one spot, gather fuel, make a fire, melt snow, and have tea ready when he came back with a goat. Lloyd didn't want to stay; he wanted to be in at the kill, so Don took him along. I stayed behind.

Fuel gathering above timber line is quite a chore. I couldn't find a thing bigger than my finger. I hurried at gathering it, laid a fire, opened the knapsack, and got out the tea can. I melted snow, made the tea, and waited and waited. There was no shot. The tea was getting cold and my fuel was all burned up. I drank the tea to save it, got more snow to melt, and gathered more fuel, but I decided not to make another fire until I heard a shot.

Then the shot came from a long ways off. I made a fire.

My men came hurrying back, both talking at once.

"Oh, lordy, Mother, you ought to see Father shoot! He shoots from one mountain to the other. I never even saw the goat. He said, 'There's one I can get!' *Bang!* And he went a-running for half a mile, me away behind, trying to keep him in sight. Oh, lordy, Mother, I'd hate to have Father shoot at me. There lay the goat—dead. Hit in the neck. Father had his throat cut and was getting his insides out before I caught up with him. Father let me carry his gun back." Lloyd laughed the whole time he talked.

"We got to get off this mountain fast," Don said as he gulped tea.

It was early July, and never truly dark at night, but there wouldn't be enough light down in the timber for either comfortable or safe going. We couldn't camp where we were because with no fuel for a fire we would nearly freeze; already we were shivering. The high places get mighty cold when the sun gets behind the peaks.

We made it down safely, Don carrying the young billy, Lloyd proudly wearing his father's gun, and me with the knapsack. As it got darker, we had to go more slowly. Pete heard us coming a long way off, and lifted up his voice in song. It was nice to be guided into camp with music. The niceness ended with the music.

Pete had no fire, and when asked why he said there were no

shavings. And the water pail was empty, which made matters even worse.

Don didn't talk while we were getting food cooked, but after we had eaten he told Pete he guessed he would want to be moving on if he expected to be in India by wintertime.

"I quite agree with you, sir, " Pete answered.

Don told him we don't carry money when out prospecting, but he would give him an order he could get cash on in town, and he said we would also give him some grub.

"I beg pardon, sir, but will the food be cooked?"

Don gave him a queer look. "Yes," he said, "the food will be cooked."

"All things come of thee, O Lord, and of thine own have we given thee," sang Pete.

Don skinned out a goat ham, made up the fire, fixed a spit, and sat the rest of the night roasting it.

Pete left the next morning after saying generous thanks and polite goodbys. He went down the river singing, "Lord, now lettest thou thy servant depart in peace according to thy word."

When he was around the bend and out of sight, we heard, "Blessed be the Lord God of Israel, for he hath visited and redeemed his people." It came back to us clear and sweet from far away.

I wonder where Pete is now. He was a lovable nitwit.

I'm cleaning up for Christmas. I've washed windows and unloaded the windowsill. My windowsill is log-wide, and everything gets dumped onto it. I have never lived in a cabin which did not have a windowsill loaded with rock, so I ended up by putting most of the rock back. Some are very nice specimens, some have nothing in them, but all are friendly and seem to proclaim a prospector is about and will be in soon to look over his rocks. I also cleaned the lower shelves and scrubbed the table and benches.

The ptarmigan are gone but the jays are back. The weasel came twice today and sassed me both times.

With the inside of the cabin properly clean, I went out to the porch and mucked it off, emptied my hockey box, and scrubbed it out. I have made good use of all this great lot of rain water, and I am thinking it is the last God will send to me this winter. The rain has now turned to snow and it is coming down thick and fast—big soft flakes. "The old woman is picking her geese," we say of this kind of snow.

I'll rest a little, then go get my tree before it becomes buried with snow. I have some little spruce spotted near the spring. I think I can get a nice one. One more day, then Christmas Eve. I still have lots to do before all is in readiness for my festivities.

22

" 'TIS CHRISTMAS, 'TIS CHRISTMAS, WE SHOUT IN OUR GLEE. WE'LL dance and we'll sing round our own Christmas tree."

Christmas Eve!

My tree is a small one, about two feet high, but perfect in shape. It grew in the open and is symmetrical. I got it just in time, for the snow is really piling up. I also brought in cedar and hemlock boughs, and went to the spring for my Christmas drinking water.

I loved being out in the falling snow. The big soft flakes hang to every twig and brush, making my world a fairyland. I was out three times, tramping around with my snowshoe crutch. I would have gone out again if I could have found the slightest excuse.

Dried apples, prunes, and dried peaches cut up fine with the scissors, also lots of raisins, went into my fruitcake. I made a pie, cookies, and candy—three kinds of candy. I was all worn out from stirring. My hurt hand rebelled and refused to stir more. The fruitcake is peaked up in the middle, baked perfectly, and it smells good.

I did myself proud at trimming my tree. Strips made from the red tops of socks look lovely in the green branches. Blue paper curls made from the wrapping of the macaroni box, colored pictures from magazines folded and pasted into odd shapes, all made nice trimmings. And I hung my diamond ring in the tip top, where it sparkles like a Christmas star. I scooped a can of dirt from down under the floor, tightly packed the butt of my tree in that, and

112

made it stand sturdy and straight. I put it in the center of the table, and I will leave it up until the last day of the old year.

I have cedar and hemlock branches up here and there about the cabin. There is a festive look to the place and a festive feeling in my heart.

A saddle of salt deer meat is soaking, and by a hocus-pocus process it will become a Christmas turkey. I need Don to carve and Lloyd to pass around the plates.

I hope this will not be a sad Christmas for Lloyd. I hope he will do as I am doing and make the most of what he has, enter into the spirit of Christmas, and try to be happy. I think he will. By now I suppose he is back East. As soon as my people learned that Don and I are lost, they must have insisted on the lad coming to them. He may not have wanted to go, surely not at first, but by now he will have lost hope, and perhaps he will be glad to go away from Alaska. This will be his first Christmas without his parents. I hope he won't miss us much, not too much, anyway. I don't want him to be sad on Christmas Day.

I want Don to be happy, too. I pray God may put within his reach a fish or a bird for his Christmas feast. We cannot be together, yet we need not flaunt our grief and sorrow. Don has the intelligence to accept the impossible and to make the most of the possible. I, too, will try to make the most of what is possible.

Every tree and shrub in the forest is robed in white; every stump and snag is crowned with a pope's miter. Big soft snowflakes are lazily falling. This is a perfect Christmas Eve.

Tradition is being kept up here in the wilderness. Christmas Eve supper is now spread with the things tradition dictates. I have made little stockings for my baby to hang up. I'll fill them with bits of candy and raisins and pretend she is already here. All my lamps are lighted. I will sing the Christmas carols and remember past years.

I am nearly well. My child moves actively and is growing. I have food and shelter, light and warmth, luxuries and a tree. With all my heart I am thankful for what I have this Christmas Eve, glad and thankful for the material things, thankful for the things unseen—my memory and my hope.

I remember my father's house on Christmas morn, and the collect we said. I can say part of it now:

" 'O God, who makest us glad with the yearly remembrance of the birth of thine only Son Jesus Christ; Grant that as we joyfully receive Him . . . who liveth and reigneth with thee and the Holy Ghost, one God, world without end.' "

I remember all the Christmas holidays with my husband and my son, and I can tell them over, one by one. I can laugh with the memory of laughter, and sing again the carols we used to sing.

" 'O come, all ye faithful, joyful and triumphant . . .'

" 'Hark! the herald angels sing . . .'

" 'Silent night, holy night, All is calm, all is bright . . .' "

I will sing and sing. I will sing all of the beautiful Christmas songs.

My whole being is being pervaded with a sense of comfort and un-aloneness. My child stirs gently within me.

" 'Away in a manger, no crib for a bed, the little Lord Jesus lay down His sweet head.' "

My own dear baby! " 'Jesus, tender Shepherd, hear me. Bless Thy little lamb tonight. Through the darkness be Thou near me.'

" 'Hush! my dear, lie still and slumber. . . .' "

Darkness comes. The carbide in my lamps has burned away.

This Christmas Eve is almost past and gone.

My Christmas Eve was good. So was Christmas Day. I fussed over dinner all morning, and the results pleased me. I had fried dried apples with salt venison.

After dinner I went for a little outing, then I played myself a game of chess; left hand against the right, with me going from side to side of the table at every move. Right hand won—perhaps I favored it. The chessmen were some Lloyd whittled out for camp use.

Don has a beautiful ivory set at home. He got an Eskimo to carve it for him, just explained what he wanted and let the carver make the designs. The pawns are seals and curltail sledge dogs; the knights are Eskimo men in kayaks with the paddle on the right or left; the bishops are polar bears and two are snarling; the castles are igloos, the kings hunters, one left-handed. And the queens are the cutest things I ever saw—Eskimo women with babies on their backs. One baby is asleep.

After the game was over, I sat at the table with my head in my arms and remembered. Remembered Christmas Days from my earliest childhood on down through the years. Pageant after pageant. The precious things of a little girl—my yellow-headed doll. Funny things—grandfather and his messmate from the Mexican War, both stone-deaf from the cannon roar, both saying the blessing into their whiskers at the same time and neither knowing the other had said it too. Happy things—the Christmas plays my mother wrote about the doings of us children. What fun it was to act them out, each child impersonating himself! I remembered visits and company, feasts and dancing, music and songs, and sleigh rides with the tinkling bells.

> "Hear the sledges with the bells,
>   "Silver bells!
> "What a world of merriment their melody foretells!
>   "How they tinkle, tinkle, tinkle,
>   "In the icy air of night!"

I do like the sound of sleigh bells.
" 'Jingle bells, jingle bells, jingle all the way.' "
Jingle for the little one under my heart.

Another Christmas and I hope to see the faces of my family—Don and our children. God will grant me this—to hold my baby and look into the face of my dear son; and to see the face of my beloved Don.

23

IT SNOWED ALL LAST NIGHT AND ALL TODAY, WHICH MAKES SIX DAYS of continuous heavy snowfall. Sam tells about the winter when it snowed for forty-six days straight. I'm sure Sam's snow didn't fall as fast as this is falling. If it did it would have been more than a hundred feet deep.

This morning I went out and played in the snow. I made snowballs and threw them in the air. I enjoyed doing such a foolish thing. Then I went all the way to the spring, but I didn't get any water because I couldn't see where it was. The walking was fun; some places were packed hard and in other places it was soft and squishy.

The snow is all of ten feet deep, maybe twelve, but it is packing. It's the kind of snow that makes good snowballs. I didn't sink beyond my waist, and in most places not much above my knees. I developed a good system for going through the snow. I get my crutch firmly down and lean well on it, then I push my right knee into the snow and let it take some of my weight. I shuffle my good foot along, tromping the snow firm under it; then I stand on my good leg, balanced by my right knee, while I bring up the crutch and poke it around for another firm place. At times I lost my balance and toppled over, but I didn't mind. Of course, if I *had* to go through that much snow I would feel sorry for myself, but in that case I would keep going and not loiter around throwing snowballs.

I am still eating Christmas dinner. Counting Christmas, this is
116

the fourth day I have eaten it. I believe it will last a week longer. I don't mind; I'd a lot rather play in the snow than cook. I had Christmas pie for breakfast—good pie, too.

It has turned much colder tonight. The wind has shifted to the east and it is driving the snow before it, piling up huge drifts. I have been sewing and watching the snow whirl. I won't be able to look out my window much longer; already it is being buried in snow. This window is on the downhill side of the cabin, and the hill drops off fast. My upper window has been a wall of white for a long time. Looking through it, I discovered the snow is stratified. It never occurred to me that snow could be, but this definitely is.

I never saw such queer weather. The snow stopped suddenly just before noon. The sun was out for about half an hour, then thick fog rolled in and sleet has formed over everything. The sleet is freezing as hard as darnicks, and is the slickest stuff in all creation. I know, for I went on the porch to examine it. Almost got a fall doing so.

I am going to the beach. I am. I am. I am! The Lord has offered me free transportation, and I'm going to take it.

I am going the first thing in the morning. I have a tremendous urge to go—a compulsion is upon me. I don't know why I must go to the beach, but I'm too busy getting ready to go to stop and reason about anything.

I don't know what I'll find at the beach, but I know what I won't find there. No food, very little wood, no bedding, a very poor bunk, precious few pots and pans, no tub, and none of many other things I have up here to use and enjoy. Still, I must go. I'll take everything I can with me.

I worked so hard today that I got a pain in my left side. I had to rest until it went away. When I was a child, I used to get such a pain when I ran fast for a long way. I think most children do. The cure was to stoop over, find a pebble or chip or bit of dirt as big as your thumb, pick it up carefully, spit exactly where it had been, then put it back over the spittle just as it had been before. The pain was supposed to leave immediately, and if I remember right it always did. Just bending over and resting probably would also have effected a cure.

I am making up bundles to take with me. I will slide them all down the hill over the slick snow; then I'll slide myself down. I have filled every gunny sack here, and I am wrapping things in canvas and tying them up tight with fuse. I am taking a little of everything and all of most things, all that I possibly can.

I found the ice creepers the men used last year to go along the canyon trail when it was icy. One is lashed to my crutch, the other to my foot. I have made three trips to the head of the draw near the spring, and I slid bundles of supplies after me. I tied them to a bush. They're all set for the trip, and tomorrow I'll have that much less to do. I must hurry and get everything ready so I can be on my way before the weather changes, before anything happens to this slick sleet.

For once in this world some good has resulted from me being just a tomfool; the trail I made to the spring when I was out playing in the snow is now a well glazed trough along which my cargo slides beautifully.

Out of Sam's tent fly I made a long roll and stuffed it with dozens of things and lashed the cross-cut saw on top. I will let it lead my pack train. I have used more than three coils of fuse tying up my bundles and packs. Soon I'll be out of fuse. I must save enough to tie them all together and then tie myself to the lot.

I wish I could picture the draw more clearly. I am sure it is steep—forty-five degrees or more—and I know it is a series of cataracts from top to bottom, but I don't know about falls and windfalls. There may be none of either, and if there are they may be under the snow. No matter what is there, I intend to go! Once I start, there can be no turning back—no second choice. It will be a mistake or a success.

More than half the night is gone, I'm sure; just a little more packing now, some sleep, then in the morning I'll finish my job here and take the toboggan slide down the hill.

24

I'M IN THE BEACH CABIN. ALL MY CARGO IS HERE WITH ME. ALL IS well and safe under this cabin roof.

Surely no one ever came down a mountainside any faster than I did, and lived to tell the story. Not one single scratch or bump! I was at the bottom before I was ready to start. I had no time to think of how I was going, or of trying to guide myself.

Early this morning I made many trips, dragging my cargo to beyond the spring, tying one bundle behind the other, getting it all ready for the caboose. After I had everything in order to travel, I put the cabin to rights, made shavings, and put a can over the smokestack.

And I put a strong protective splint on my leg and the cast on my arm. I put my eiderdown in a packsack and carried it on my back. The deerskin bedside rug was tied around me—over my bottom—for added protection. I was bundled up worse than a clown.

Then I put the primers into the powder, lit the fuse, and threw them into the canyon. I think they slid clear to the bottom; the blasts sounded as if they came from there. The three shots rang out loud and clear, echoed and reechoed: A farewell to my good cabin, a thanks for shelter and warmth and comfort, a salute to the things we have done here.

My cargo was waiting, all lashed together, pointed into the draw, and tied to a little bush to hold it until I was ready to go. I had just tied the fuse to my belt and was trying to work my

119

crutch under the lashings of the last bundle when my movements made me slide into it. The bush snapped off and the cargo started downhill—me with it. I grabbed for brush, a jerk broke my hold, and then came speed and more speed. I wouldn't have stopped until I hit the bay except for huge snowdrifts the east wind had piled obliquely across my way. Up and down, roller-coaster style, I went over a few of them, gradually losing momentum until I came to a stop not more than three hundred feet away from the beach cabin door.

I think I never took one breath between the top and the bottom. I felt as if I were flying through the air, and part of the time I probably was. There were lots of drops but no bumps. All the way the snow was hard and slick and steep. I came mighty close to brush and trees, but neither my cargo nor I touched a one. Out from the draw and into the timbered flat, I kept veering to the right, toward the cabin. The snowdrifts were not square with the draw, but angled a little and turned me the way I wanted to go.

When I finally stopped, I just sat there and laughed. I laughed like an idiot, and I'm still laughing. There I was, all the way down and out into the flat before I was even ready to start. I think it the funniest thing ever to happen to me. Lloyd would have loved it, if only he could have been with me. We would have laughed together until we got the giggles.

For a while I sat there in profound appreciation of the situation, then I untangled myself, took off the leg splint and the deerskin wrapping, pulled my crutch out, and made my way to the cabin, dragging bundles behind me. I made trip after trip until the last thing was brought and dumped in the middle of the floor.

Goodness, there's an awful lot of stuff: I didn't realize there was so much. This cabin is much smaller than the upper cabin, and the floor space is so taken up that I hardly have room left to get around.

The cabin is just as I left it; no one has been here. Snow is above the eaves on the upper side, but wind has left the front fairly clear; not more than two feet of snow before the door.

The big old leaning cedar has been blown down. It split off about twenty feet up and left a ragged snag. Lots of wood there, but it is mired in the snow.

I must get wood; very little is here in the cabin. I must get some today—as soon as I've rested a little. Where in all this snowy world am I going to find it. Find it I must, and I will, too.

Mercy, but I'm tired! And my bed not fixed! I've got to get horizontal before I drop.

A varied thrush came and paid me a call, welcomed me here. He stood upon my windowsill and cocked his little head, fluffed his feathers, turned about this way and that, showing off his fine black collar and his bright orange breast. I rummaged round and found the cookies, and crumbed one for him. I hope he finds it. I do hope I'll see him again; he's so modest, and as pretty as can be.

Don could call birds by softly whistling to them. The way he could catch live birds in his hands was beyond belief. Many times he has brought me a live bird. He's come in laughing and singing, "Birdie, birdie, pretty birdie."

He showed me how to stroke a bird gently along its back to hypnotize it. After being stroked a few times, a bird can be put down for a minute or so, then picked up again, and it will not struggle or try to fly away. I always wanted Don to build a bird cage for me, but he said it wouldn't be fair.

"It's enough to hold the birds in your hands for a little time," he told me, "then let them fly away. Wild birds would be unhappy in a cage, Martha. Besides, we couldn't find their native food, and they would surely die."

While I was out gathering wood, I found a wonderful treasure. The old cedar is full of moss—great lots of fluffy soft moss. I quickly gathered two canvas loads and dragged them into the cabin. Right now it's a mass of sleet and snow, but when it has dried out I will have a bed fit for a queen.

It wasn't too much trouble finding some wood. I got lots of dead branches from the cedar; they stuck up handy and broke off easily, with a loud snap. Some, though, didn't break at all, and are still there. I did some of my wood gathering in a direction toward the boat so I could take a look at it without making an extra trip. The pilothouse door is open, which is the way I left it. The boat seems low in the water. I know it needs pumping. I wish I had some way to take care of it. That boat cost a lot of money, and we were all so proud of it. Even Sam bragged. The dinghy is swamped. I suppose it's full of rain water which has frozen, snow on top of the ice, then this sleet. It is made of Port Orchard cedar, and it's a dandy—light and well balanced. If I could only get it, it would be so useful to me. I could go along the beach in it to find driftwood, haul the small pieces home and tow the big ones.

There is ice between the island and the boat, but not up to the boat. This side, the water is open. The current and breeze will keep it open unless the whole bay freezes over, which it does some winters—about once in every four or five years, so they say.

On the way home I found a right good-sized log. It looks as if it had been a skid log; much of the bark is battered off. It hasn't been in the water long, maybe a month or so; the ax marks are fresh. It's hemlock, and not very good firewood until it is dry; but it's a gift of God, and not to be wasted. I tied it up.

In the stove ashes I found a big crooked spike. It must have come from some old plank we used for firewood. I've improved my crutch with the spike. I took off the snowshoe, which wasn't very satisfactory on the beach, carved a notch for the spike to fit, and fastened it home with nails I took from a milk case. The spike sticks down about a quarter of an inch, and will keep my crutch from ever slipping on the ice.

I'm proud of that job.

25

I WAS OUTSIDE MOST OF TODAY, AND BROUGHT IN A BIG SUPPLY OF wood. I plan to gather all I possibly can while the good weather lasts. When the next storm rages, I'll cut it down to stove size.

I also found three more skid logs, and have made them secure.

I thought of the way I looked, and I had to laugh at myself. There I was, hobbling along with my crutch, going under the trees, looking up for dead branches which I might be able to pull down, searching along the beach for anything the tide may have brought in, dressed in Sam's big old work pants and his mine shoepacks, Don's old Dux-bak coat, and a miner's cap with my short hair sticking out every which way. My own mother would never recognize her child. If anyone mistook me for an old Indian squaw, I would not have been offended, for I know I look worse than a squaw.

I will be very proud if I am able to match the abilities of an Indian woman. I have seen many of them, when we passed by Indian villages, packing wood, drying fish, dressing skins, gathering berries, and doing all manner of things; but I didn't get acquainted, never thinking that some day I would be doing the same things myself. Then I did not properly respect the Indian women, but my opinion of them is changing fast. Any people who can live in this wilderness and off it, who can wrestle the necessities of life from the raw hills and the savage ocean, deserve profound respect.

I left my ring on the Christmas tree—my beautiful diamond

ring that Don gave me, my engagement ring. I feel so bad about it. I never did wear it in the hills, but kept it on a silver chain around my neck along with my wedding ring. Last night, in bed, I happened to touch the chain, and felt only the wedding ring there. I'm just sick about it. How could I ever have done such a thing? What in all creation made me put it on the Christmas tree in the first place? It was Don's mother's ring, and his father's mother's engagement ring before that, and some day it was to have been Lloyd's to give to the girl he will love. I can't understand how I treated a lovely ring so shabbily, going away and leaving it behind as if it were nothing but a piece of glass. Don's grandfather had the ring made in London; three generations of Martins have been proud of it.

But I'll get my ring back; it isn't lost forever.

In less than two months I will have my child in my arms. I feel fine; get a little short of breath now and then, but otherwise I am quite well. A little pain in my side when I overwork, a bit of an ache in my leg when it gets cold, and a lazy arm that wants to be pampered does not mean ill health. I am hungry all the time, and eat enormous amounts. I eat five or six times every day. Even so, my stomach doesn't hold enough to last from one meal to the next. I carry the child high, and I am sure she is crowding my stomach.

My baby is doing well and has grown until now she has a human shape I can feel with my hands. I can feel the roundness of her little head, and feel the arms and legs when she takes her exercise. I am sure she is perfectly healthy, for she takes quite a lot of exercise.

My thrush came twice today—early morning and again just before dark. He picked at the crumbs I had put out for him, fluffed his feathers, and hopped about on the windowsill. He is a proud bird, stands very tall as he looks about, and he has nice table manners. He doesn't gobble his food, but takes dainty pecks. He wasn't afraid when I moved near to the window to see him better, and cocked his head to inspect me. Approval seemed to have been mutual, for neither of us went away until all the crumbs were eaten.

I have been scheming and figuring out a way to get to the boat, and now I know what I am going to do. I'll build a raft and ride it to the boat. My raft will be made from the skid logs, and all told I have already collected five. A dandy one came in today. It's spruce, and almost twenty-five feet long, two inches through at the top end and about seven inches at the butt end. That log told me a lot. It's a topping log—the top end the loggers saw off their timber after they get it out of the woods and down to the water. Somebody is either logging in this Arm right now, or was logging here not long ago. I know they aren't far away because these toppings haven't been in the water long, haven't banged around on the rocks. They all came from the same place and drifted here in the same tide currents, which means that the loggers are working on this side of the Arm, for the current sets in on this side; on the other side the current sets out.

Logs are easier to get out of the woods if the tops are left on and trimmed down to the very tip end of the tree. This makes it easier for the logger to get a skid under as he works the log out by hand. When the hand logger has enough logs to make up his raft, he goes around and saws off the tops. Every one of my logs has been so sawed. There's not one with an undercut mark on it, proving absolutely that they were not fallen as trees and that they are toppings.

I pity the men who are trying to get logs out in this deep snow. I bet they do a lot of cussing. Of course, they may have been logging for the last two months, got all their logs to the water before the snow came, and just recently rafted them and towed them away.

I got a lot done today; I really worked hard, and I am very tired. All five logs are cut down to raft length, and I have six cross pieces and a jill poke. I know I can finish my raft soon, if the tide doesn't scatter it from here to Jericho. I plan to lash the logs together with fuse, for I have no spikes. It's slow work, but the raft will be plenty sturdy for my purpose.

The weather remains fine, and for that I am thankful. I have worked outside almost all day long. I have brought great quantities of wood and more moss. I burn very little fuel, have a fire only at morning and night. I eat cold food between times, go in the bunk to rest, and cover up to get warm.

Perhaps I can finish my raft tomorrow.

26

THE RAFT IS FINISHED. GLORY HALLELUJAH!

It is a wonderful raft—wonderful beyond my dreams. I got all the long logs in place with the jill poke, and the crosspieces are well spaced and firmly lashed. It took a lot of lashing, and I was glad I had enough fuse. I pried four pieces of puncheon from the cabin floor and made a platform on my raft. I worked fast to keep ahead of the tide, and so got it all done.

I tried it out when the water was deep enough. It's a dandy raft, and holds me up just fine, but I got wet to the knees wading around in the water. I had to do it; the tide came in faster than I expected, and it's still coming in. It seems higher than it should be at this time of day. Perhaps a storm is brewing up far out in the ocean and pushing the tide in ahead of it. I didn't like getting wet, but my job was so nearly done that it seemed wise to finish it and launch my craft on this tide. Doing so has saved me a whole day.

In celebration of the launching I have built a big fire and have the bottom parts of my clothes off and drying over the stove. I'm wrapped in an old sugan and just sitting here rejoicing over my wonderful raft.

I don't think any harm will come from the wetting. I wasn't in the water for very long, but it is still as cold as ever—maybe colder. Baby is quiet now, but she sure wiggled when I was dabbling around in the water. I guess the little lady doesn't like her mother to get wet. I wish my clothes would hurry up and get

127

dry. I do want to lead my raft around to the boat, and get aboard today.

I should clean up this cabin. It looks awful—everything right where I dumped it, wood and moss piled on top of the lot. It will just have to stay that way, though, while the weather is good.

I'm going to the boat when the tide goes out. I have a dour determination to get the dinghy this very day. But I'm going to crawl into the bunk and sleep while I wait on the tide.

Well, I got to the boat all right, but again I got wet to my knees. For the second time today I am drying out my pants and drawers, socks and shoepacks. I have another hot fire going. I've been very extravagant with wood today, burned more fuel than in any day all winter. A hot fire is a luxury I surely do enjoy when I can.

This is a beautiful night—the half-moon up above the hills. There isn't a cloud in the sky. The mountain peaks stand tall and sharp, and the water glimmers with flecks of gold as a scant breeze tickles the surface.

When I woke up from a fine nap, this afternoon, I saw the tide was out almost to my raft. I jumped into my clothes fast, took up my crutch and the jill poke, and went to work. I poked and led the raft along the shore to the bar. Then I climbed aboard it, being careful to stay in the center. I balanced on my knees and poled until the water got too deep, then a bit of urging with my crutch for a paddle and I was alongside the boat. I tied the raft at both ends and climbed on board.

The deck was all ice, and as slick as glass. I didn't dare stand up. The long dinghy line was frozen stiff, and I had to bring a wrench from the pilothouse and beat it and pound it before I could untie it. I dropped all but the very end of the rope into the water and let it soften up while I was doing other things.

There is lots of water in the boat, way up over the floor boards, above the engine pan, and the pump was stuck fast in ice. I pounded and pounded the pump before the plunger came free. I pumped until I was so tired I had to take a rest; then I pumped some more, and it still looked as if there was just as much water as when I started.

I hung the binoculars around my neck, took the guns off their pegs, wrapped them in my coat which I had left in the pilothouse, and got back onto my raft. I tied the long dinghy rope to the crosspiece and was about ready to shove off when I spied the pike pole hanging in the rigging. I needed it badly, so I climbed back aboard and got it.

A push against the boat with the pole to start me on my way, and, in what seemed no time at all, I was back on shore again. I tied up the raft, untied the dinghy, took the guns and pike pole, and started along the beach for home.

My arms were so full I had a bad time managing everything, but it was already night and I didn't want to make a second trip. As I walked along, I wished I had left the guns on board. And I remembered what my father used to tell us children when we overloaded ourselves to keep from making a second trip:

"You children are plain lazy. You're like the man who broke his back carrying everything at once because he was too lazy to put his load into two lots," and Father predicted we would break our backs in the same way if we persisted in being so lazy.

By a system of relays I did manage to bring everything in one trip, and I didn't break my back either, but I certainly did get my feet wet. The dinghy was heavy and contrary and kept hanging up on the beach. Sometimes I couldn't free it with the pike pole, and just had to get into the water and push.

I am waiting for the night tide to come in enough for me to pull the dinghy up to where it will be high and dry tomorrow. Getting all that ice out is going to be a bit of a chore, but once it is out I'll have a good rowboat to use. That's a most comforting thought—to have a rowboat. My raft was good and it did serve a very useful purpose, but I have no love for a raft; a dinghy will be a world better.

The tide is over half in now. I'm too sleepy and weary to wait longer. I'll go now and pull the dinghy up as high as I can, and that will just have to be far enough.

27

THE BOAT IS UNLOADED. I HAVE BROUGHT EVERY BLESSED THING THAT might be useful to me here. The raft is home and tied up high and dry. It will become stovewood when I get around to sawing it up. The dinghy is still full and down at low-tide line.

I will sleep a little, and when I wake I'll go pull it up and unload it. The dinghy leaks worse and worse. I only need to bring that one last load, and then my hard labor will be over.

A record should be made of the condition of the boat and some of the things I took off it. The boat is in bad shape, and poor Don would be so unhappy if he could see it now. I had left the door open, and rain and snow blew in and leaked through onto the engine, but the engine was already ruined. The reason it had stopped was because it got hot. Don always oils up every two hours. That engine ran for two days without oil, and it burned up. The paint is blistered and the flywheel is frozen.

I took the compression off and tried to turn the engine over. Paul Bunyan couldn't turn that engine over now. After the engine stopped, the gas kept right on running—maybe a hundred gallons ran out into the bilge. The tanks are empty down to the level of the carburetor.

It took me three days to pump the boat dry. Water was over the floor boards and above the engine pan. Of course, I didn't pump every minute, only until I got too tired; then I did something else while I rested enough to pump again. I didn't keep
130

count of the strokes, but I think there must have been far
more than a thousand.

I closed the door the first time I went aboard, and when I
got back next day the boat stank so much it made me sick. The
bilge stank, and I couldn't figure out why. Our boat has always
been nice and clean, and never did smell bad. I couldn't understand why it should now. Then I opened the hatch, and there
was that buck! It was rotting, and green water was oozing out
of it.

I had forgotten all about the buck Don had put into the hold.
Strange I could have forgotten all about it. Well, I had to get
it out of there, but I had to do some thinking about it first.

Suddenly I remembered the boom stick. It would be just the
thing. I got the boom stick down after considerable trouble
with stiff lines and frozen blocks. I got a cargo sling around the
buck's horns and prayed the Lord to let his head stay on. It
stayed on, all right, and I pulled him out of the hold and dropped
it overboard. That night I left the hatch cover off.

I didn't dare make a fire for three days because of the gas.
After I had pumped the boat dry, I opened the valve of the
fresh-water tank and let the water out onto the galley floor; then
I got busy and pumped that out. If I had had the energy, I would
have dipped up barrels of salt water and scrubbed the boat well.
I opened two portholes and left them open.

I brought off all the food. There was quite a lot, and most of
it was in good shape. There was half a sack of spuds, about ten
pounds of onions, and nearly as many carrots. They were in a
locker and down below the water line, both the outside water
line and the inside water line, and they stink of bilge. I washed
them, churned the bags up and down in sea water, and now
they're buried in the dirt down under my floor. Maybe the good
earth will absorb whatever bilge smell is left on them. I surely
hope so.

I brought all the bedding, towels, clothing, the guns and gun
shells. Brought charts, writing paper, sewing kit, compass, barometer, tools, soap, and Don's shaving outfit. I'm so happy to have
more paper to write on, for I could see the end to what I had.

Brought the handsaw, hammer, hacksaw, blowtorch, a can of nails, bottle of copper tacks, carbide lamp, and a ten-pound can of carbide. I already had the two lamps and a lot of carbide from off the hill. Surely I'll never be without light now. Also, I got the lantern—which is useless because I didn't find any kerosene— the brace and bits, and a case of fine drills and other special tools. I got the retort sponge and most of the specimens, but I left all the samples aboard. I brought the sourdough pot and the hotcake griddle, the iron frying pan and the washbasin, deck pail, dishes and cook pots, and many other things—too many to mention. Oh, I must mention the cargo shore boards: I took them to make shelves for this cabin. And the mattresses, I got two of them.

My mattress in the pilothouse bunk was wet from the rain and snow that had blown in on it. I left it there, but I brought the other two and dried them out behind the stove. Now I have a wonderful bed. I took out all the old boughs clear down to the poles, spread a canvas and covered it deep with moss which had been drying out for several days, pulled the canvas back, covered the lot over, and tucked it in all around. Then I crowded in the two boat mattresses side by side, spread a woolen blanket, put on the old eiderdown opened out full width, covered it with sheet blankets, and then added my new eiderdown, also opened out full width. On top of all this went another canvas. I have three grand pillows. Surely I will rest well; and I need to, for never before in all my life have I worked so hard and for such long hours, and I've a hurting in my side.

28

GRADUALLY ORDER IS COMING OUT OF CHAOS. AS I BROUGHT LOADS from the boat, I quickly dumped them on the floor and hurried back for more. What I had brought from the hill was already in the middle of the floor, plus my wood, plus lots of moss. What a looking place! The cabin was so cluttered I couldn't even walk straight from the bunk to the stove.

Now that all my wealth is under the roof, I work in the cabin all day, and go outside only long enough to tend my needs and bring a pan of snow to melt. For days I haven't even gone to get a stick of wood, which is breaking my own law. But I've been so busy. Actually, the work wasn't very hard; not all of it was labor. I did a lot of puttering and gloating over my loot. I am rich beyond words. I now have plenty of everything I need, and luxuries besides.

A wind came up last night, and all today the sun was hidden. The sky warns of coming bad weather. It's much warmer, and three deer were out on the beach.

My nice little thrush, who has been coming every day and sometimes twice a day, was here late this afternoon to get his grub. A mean old jay came and drove it away. The jay pecked the thrush—pecked so hard he pecked a feather out. I'm so mad at that jay, I'll not feed him. Let him starve!

Well, the bad weather came today—rain and hail and plenty of wind. It was a real stormy day. I was outside for a little while

133

during a lull, and I actually sawed one block of wood off a raft log. That's the first block of wood I ever sawed all by myself. If Pete were here I'd have him decorate it, and I'd treasure it along with my first schoolbook. But I won't be foolish; my first block of wood is going to be burned. For one reason, it looks too much like the work of beavers for me to brag about it. I had some trouble with the big saw, but I did get the block off. Now I know I can saw, and I feel sure my skill will improve with practice.

Between doing my housekeeping chores and sawing wood, I walk the beach after high tide to see what fuel the Lord has sent to my door. I must never, never be guilty of neglecting to gather the gifts God strands on my beach.

While I was out on the beach, I saw an eagle eating something, so I went to investigate. It was a sort of sea monster, something I had never seen before, or even heard of around here. From the tip of its square nose to the tip of its long round tail, it was about four feet long. The tail was about half of the over-all length, and was rounded like a piece of kelp. It was finned at the tip and had two rudder-like fins near the end. It didn't taper much, the whole tail being nearly the same diameter, and the body was square. Where the body and tail joined, there were two fin-like parts, but they were not true fins. There was a bit of spinal ridge and a slightly raised part for the head. The general appearance was quite flat. The eyes were set far back, and the eagle had eaten both of them. The top or back of the monster was a brownish gray, somewhat the color of halibut, and it had skin, not scales. The underside was very white. The mouth was far back, rather wide, with no teeth. Instead of teeth there were many spines. The whole underside of the nose was covered with spines, too. Where the eagle had torn into it, it showed white meat somewhat like crab meat. It looked good to eat, but I didn't want it, so I left it for the eagle to finish. I remembered seeing pictures of fishermen in Florida with square-looking fish. I think they were called sting ray. I wonder if this was a sting ray.

I have no salt. I didn't think to bring some from the hill, and the salt on the boat was dropped and spattered all over. Salt is absolutely necessary to make my food fit to eat, so from now on I'll have to dip up a pot of ocean water and cook my food in it. It's a good scheme in more ways than one; it saves melting snow.

The topping logs keep coming in. Now I have fourteen tied up, and three more are floating around out front. I should row out and bring them in, but the dinghy leaks like a basket. Also, it's still windy and squally. Let them go! There's too much work here.

I have been using the brace and bit to bore holes in the logs for pegs to put my shelves on. It takes more skill than I have to get the holes straight and in line.

A bitter disappointment came to me today. I can hardly bear to think about it. Looking up from my work and out the window, I was sure I saw a man in a skiff coming around the point.

Don! At last Don was coming!

The weather was terrible—snow squalls blowing all the time.

I got so excited and confused. I saw the object clearly: a man rowing a skiff. Then a snow squall blotted it out. I ran out of the cabin and yelled and hollered, not realizing he could never hear me in this wind and that far away.

The snow raced on past, and there was the man and the skiff a mile away. Plain to be seen, and coming toward my cove. It was Don; I could tell by the way he sat in the skiff.

How glad I was! And so anxious to make him know I had seen him. He would hear gun shots. "Fire the gun," my brain shouted. Back I rushed to get the gun. Hurry. Hurry. Fire to tell Don I was still alive and well, to tell him to hurry to me.

Find the gun.

I found it. The magazine was empty. I dropped it in the middle of the floor and rushed to the window. Don was still there. He hadn't gone away. I wasn't imagining things.

How wondrously good it was to see him, even a mile off and through misty snow flurries.

The binoculars. Find the binoculars the better to see him.

I hurried and trembled and fumbled. Had no more sense than

a chicken. I couldn't find the binoculars. I upset everything. Scrambled things about in my haste. Rushed back to look again. He was still there. Hurry. Hurry. I trembled and dropped things.

A box of shells. Thank the lord!

My hands shook as I lammed one into my gun. It stuck. It was Don's 30.06, and too big for my Krag.

In helpless rage I threw the gun down, picked it up again, and turned to the window. He was still there. He wouldn't go away and leave me. Don was coming, coming to his Martha. How miserable to be out in a skiff in such terrible weather. He would be cold and hungry. Where was my sense! Larny up the fire. Get coffee cooking. Get some of the junk out of the middle of the floor.

Control myself. Don't look like a witch as I meet him. Don't stutter as I greet him.

Once more I look. Through the snow I see him. He's still there. Grand. Wonderful! Saved!

Urge the fire; poke at it. Put on coffee water. Spread my bunk. Pick up some of the litter. There they are—the glasses. Grab them. Now I would see Don, confirm what I already knew.

All I saw was snow—a great white curtain of snow. I looked and looked, unable to find the man in the skiff. My hands shook as I held the glasses, and I mumbled as I watched the snow clear.

I would not believe my eyes. The man in the skiff was only a snag with a limb sticking up.

I was completely worn out with the great excitement and the awful letdown. The cabin is in a worse mess than ever, and I haven't the will to clean it up. I feel sick now from writing about the terrible disappointment.

Don was not coming for me. Maybe he will never come.

Maybe no one will ever come.

29

I SAWED THREE BLOCKS OF WOOD TODAY AND SPLIT ONE. SPLITTING is a real task. If I don't hit the block hard, there is no hope of its splitting; and if I hit it too hard the ax often gets stuck, and it takes a lot of energy to get it out. I have decided one thing: I am not going to try to split wood outside in all this snow. I'm going to do my wood splitting right here inside the cabin. I took up some puncheon, fixed myself a chopping block, and from now on I will do my work in comfort, near the bunk, where I can rest properly between efforts.

I made myself a fine toilet, much better than the one at the upper cabin. It's just inside the door, with the table for a back rest. I use the deck pail for my honey bucket. Taking care of my necessities up to now has been inconvenient, sometimes an ordeal, and I do appreciate the improvement in my living.

This cabin is well built and warm. Sam did a fine job of chinking it. The ever growing cord of wood along the wall behind the stove assures me of fire for the cold days to come. The solid cabin walls, made of yellow cedar logs, please me with their fragrance and give me certain knowledge of safety when the cold winds howl and winter storms rage. I am snug and warm, safe and cozy, and I should be well content. Well, I'm almost content, yet there is an idea gnawing at me, and I can't get rid of it.

I know beyond the shadow of a doubt that somebody is logging in the Arm. Every tide brings chips, toppings, or cut branches to the beach. The wind right now is favorable for bringing anything ashore. Because the tide current has ever set in along this side, things end up here from miles away, but nothing like these toppings and chips. These haven't come very far. I must think this over very carefully. I must plan.

There is a big stand of timber in Grand Fall Cove, which is the next cove down from here. It's only three miles away. Don could row to it in an hour, and I could row there in two hours, even in my present condition.

But with this wind, and my leaky boat, how can I row there in a whole lifetime? I must try to fix the dinghy. It seems to be leaking more and more. Last time I used it to go pump the boat out, I had to bail every few minutes. It leaked almost as fast as I bailed. In clearing the ice from it with the ax, I must have loosened up some of the seams.

I should try to go to that cove, though. With help so close I should not risk being alone when the baby comes. I know the loggers are there and I know they are rafting their logs. I saw half-circles from auger drillings today on the beach. They must be using a two-inch auger to bore the boom chain holes. They are getting ready to make up the raft, and they'll be leaving as soon as it is ready and the weather permits them to cross open ocean.

It will take quite a while to make up the raft; swifters will have to be put across and cabled fast, because the raft must be towed out among reefs and rocks, through open ocean, and back in through a narrow pass with hazards on every side; and right now the swells are pounding in that place so hard no sane person would try to get a raft across.

Sam and Lars lost a raft of logs once in.heavy seas; almost lost their lives and the boat, too. The swells pushed their raft ahead, and the slack cable got into the propeller. They were terribly close to the breakers between their raft and the rocks, and there were big swells and an onshore wind. They had a fifty-fifty chance to get out of that bad spot: speed the engine, slam home the clutch, and either break the cable or the crankshaft. The cable broke and they lived to tell the story, but the logs went to China. Sam is still cussing about it.

That stand in Grand Fall Cove is the only timber out this way

which is big enough and handy enough to be worth taking out
in the wintertime. I remember Don and Sam talking about it.
Don said a couple of hand loggers could make some easy money
there, and Sam agreed with him. But no timber in the whole wide
world would be easy to take out in all this snow.

Those poor loggers will have an awful time. If they drop a
wedge it will take half an hour to find it again in the snow. Of
course, the snow wasn't here when they started; nobody would
be foolish enough to start logging in six to ten feet of snow.
I am sure they would stop falling timber when the snow got deep.
They may have run back to Big Sleeve to wait for better weather.
At Big Sleeve the mine superintendent may have been short of
timbers, and he may have asked them to bring in what they had
ready. Very likely that is what happened. Or maybe the loggers
went in for Christmas and came back just a few days ago.

This much I do know: they will stay right where they are
until the weather changes. There should be a change on the new
moon, which is four or five days off—not more than a week.
The new moon will also bring high tides, the big winter tides.

The ground was soft and getting mucky around my chopping
block, so today I started bringing beach gravel to put over the
dirt. I'm going to bring in a little every day.

I must do something about the snow around my door. There
is a shovel at the water hole, but under all this snow I can't even
find the water hole, much less the shovel. Still, I must clear out
from my door.

I did a little sewing for the first time since coming to the beach.
I have been neglectful of my child. I even neglected thinking
about her. I'm ashamed and contrite. Poor little darling, not
much has been done to receive her. You blessed, precious baby,
I will do better.

The poor deer are having a hard life with this vile weather.
Five of them came past the cabin. They looked scrawny, and
were nibbling at seaweed. I put out all the bread I had and cut
up some potatoes. I hope they will find my offering.

My little thrush has not been back, and I don't think he will come again. I'm sorry. I do wish he would come. The jays are here, a whole tribe of them. The greedy, gluttonous things grab for every scrap, and they swear at me like a bunch of pirates.

I have had a bath and changed clothes. I washed and scrubbed my head and took the splint off my leg. I didn't put it on again. My leg feels light, coolish, and lonesome without the splint. I think it's about well. I can walk on it, but I won't, not yet. I'll use my crutch, and keep on using it, when I'm outside, for quite a while.

The hurting in my left side comes more and more often. I don't like it or understand it. It comes when I work hard, and goes away after I have rested. Hot rocks ease the pain. I keep rocks on the stove all of the time, and hold one to my side when-ever I rest. I take them to bed with me, too. They're a great comfort. I didn't know about hot rocks when I went prospecting the first time. Lots of things I didn't know much about in those days.

The second summer I joined Don, I decided to live in style. I took along so many luxuries it's a wonder Don didn't stop me. I just blithely put all my things in his pack—I didn't have one of my own—and the poor man staggered over the hills and never complained. Once I asked him why he did it, and he said, "Well, you wanted them." That was Don, always so good to me.

Among the many useless things were sheets and a hot-water bottle. Sam took one look at my outfit that first camp night, then moved his bed as far away from us as possible. He even made himself a private fire. He mumbled all the time. Nobody told me anything was wrong. I was enjoying life, was happy and helpful and took pride in fixing our bough beds. First we would clear off a level space, under a sheltering tree, place the boughs nice and orderly with the branch end stuck down and under, cover with the tarp and a heavy blanket, and then I would put on my white sheets. Another blanket and the tarp folded back over it completed the operation.

One evening a bewhiskered, dirty, ragged old codger came visit-ing. The men hailed him like a long-lost brother. I acknowledged the introduction and stood on my dignity. The old feller talked to the men a mile a minute for a while, then he sort of looked around at our camp and spotted the sheets.

"Great guns," he said. "White sheets in the woods! Bet you got a hot-water bottle, too." He looked accusingly at the men, but neither one said a word; they hung their heads and looked ashamed.

"I knowed it," he twitted. "Ha, ha, haw!"

After he had left, I took the sheets off the bed, rolled them into a tight bundle, and poked them under a root. They are there to this day, if the mice haven't eaten them up.

I am not very big for nearly eight months pregnant, but I am carrying the child high, so high my innards are being terribly crowded. I know my stomach holds less and less. I have to keep eating all the time—wee small bites, a tiny sip of tea—to get the equivalent of three good meals. I think the hurt in my side comes from pressure. The pain starts up under my ribs and extends downward.

Tonight I sleep in pajamas for the first time since Don and I slept on the boat. I feel so civilized—wearing pajamas.

30

I HAVE REPAIRED THE DINGHY, AND IT IS LEAKING MUCH LESS. IF I could turn it over, I am sure I could fix it quite well, but that is far beyond my puny strength. I put in several nails and did some calking. It still leaks, but not an alarming amount. It is in good-enough shape to carry me to Grand Fall Cove. I'll go as soon as the weather will let me make the trip.

The mice have gotten news of my whereabouts and have moved in on me, bringing their families along. They are welcome to what they can find on the floor; I have no broom anyway, but they'd better let my supplies alone. I am going to arrange my supplies so I can be sure the mice can't get at them.

My cabin has such a nice lived-in look. Things hang neatly from the crossbeams and on the walls. My shelves are well arranged. The place is cheerful and clean. I've scrubbed things— even washed my window inside and out. I found the shovel and cleared away the snow from my door.

Rain and hail pound on the shake roof and hiss down the smokestack. Angry waves gnaw at the shore. All day it has stormed hard, and there is much water running over the ice in the creek. I hope I can find the water hole, or make a new one. I never want to melt snow again. Silly, how I object to melting snow for water.

I scrubbed clothes today. Everything here is now nice and clean. I have three fuse lines across the cabin, and my laundry is drying on them. I used a lot of wood heating the wash water, and

I am a little worried. It wouldn't take many such days to use up my fuel supply. I hope a lull comes soon so that I can ease my conscience and bring in a little wood.

Thank heavens, the weather has let up a little. I sawed seven blocks today and brought them in. I am getting the knack of sawing, and the saw sings to me. Today it sang to me as Don sometimes sang when we climbed the high hills together.

The thought of Don did not make my heart sad, and I wondered why. Since the bitter disappointment of the floating snag, I haven't thought of him very often, and I haven't been very sad either. I didn't want to make myself sick, or unable to do my work, and I just had to put the thought of him out of my mind; but I didn't mean to forget him.

Am I forgetting Don? No, I don't think so. I know I love him with all my heart and soul, all my mind and body. I love his memory, and it will always be precious to me, yet whole days go by and I don't think of him at all. When I do think of him, I'm not sad; in fact, I'm often glad. I know Don would be proud of the things I'm doing. He would smile and praise me for some of the nice work I've done. Sometimes I'm happy with the feeling that he will come and say I have done well. Always, my heart expects him to come, but my reason would deny it—if I listened to reason. But I won't!

The wind shifted and the rain turned to snow, and all night long great quantities of snow fell; then early this morning the storm blew itself away. When the wind had gone and the waves stopped pounding on the beach, the whole earth seemed so silent and quiet. The sky is still overcast, high overcast, but the snow has stopped falling, and there is not a breath of air stirring.

Many deer have come onto the beach. The poor things had to struggle through soft snow to get out of the woods. When I was out gathering wood, I came upon a sleeping fawn. He was in the snow, and back just a little from the tide line. I was quite near before I saw him. He didn't move, and I knew he was asleep. I got the idea of catching him, so I crept right up to him, making no sound in the soft snow. Just as I was reaching out to take him by the ears, he jumped up and right into me. I went tumbling backward. By the time I had picked myself up, he was almost to the woods, leaping through snow that almost buried him.

I have decided to row to the loggers. I will leave at first daylight tomorrow. The dinghy is free of snow, and washed down with salt water. I will take my sleeping bag, the ax, a carbide lamp, and lunch, but nothing more. If the weather remains good, I can easily make it in three hours—probably in less time.

The men will be surprised to see me, and they will be so good to me, vying with each other to do little kindnesses for me. They will be sorry for all my troubles, and silent in their sympathy.

Suddenly I feel terribly lonesome, just thinking someone is near and I will see them soon. When I knew for certain I was all alone and it was impossible for me to get to any other person, I didn't feel so lonesome. I didn't feel lonesome in the bad weather, either, because I couldn't possibly go anywhere. I just accepted it— there was nothing else a sane person could do. Now the storm is over, I can go to someone, and I am anxious to be on my way to find another human being.

I shot my gun twelve times today. I hope the sound carried in this still air. Maybe somebody will come tonight, but I don't expect it, only hope for it. It's so dark it would be foolish for them to come. If the weather holds, I'll go tomorrow morning early.

All Alaskan men are good to women; there are so few of us in wilderness places, and we get pampered and no end spoiled. The consideration we get is enough to turn any woman's head. I have come to like these rough, dirty-looking men, and to respect them above any group of men I have ever known. Often bewhiskered, dirty, and so ungainly in their dress as to be comical, they're shy when a woman is around, and very careful of their manners, most awful careful not to cuss in a woman's presence; but they are so in the habit of using cuss words they often let one slip unnoticed. Then they become embarrassed, and apologize. I have learned to be stupid, hard of hearing, absent-minded, and dreamy when that happens. As soon as I know an apology is coming, I say:

"Ummp. Excuse me. I wasn't listening. What did you say? I was thinking about what I should cook for dinner. I have a one-track mind. I'm so sorry. I didn't hear you," or some such thing.

They are no end pleased to think I missed their cuss word.

Most of them have radical political ideas, and they can talk for a long time over trifles. They pretend to have no use for churches and "old preachers," yet they are godly men: the life they lead makes for a feeling of brotherhood. You can't guess their ages; they all look about the same age, which might be anything from forty to seventy. None are really young. They have little regard for the laws of man beyond the desire not to get caught, but I have never known one to break the laws of God. They are fiercely proud of their independence and freedom, proud to call themselves prospectors, and would scorn the name my mother calls them: "explorers." They are the most optimistic people on earth; there is no end to their faith. Every one of them is dead certain he will find "the richest mine that ever lay out of doors"; but in the meantime he may be persuaded to take a job logging or mining, but only on a contract, and where he can be his own boss. One and all seem to hate a boss and "big corporations."

Oh, the loggers will be good to me. I'll be treated like a cross between a helpless invalid and a reigning queen. I am anxious to go. I wish I had gone this afternoon. Please God, make good weather for tomorrow.

As I write, my child is wiggling all over the place. She must be a chip off the old block—like the Martin family, overjoyed to be going someplace. Lie still, you babe! You'll get your trip, and maybe collect yourself some grand old uncles. What a lucky thing for me that I can carry you inside. I shouldn't like starting out in a rowboat in the middle of winter with a tiny baby in my arms. How could I ever row and hold the baby? You just stay put, young lady, and we'll soon be on our way.

Time drags, and I wish the present would fly. It would if I went to bed and to sleep, but I'm still too excited and restless.

Just before dark I looked out and saw the farther shore reflected in the still water. I could hardly tell where the shore ended and the reflection began.

It's still cloudy and warm. I hope it stays warm until tomorrow afternoon. I'll be close to my destination by then—or perhaps already there. A few degrees' drop in temperature with no breeze, and this Arm will freeze over clear down to where the ocean swells come in.

Sam might be with the loggers. He has worked in the woods a lot, and is a good man at getting logs out by hand. I hope he's there. It would be logical for him to be. I know he took the loss of Don mighty hard, and I'm sure he would seek arduous work, hoping to ease his feelings, to sweat out his grief.

Even if Sam were working within three miles of here, he wouldn't return a second time to the cabin. I can almost hear him say, "What's the use?" Sam will never want to come back here. He'll sell his interest in the mine for a song, go far away, and start prospecting somewhere else. Sam is tenderhearted that way. He and Don were closer than brothers.

In all the years Sam and Don were partners, they never had a quarrel, yet they often disagreed—growled at each other every day. At one time it looked as if there might be a quarrel over Lloyd and me tagging along. But then they found this good mine, and Lloyd and I survived all the hazards of the wilderness, adapted ourselves, and became useful. I know Sam would do all in his power to help me. If he thought I was here alone, he'd risk his life to come to me.

I just looked out my door. It's snowing again, but there is no wind. I'll go tomorrow anyway, even if it does snow. Snow shouldn't be a bother for rowing. But I dare not try to go if it's windy.

I'm going to bed now. I pray for one more day of good weather.

31

HOME AGAIN. WEARY UNTO DEATH. SAFE. THANKS BE TO GOD!

Two days and three nights I have lain in my bunk; didn't even make a fire. Today I made a fire and cooked and ate hot food.

This is the sixth day since I left to go to Grand Fall Cove. Two nights I slept in the woods. No harm came to me, only a very great tiredness. The child moves, and all seems well.

It was a nice winter morning when I left the cabin. Only about two inches of snow had fallen during the night. The air was still and fresh and sweet. I loved being out, going someplace, and I was excited and hopeful about the trip.

It was about quarter incoming tide when I left, and I had to buck the current getting around the point. From there on the going was easy enough for a while. Then the dinghy began leaking more than I thought it should, and soon my side began to bother; my leg was cold and aching, but I was determined not to give in. I refused to recognize my pains, and resolved to keep going.

But I found I couldn't keep on. I had to rest, and the dinghy had to be bailed.

The weather grew colder and tiny wrinkles of scum ice appeared. A far-away cold sun came through the haze, and my way was heavy with silence.

Every time I rested, I got colder—almost numb with cold, and the dinghy kept on leaking, and drifted back toward the cabin.

147

Time after time I rested, bailed, righted the dinghy, then rowed a little farther. I rowed until I could row no more.

I was nearly to the mouth of Grand Fall Cove. Only one more point to round, and I could have looked into the cove. I wanted desperately to make the point, and I struggled until the tears came and I was breathless. I got fumbly because the cold numbed my hands. All my efforts were wasted. I just had to rest and get warm. I had to get the cold and stiffness from my body, and find relief from pain.

There was nothing for me to do but go ashore and make a fire. How I wished I had brought kindling with me. How I needed my crutch. With stiff hands I picked a few dead branches from the alders, pushed away the snow, and carefully laid a little fire. I spit in my carbide and made enough gas to light the lamp and get my fire burning. It was so good to hover over my small fire.

As I rested and warmed myself, I wondered how I could help the aching in my leg. If I could keep it warmer, it would be less troublesome. I decided to take the sock from my good foot and put it on the complaining one.

I had my shoepacks off and one sock off, and was holding it over the fire when I heard a boat engine. I was frantic. The boat would go away and leave me! I started to the dinghy without my shoes, turned back and put them on; but my feet were snowy, and it was so hard to get my packs on in a hurry. I didn't bother with the laces, just left them dangling, and I tripped over them as I rushed to untie the dinghy. My gloves! Beside the fire. Oh, leave them there. No! Get the gloves. Trip on shoelaces. See the carbide lamp. Leave it.

I rowed with all my might and main, straining at the oars with every ounce of energy I had. Far too much water was in the boat, but I disregarded it with the courage of despair. I disregarded it until the dinghy began to sway and roll. Then I had to stop and get some of the water out. I bailed in a frenzy, grudging every moment of lost time.

All the while I could hear the engine. "*Chuc-it-te-chuc, chuc-it-te-chuc.*" It was a three-cylinder engine. I wished it would stop. I hoped it was a contrary engine and would take a long time to warm up. I heard a man shout. The engine slowed. More shouts. The clutch went home, the engine was at work, and the boat was moving, slowly getting under way. Still I had not come to the point.

I rowed and rowed. I prayed for God to have mercy and let me go fast. The minutes dragged by agonizingly. I wondered if it would take to the end of time for me to get to the point. The sound came nearer; the engine was laboring. They were towing the raft; that's why it labored. I prayed that the raft would be heavy, or would swing ashore and hang up. I wanted every log in it to be a sinker. The sound of the boat came on.

I strained at the oars, and shut my teeth on my lip until the taste of blood was in my mouth. The point was near—just a few more strokes.

I rounded the point. There was the boat coming out of the cove, swinging in a big arc, straightening out, dragging a raft of logs on a short towline. Two men were on deck, and one of them was Sam. Good Sam. Blessed Sam. Oh, how I loved Sam that minute. I know it was Sam. His hat was cocked sideways, and all his movements were quick. That's the way he always looked and acted. I saw him go to the stern of the boat, lean over, and do something to the tow cable. Then he stood there watching the raft swing around and ease into line.

I screamed, but my voice was no more than a mouse squeak. I floundered to my feet, stood and waved my arms, gulped for breath and shouted. The dinghy had a dangerous amount of water in it, and rolled, threatening to swamp. I staggered drunkenly, knowing the risk yet disregarding it because of the greater risk —Sam might not see me. I had to risk my life to save it. I stood and waved my arms, shouted and called, screamed and hollered until I was out of breath and exhausted.

Then I could no longer ignore my rowboat. I had to bail, and bail fast.

Sam stayed at the stern and stood there like a lout, never once raising his head for a look around. Another man came out on deck. Sam turned and went up to him. There were three men, and they stood together a minute or so, then one went back into the pilothouse. Sam and the first man pulled their skiff on deck.

They had not seen me. There I was, not half a mile away, screaming and begging them to stop and take me with them.

I saw them working near the mast, probably making the cable fast, cinching it with cable clamps. Again they came to the stern of the boat and worked over the cable, letting it out, lengthening the towline. The third man stuck his head out of the pilothouse door. The boat slowed and the engine idled. I was sure they had seen me.

Frantically I waved the bailing can, stood up on the thwart and screamed.

Nothing happened. They went about their business; carefully they put something over which looked like a small anchor and which was made fast to the tow cable. The skipper threw in the clutch, eased the boat forward. Sam and his helper did things to the cable. Again the engine idled. I stood and waved and shouted some more. The men kept right on tinkering with the cable; then the clutch went in, and the boat moved ahead. Sam stayed at the stern, easing out more cable over the chock. The other man began to stow things and lash gear down, for soon they would come into open ocean. They had put the anchor in the middle of the towline to take the strain in ocean swells.

They had not seen me.

They moved slowly, slowly away from me. I thought I could catch up with them. I prayed they might still see me. Again I rowed—rowed for my life and the life of my child. Again I stood up and screamed and waved. It was no use. My voice was lost in the sound of the engine—lost in the swish and splash of the moving boat.

The boat kept right on going, nosed behind the island, and slid out of sight, with Sam still standing there at the stern, watching his measly old logs.

I was furious. If I had had a gun, I'd have shot them dead. Those lazy, stupid men kept right on going and left me alone. Not once had they looked in my direction, and me needing help so bad. I was so mad at them that I cussed. I screamed cusses at them until I was hoarse. I said all the bad words I had ever heard in all my life, and I invented some new ones, too. I wished the towline would break and they would lose every last log; wished their old logs would go to China. I stood up and shook my fist at the disappearing boat.

When it had gone from sight, I dropped down and cried. I shed tears of helpless rage and of utter defeat.

32

I DIDN'T WASTE MUCH TIME CRYING. THE LEAKY DINGHY SOON
reminded me that I was alive and still wanted to stay that way.
Now that the boat was gone, I told myself it was no longer my
life. The cabin once again became my life. I had to get back
there, back to my good cabin. I had to return to my cabin!

I worked back to shore, paddling slowly and painfully to my
camp site. The fire had not gone out; smoke was still rising in
tall white plumes. Why hadn't those men seen the smoke. The
stupid fools! I never heard tell of such stupidity.

I pushed the fire together and unrolled my eiderdown. I didn't
open it, just lay down on top and covered myself with the canvas.
I was too numb to think. I felt drained in body and mind. After
a while I found myself crying again. I felt so God-forsaken, so
terribly alone, with a heavy, burdensome aloneness. It seemed to
me that some demon must be after me and bent on my destruction. I had done my best, planning and working. I had tried to use
every grain of intelligence God had given me, and I had kept my
faith. I had tried to accept my fate, and not complain very much.
Always I had been thankful, thankful to be alive and to have my
good cabin, thankful for food and warmth. Why should so much
tragedy and sorrow and suffering and pain come to me? Why was
I compelled to remain in this wilderness all alone when I needed
help? Why must this evil fall upon my unborn child—my inno-
cent baby? All these thoughts came with my tears, and again
I became rebellious. I cussed some more, shouting my invectives at
the lonesome sea and at the mountain wall.

152

The words echoed back to me, and suddenly I realized it was my own voice saying those awful things. I was shocked and ashamed. I thought of Don and of how humiliated he would be to hear me cuss. Don has never heard me say one bad word, not one.

I cried again, this time in shame. I felt unworthy, undeserving of my good husband. And I was afraid. I was afraid of the unseen, the unknown; afraid for myself and afraid for my child.

I remembered my grandfather who had been in two wars—the Mexican War and the Civil War. He was a rebel in the Civil War, had been in many battles, and was wounded three times. He told us that he was always afraid, and that he believed all soldiers were afraid when they went into battle. He said the only difference between a brave man and a coward was that the brave man went on in the face of his fear, while the coward just gave up and let his fears get the best of him.

As I remembered, I thought maybe it wasn't too wrong for me to burst out in angry protest and to be afraid, so long as I did not give up and quit trying. Maybe it was all right that I hadn't reached the loggers, all right that Sam hadn't seen me, all right for me to be alone. I knew full well it was no one's fault they hadn't seen me. I realized how terribly the men would feel when they learned some day how near I was to them. I regretted my cuss words, and felt sorry for the men, not for myself. Those poor men would condemn themselves, heap blame on their own heads. I was determined they should not, for I would never tell them—never! Thinking I would save someone else from distress comforted me. I felt so much better that I sat up and ate some of my lunch.

The tide was going out, and the stern of the dinghy was barely in the water. I pulled the plug, then carefully looked to see if I could stop some of the leaks. Tearing off a strip of canvas, I did some calking, and with the ax head I tapped some of the nails tighter. It was an improvement, and one step further toward my cabin home and comfort. The charred ends from my fire went into my boat, and I was ready to start when I spotted a big dead branch hanging in the alders, and went back and got it. I hoped I wouldn't need another fire, but I meant to be prepared. I also took a hot rock from the fireplace to hold to my side.

Big spots of scum ice were forming all over the water, wrinkly patches of a different grayness from the grayness of the open spaces. Two sundogs came out and traveled with the pale cold sun. As day wore on to late afternoon, it became much colder, and scum ice was all over, leaving no open lanes. But the ice wasn't hard yet. It broke to the oars with a tinkling sound.

I got awfully tired, and often had to rest, but I didn't go ashore. I rested by leaning my head on my knees and pressing my hands to my side. My repairs did help a lot, and I didn't have to bail nearly so often. I got cold, so I unrolled my eiderdown, wrapped it around my body and down over my legs, and draped the canvas across my shoulders.

The ice got thicker and thicker. I had to hurry, but somehow I didn't hurry. I knew I didn't dare exert myself to the point of exhaustion. Gradually I developed a slow easy stroke which made progress, yet still gave me a breathing space between strokes. I'd lean far over as I lifted the oars, lay my aching side against my thigh for a few heartbeats, dip the oars with a thud to break the ice, then pull a long stroke as I raised my body. It was a good system, and it worked fine until the ice got so thick it wouldn't break to the oars. Then I had to stand up, reach ahead to break the ice, and pole or paddle along.

Something, perhaps my moving about, started the leaks again, and they were worse than ever. I had to bail and bail. Still I moved along. Slowly, surely I neared the cabin. I was almost to my home point; just around the point I would see my cabin. I prayed for strength enough to get past the high steep cliff which makes the point. That's all I wanted—no more. Just to get past that point.

Forty yards more. I kept going. I didn't give up. I wouldn't give up. Slowly, slowly I moved on.

Thirty yards more and I would be where I could walk the beach to the cabin. There was a dangerous amount of water in the dinghy, and I was fumbly with tiredness. I knew I had to rest, bail, then make the final effort. Rested, the effort need not be too great.

It was so good to rest, just to sit and make no move. As I rested I ate raisins. I told myself to hurry and get the water out—get going. Night was near. I dared not rest too long.

I reached for the bailing can. I had left it on the thwart, and it had become coated with ice. It slipped from my hand and went over the side. It did not break through the ice, but went sliding and rolling far out of my reach. I knew fear then—stark, naked fear. Because I had put my feet up on the thwart to keep them out of the water, I had not realized how fast the skiff was filling. The amount of water in it frightened me. Could I keep the dinghy balanced while I broke the few feet of ice which separated me from the shore.

Well, I did! It was nothing less than a miracle. I thanked God with all the breath I had, thanked Him from the bottom of my heart, and asked no more than to be able to thank Him. How good was the firm shore, the ice-coated rocks!

The beach was steep and rocky, and the tide, almost low, had left the rocks covered with ice—thin ice that broke at my step like cracking glass, yet made the rocks treacherous. I had come ashore at the very edge of the cliff.

I pulled the nose of my boat as far ashore as I could get it, then tied it up. I took the eiderdown sleeping bag and the canvas, shook the water off them, carried them up to the edge of the snow, and then went back for the ax and firewood.

I looked about for a place to camp and found a perfect nook. The blunt face of the cliff was the end of a ridge, and on either side was a little draw. On my side the rock wall tapered back into the draw irregularly, at one place making a small recess. There I would make my fire. The little nook was above the present high tide, but it had been below higher winter tides and was clear of deep snow. Also, some driftwood and debris had caught in it. No weary person could have possibly found a better place for a night camp.

I made my fire, using the driftwood at hand. Wrapping the canvas about me, I sat toasting myself, first one side, then the other. I nibbled sparingly from my lunch. As I ate and warmed and rested, I took stock of my situation. I hoped I could use every grain of sense I possessed, and think carefully of what should be done, and in what order, and try to foresee the results.

My unhappy day was the result of an attitude not unlike that of the five foolish virgins in the Bible story. Looking back, I saw how I might have avoided some of the tragedy. Even another pair of socks, put on before leaving the cabin, might have made the difference. A little more calking certainly would have helped. And why hadn't I taken my gun? That was almost too painful to remember. A gun shot would have attracted Sam's attention.

Many times I have heard prospectors talk of making emergency night camps in the far north in weather way below zero. Their stories didn't sound as if they had endured any great hardship. I knew that I, too, could make myself comfortable for the night if I kept my wits about me and didn't do anything foolish. So I thought out all the chores, pictured myself doing them, and visualized the results.

When I felt somewhat rested, I got up and went to work. I chopped down a brushy little spruce, dragged it beside the fire, and spread my eiderdown over it to dry. I found boughs and brought them to my camp site. For kindling I hunted dead branches, and soon gathered enough.

I stirred up the fire, rested, warmed myself some more, and then went to the beach to find the right size rocks to heat for bed warmers. The tide was low and the dinghy was dry. I was going to pull the plug and drain the water, but there wasn't any water; it had all leaked out—all that hadn't turned to ice, that is.

Back at camp, I selected the spot for my bed, leveled it off, cut my boughs, and placed them over the snow. I didn't need many. I made my bed as close to the fire as I dared. I spread the canvas so that half would be under me and the other half could be pulled over the top of the eiderdown. Then I fixed the sleeping bag, and all was ready for me to go to bed.

The nook was snug, and the rock walls reflected the heat from my fire. I was rich in driftwood, so I made up a good fire. I put my gloves out to dry, took off my packs, pulled out the wool insoles, and put them beside the gloves. I made the now boughless little spruce into a leaning pole within reach of my bed, and draped my socks, pants, and coat on it. I crawled into my bed just as the last glimmer of day faded into night.

The person who said, "The harder the toil, the sweeter the sleep," never had toiled to the end of his endurance as I had. I needed much rest before I could sleep, and even then my sleep was troubled and I woke often. Not until toward day did I sleep naturally and sound.

My bed was good and I was warm, with a hot rock at my side and another easing the aches in my leg. Tinkling sounds came from the water as the tide disturbed the ice; cracking and popping noises came from the woods as the timber protested the cold. A whiff of driftwood smoke was in my nostrils; the stars were dim and far, far away. I dozed and wakened, dozed again to dream strange, unrememberable things, dozed some more, then became wide awake to see the stars were brighter. They didn't seem so far away.

I lay thinking of how I would get home to my cabin. I held no hope or faith in the rowboat, and wasted no time thinking about it. I knew I must go over the ridge; somehow climb up the cliff and get down the other side. The ridge was heavily covered with brush and timber, and it should not be too difficult, but before I could reach to the hand holds in the timber I would first have to negotiate fifteen or twenty feet of sheer rock wall. I had either to go up it or around it.

While I thought of the way I had to travel on the morrow, my baby moved quite a lot and took her exercise. If she had moved during the day, I hadn't noticed, being much too occupied with other things. I held my belly, felt her move against my hands, and was filled with gladness. I thought of the climb ahead, and was more than thankful I still carried my child in my basket instead of in my arms. Then I slept soundly.

It was day when I awoke, and I was not nearly rested enough. I would have liked nothing better than to stay in my bed. I dressed quickly, ate a few bites of my much-diminished lunch, rolled my bed, slipped my arms through the pack straps, tied the ax to my belt, and left camp without making a fire.

I looked for a break in the rock wall where I could start my climb. There was such a break in the draw near my camp, and I studied it for a long time. It didn't look like a bad climb at all. Many times I have gone up and down much worse places. If I had tackled it at once without thinking, I feel sure I could have made it, but I stood there looking at it. The longer I looked, the more afraid I became of falling. I lost all confidence in myself for cliff climbing.

I decided to find a way around it—an easier way. I went along the beach looking for an easier way. At first the cliff came down to near high-tide line, with only a wide shelf, strewn with huge broken rock—alders and stunted trees growing among them— between the cliff and the water. After a way it curved back and became a little flat covered with timber. Going over the broken rock was arduous work, and wading through the snow in the flat was a continuous struggle. How I missed my good crutch! That was the first time I had taken more than a few steps without it, and I missed it sorely.

I found a way up, steep, but no sheer climb, and very brushy. I traveled obliquely up along the hillside. Not once did I trust myself to a brush until I tested it, and not once did I let go one hold before I found another. The snow was firmer, had settled some and frozen some. The frozen snow was troublesome indeed. The crust was not strong enough to hold me, but too strong to push through. I had to use the ax to break my way.

I became very tired. There was no level place where I could sit down. I had to rest leaning into the snow, always holding on. Sometimes it was a good place where I could crook my knee or elbow round a small tree; sometimes it was a bad place where I had but little more than a fingerhold. I rested often, trying to save my strength; but I had so little, and aches and pains tormented me.

I looked at the sun when I came to an opening where I could see the peaks on the peninsula, find markers, know directions.

The sun was past south and going into the west. I was nowhere near back to the point. I wasn't half to the point. It would be insane to try to struggle on. I turned back.

It was getting dark when I staggered to my camp site. I dropped on the boughs and just lay there. I didn't care if I got cold; I didn't care about anything in all creation. After a while I began to care a little bit, but not very much. I unrolled my sleeping bag and crawled into it; I didn't take off my hat or untie the ax from my belt; didn't even take off my packs. I slept with my shoes on just like an old horse. I was stupid and dumb and numb, bereft of my senses and of all sensation. I don't think I slept, and I know I was not awake.

When it was broad day and the sun was shining, I sat up and looked about, looked toward the water, and saw a crack of open between the ice and the cliff. I watched it grow wider, saw small pieces of ice floating, and I remembered the current of the incoming tide sets against this shore. It comes strong against the cliff. I could get around the cliff in the dinghy. Praise be to God!

I made a fire and waited. It was a long wait. I had to wait until the tide came to the dinghy; I hadn't the strength to get it down to the water, and yesterday's tide had left it stranded quite high. It was in a good position for me to hunt for leaks—or rather, I thought it was. I found no leaks; it was coated inside and out with ice. Ice should stop leaks for a while, at least until it melted, I convinced myself; so I didn't disturb the ice.

I went near the water's edge and threw rocks out to break up the ice and enlarge the open spaces so I could start without first pounding at it with an oar. I broke the ice all the way to the open space, making a clear lane. The current carried the floating pieces past the point, out of sight.

Then I went back to my fire and lay beside it, waiting for the tide to come to the dinghy. I was weary and feeble, and my body felt heavy beyond my strength to raise it. If the little effort of throwing a few rocks had used up all the energy stored during a long night's rest, how then would I ever get through the ice I knew I would have to fight on the other side of the point?

Food! I was starving. That was what was wrong with me. I was starving, and didn't even feel hungry. I ate the last of my lunch, all except a handful of raisins, ate slowly, my hand bringing each bite to my mouth as if it were a heavy weight.

The tide came in so slowly, it seemed to take forever for the water to rise to my dinghy. I was both glad and impatient: glad not to have to make an effort, impatient to be on my way. I brought the oars to the fire and melted the ice on them. I rolled my bed, put the bedroll and the ax in the boat, then sat by the fire and waited.

Finally, it was time to go. I got a good push off in the right direction, and the current took me on. I was half past the cliff before I had the oars into the oarlocks.

On the other side the current had cut a lane in the ice for a thousand feet or more. It led toward my cabin, but the end of the lane was quite far from shore. I debated about using the open water. It would close when the tide turned, for the outgoing current sets to the far shore. If I couldn't break a path to my home beach, I would be left locked in the ice over deep water, and no doubt the dinghy would soon be leaking like a basket. I remembered yesterday's trudge in the snow, and decided if I was to save my life I must risk it again.

Quickly I came to the end of open water. The ice I had dreaded so much was not thick at first, and I made good progress. The last half of the way was harder; the dinghy was beginning to leak, the ice seemed thicker and stronger, and my strength was ebbing away. But the shore was nearer and nearer; unlike the men and the boat, it would not move away from me.

What joy and gladness I knew when I reached the shore and could see my good cabin! I had wandered in the wilderness and been led back safely. I tied up my rowboat, ate the last of the raisins, and went slowly home.

33

ANOTHER DAY OF REST AND RECUPERATION. I WENT ONLY TO THE water hole, chopped away the ice, and brought half a pail of water. I did not gather wood or cut what is gathered. All I did was cook a little, eat a lot, then sleep and rest again.

My child has suffered no harm from all my weary journey; she moves, takes her exercise, and seems to have grown in these few days. Something has happened to her position; she is lower, and my abdomen protrudes enormously. Now I look very much pregnant, and Sam's old work pants barely meet across my belly. The pain is gone from my side. I have not suffered it since I returned to the cabin, and I am less short of breath.

The bay is frozen across from shore to shore. I am truly alone now, and I will remain alone. No one can possibly get to me, and I cannot get to anyone.

The weather is cold—must be below zero, which is awful cold for this coast; it doesn't often get down to zero. I haven't seen any deer on the beach, but the jays come every day. They don't stay long, just look for a few pecks of food, then hurry back to wherever their home is. I heard ptarmigan when I went for water, but I did not see them.

I stay at my sewing, and little by little I am getting many things made. Among my dress-up clothes are several things I can convert into garments for Baby. I am glad I brought some good clothes out here to camp.

Don does not like me to wear skirts in the hills, and he

absolutely forbids them on the boat. He knew one woman who got hung up with her dresstail fast to a cleat and was almost dead before anyone could rescue her.

I wear overalls in camp and on the boat and Dux-bak for climbing around over the hills. I do like to get into women's clothes now and then. Sometimes I dressed for dinner, and always I wore dresses when we were in Big Sleeve.

Every day I feel better. It is a wonderful relief not to have that pain in my side tormenting me.

Is there anybody in all the world who would believe wood can freeze? Well, it can! My topping logs are frozen as hard as bone, and I cannot possibly saw them. I can hardly believe it. I don't remember ever hearing Don say logs would freeze. Since I can't saw, and since ice keeps the tide from bringing me gifts of fuel, I have to go into the timber to find wood.

The crust on the snow is strong enough to bear my weight, so I put on the ice creepers—I didn't really need them, for the snow is not slick—and went moseying through the timber. It was a nice outing, and so easy to get around. I found quite a lot of dead branches and dragged them home. With the handsaw I cut them into stove lengths. I have considerable wood now, but not a splinter to spare. Every day I must bring in some fuel, no matter how little.

I found a big spruce windfall, and it is literally full of moss, just as the big old cedar was. I gathered a load, shook out the waste, and brought only the long strands. Fresh moss smells so good. I found an eagle feather lodged in it; it must have hung there for months, as this isn't the time of year for birds to shed their feathers. It is still glossy and undamaged by the weather. I brought it home and stuck it up on the wall.

I also brought a few cedar boughs to put about the cabin to take the place of house plants. I dropped them outside the door until I could find time to fix them. When I opened my door and looked out, there stood a deer eating them. He was the same one who visited me at the upper cabin. I could tell because he has the scar under his throat. He didn't seem afraid of me, just stood there and looked. I turned back in the cabin, got some old hot-cakes, and threw them to him. He moved away a little, then came forward, smelling around. He found a hotcake, ate it, liked it, and looked for more. He ate every scrap I had thrown to him. I have named him Sammy, and I think Sam would feel honored if he knew. Hereafter I'm going to make lots of hotcakes so I will always have something handy for any deer who offers me his friendship.

The jays were around again for a little while, looking for scraps, but my little thrush has never come back since the jays beat him up. I never did like Steller's jays very much, and I like them even less now. The varied thrush was such a pretty bird, with bright orange markings, and so gentle and well mannered. The jays are noisy; they jeer and swear at me.

I hurried with my chores, then got at my sewing. I am making a bed pad for when Baby is born. I am using two hundred-pound sugar sacks, padding them with moss, and quilting with string. I like to work with the moss, and I feel so fortunate to have such lots of it.

I felt happy today as I walked through the woods, and a song welled up from within me. "Joy to the World, the Lord Has Come," I sang. It was good to hear my own voice ringing through the timber.

34

I KILLED A SEA OTTER TODAY. I ACTUALLY DID KILL A SEA OTTER. I killed him with the ax, dragged him home, and skinned him. I took his liver out, and ate part of it. I'm going to eat the rest of it, and his heart, too. His liver was quite large, bigger than a deer's, and it had more lobes to it. It was very good liver, and I enjoyed it.

Most of today was devoted to the sea otter; getting the hide off was a real task. It's a lovely skin, the softest, silkiest, thickest fur I have ever seen. I am going to make a robe for my baby out of the beautiful fur. My darling child may be born in a lowly cabin, but she shall be wrapped in one of the earth's most costly furs.

It was such a splendid piece of luck. Lucky in more ways than one. The otter might have killed me, although I have never heard of such a thing.

This morning I went to the woods to gather a load of limbs. As I was coming home with them, I saw the tide was nearly out, and I thought I'd walk over to the bar and take a look at the boat. I put my wood down and went across the beach toward it. There's lots of scattered ice on the beach; in fact, it's all over, but broken up so as to leave ample space for walking between the chunks of ice, and the beach is covered with brownish seaweed.

I was going along, swinging the ax in my left hand, managing the crutch with the right hand, more or less watching where I placed my feet, not thinking of anything in particular, when right beside me I heard a bark. It was like a dog bark; not a bow-
164

wow bark, more of a yip. I looked around and saw a huge creature reared up on its haunches. I saw its white teeth.

Without thinking, I swung the ax at the side of its head, saw it hit, felt the jar in my arm, heard the thud. As I swung the ax, I turned and tried to run. I was so terrified the thing would nab me from behind that I could hardly move. I glanced over my shoulder to see how close it was. It hadn't budged from where it dropped.

I went back very gingerly. Picking up a rock, I threw it and hit the brute. It never moved. I mustered up more courage, went a little closer, threw more rocks, and still it didn't move. I got real brave and walked right up to it. I heard it breathe, and saw a twitch or jerk. I didn't lose much time pounding his head very thoroughly with the ax. Soon it was quite dead.

I got down on my knees and examined it from one end to the other. First off, I noticed the lovely fur. I took off my glove and ran my fingers through the nice silky coat. I decided right then I would have the skin. I saw it as a baby blanket.

The legs were short, the front ones held rather far apart by a wide deep chest. They fitted to the body very much like a dachshund's legs. The toes were webbed, and the web was covered with fur. There was fur between the foot pads. The tail was a bit short for the length of the body, in proportion much shorter than a land otter's tail. It was a nice tail, somewhat bushy, but not nearly as bushy as a foxtail. The body was over a yard long, rounded and firm. The ears were small, well back, and close to the head. It had whiskers, and I think the top of the face must have looked somewhat like an airdale with fur around the eyes. The nose and chin were more like a dachshund. The jaws were strong, and the teeth were doglike and very white.

It was a female, and although I had never seen one before I knew it was a sea otter. It just had to be, because it was of otter build, yet it was not a land otter; I have seen many land otters, both alive and dead, and I know this was not one.

It is very much against the law to kill a sea otter. Right now I don't care a rap for law. I'd like to have a picture of a game warden who could arrest me now. I am safe enough from the

law, and I think I always will be. Under the circumstances I
doubt if any judge would send me to jail for what I have done.
He might take the beautiful fur away from me, though, which
would be almost as bad. Maybe a judge in the States would, but
an Alaskan judge wouldn't.

I'd never deliberately hunt a sea otter, or ever kill one under
other circumstances. They should be given rigid protection. A
hundred years ago thousands upon thousands of sea otter lived
along this coast, and now they are almost extinct. It was sea-otter
fur the Russians were after, and it was largely they who destroyed
the great herds.

I dragged my kill home, and was a long time doing so. I'll bet
the creature weighed a hundred pounds. I worked and worked,
rested, pulled, and dragged, rested some more, and by and by
I reached the cabin with my prize. Soon I had it inside. I made
up the fire, had some hot tea, and sat there admiring the fine fur
and considering how to go about getting the skin off.

I decided to skin it exactly the way the men do a deer. I have
watched them many times, but I never helped or paid much
attention. I didn't know very much about skinning a fur-bearing
animal when I went to work on that creature. How I wished I
had an Indian squaw to instruct and help me.

Well, I laid it flat on its back and fixed it as straight as I could.
I sharpened the smallest-bladed knife, then went to work. I
slit the skin straight across from one front paw to the other,
then from the anus to each of the hind paws, then from the chin
to the anus in as straight a line as possible. That gave me several
corners to start on.

I had plenty of trouble. No place would the skin pull off like
a deer hide. Every inch of it had to be cut off. The animal was
terribly fat. I got all the skin loose from the under parts, turned
the otter on one side and got it off there, then off the other side.

The head was a mess, so I just cut the skin at the neck line
and let the head fur go. I chopped off the feet and threw them
in the stove. After I got the legs and sides skinned, I turned the
otter on his belly and worked the skin off his back down to the
tail. I had more trouble with that tail than I did with all the

rest of the animal. I wanted it for a neckpiece, and I tried to get the bony tail out without slitting the skin. It can't be done. Finally I cut the rest of the skin off at the tail and moved it out of my way. I simply had to slit the tail clear down to the tip end. Soon the tail skin was off, and there on the floor lay the "naked" animal. It looked much smaller with the hide off. I pulled it outside, then thought of the liver. I opened the belly and got the liver. I got the heart, too.

I was curious about what food a sea otter could find to eat in all this ice-covered water, so I opened up his stomach and looked in. The stomach was nearly full. All the feed looked like shellfish. Some things I definitely identified as clams. Others I thought might be sea urchins. Most of it was chewed up and partly digested. I had no idea what it was, except perhaps some sort of meat, not vegetable matter like grass or kelp.

My hands got awful cold examining the innards, rather smelly, too. I had let the fire go down, and there wasn't enough hot water for me to scrub properly. I made up the fire, washed a little, and then sat down to rest and gloat over my wonderful sea-otter fur.

Suddenly I felt I had done enough for one day. I doubled up the hide, folded the skin side in, wrapped it all in canvas, and put it outside on the snow. I cleaned up; then I cooked the liver. By that time it was dark, and I had had a full day.

I woke up in the night, and felt rested, so I got up, lit the carbide lamp, and sat here writing all about my sea otter.

35

I HAD PLANNED TO WORK ON MY OTTER SKIN TODAY, BUT WHEN I looked out this morning I saw Old Nick was flaunting a plume. It was a very small plume, but ample warning that the cold Taku is going to blow. I know how much wood will be needed to keep warm in cold windy weather, so I put all my energy into gathering wood and left the skin alone.

I did remarkably well, and brought far more wood than I have ever gathered in any two days. I didn't bring it into the cabin because there is no need to; it will neither snow nor rain while the Taku blows, and that might be for a month. I dropped the wood outside the door where I can reach it easily for chopping and sawing. I worked pretty steadily until late afternoon. I'm so glad to have all that nice fuel. They're fine dry limbs, and will be just the thing to mix with some of the soggy stuff which I brought from the beach weeks ago and which hasn't dried out yet. Also, it will be good with the green wood from my topping logs.

Before I got back with my last load of wood, the wind was howling, and it seemed much colder. On the way home I considered how I might keep more cold out of the cabin and thereby save fuel. I thought of a storm door, and after I had eaten and rested I got busy and made one. Made a good one, too, and in the cold windy days it will save as much wood as I could gather in a whole day. I nailed a double canvas across the top of the door on the outside and all down one side. I tacked a heavy stick to the bottom and fixed a bent spike to catch the end and hold it

168

snug. My storm door is a dandy, and will keep out lots of cold. Tomorrow I will see what more can be done.

Goodness, I have lots of work to do before I am ready for my little darling. I must get the fur finished for her. I am determined my child shall have a priceless gift.

Now to eat again, then bed.

I worked most of today fixing the cabin, and I really did a wonderful job. Already I can feel the difference in the warmth, and it looks better, too. I made a decking of the big tent fly, and it wasn't as much trouble as I thought it would be. I started in the corner over the bunk, drove in a nail, hooked an eyelet on it, stretched the canvas tight, drove another nail for the next eyelet, and so on all across the cabin as far as the fly reached. Then I nailed a long thin cedar limb firmly to the canvas and tight against the log.

I tied fuse into the eyelets at the other end of the fly and threw them over the crossbeams. Then I pried up a few puncheons, and cinched the fuse to the sill to hold the canvas tight while I nailed on cedar poles. I stood on the table to do the nailing. My ceiling didn't sag much, and there was only a little canvas left over, so I just threw it back out of sight along the crossbeam. The logs for the cabin were cut sixteen by twenty feet, making the inside measurements nearly eighteen by fourteen feet. The canvas fly is twelve by sixteen, and made a nice decking, with barely room on one side for the smokestack. The end which isn't covered is next to the door and away from the stove. That fly is a pretty fine fit.

I nailed a sugan to the wall at the side of my bunk, and a blanket at the head. Then I calked up around the window, and now I'm snug and cozy. Let the Taku howl!

The wind is cold and wild, and even the jays have stayed home. The full force of the blast doesn't hit here, but backlashes and downgusts hit hard. It's an awful cold, biting wind. I nearly froze chopping out the water hole.

This must be the kind of winter old-timers tell about, when the Japan Current shifted to miles and miles offshore and all this coast got as cold as Labrador. But why does it have to come this winter? Why couldn't it have been last winter? or next winter?

Poor Don. My heart is filled with anguish for him. How he will suffer in this savage weather. Surely he has made himself a hovel or a yurt. If he only had a shovel, he could soon make a good yurt; still, the Eskimos made them without shovels. Don is handy. He can make so many things. He will have shelter. I know Don will have shelter. Oh, Lord, have mercy on Don; temper the wind to the shorn lamb.

I am thankful for the protection this deep snow gives the cabin. A small fire keeps me comfortable. This is a good warm cabin. While I was away on my wandering journey, nothing froze, not even water in the pail. Of course, it wasn't nearly so cold then as it is now, and it does take a little time for cold to penetrate into a snug log cabin where there has been fire for several days.

I've begun scraping off the fat from my otter skin, and it's about half done. I have learned a few things about scraping skins: they scrape better when they are stretched tight over the end of a block of wood, and the fat comes off easier when it is cold. Another thing, when a skin looks scraped, it still has lots of fat on it. I know I'll have to go over the whole hide at least twice.

And I've made another discovery—sea-water ice is not salty. I use sea water for cooking to get the needed salt, and have been bringing ice instead of water because it's so much easier just to pick up a chunk of ice than it is to push away the ice and dip up water. Besides, the ice is all over the beach, and I can get it at any tide; at low tide the water is quite far out.

My food wasn't tasting salty enough, and I thought I might be getting scurvy. Craving salt, the old-timers say, is the first sign of scurvy. I examined my gums and found them sound, not at all sore nor redder than they're supposed to be. I've been eating well—raw carrots and onions, potatoes cooked in the jackets—I eat the jackets, too—several cans of tomatoes, and raw dried fruit, so there was no reason for me to be getting scurvy.

Today I got my cook water at high tide. It happened to be

handier to dip up water instead of picking up a chunk of ice. That's how I learned that sea-water ice is not very salty.

At last I have finished scraping the otter skin. It is all very nicely done, and not one single hole did I cut in it. I was afraid it would be in tatters because the fat was so hard to get off. I am going to scrub it well in lots of warm soapy water. Right now it's as greasy as a Finn cook. I could never wrap my darling in such a greasy thing. The tail isn't scraped yet; it's still lying out in the snow. I'll get at it after I tend to other chores.

Goodness me, I have more chores than a farmer.

I'm going to bed early tonight, so I can get an early start with the skin and finish with it tomorrow.

Hurray! My otter skin is nailed to the door. It's the biggest thing—much bigger than I thought it was. It nearly covers the whole door. The animal was probably a little less than four feet long, and I threw away at least six inches of head skin; but now the skin has grown, or rather stretched, until it is almost six feet long and nearly as wide as the door.

It took a deal of carrying to get all the water I would need for scrubbings and rinsing. I was so glad I had brought the tub from the upper cabin. I don't know how else I could have washed that big otter skin. Well, I filled the tub, the dishpans, the pails, and every cook pot and the teakettle. I wanted to do the scrubbing in one day and get it over with, but I soon realized it would take half a cord of wood to get all that water warm, since it was only a few degrees above ice to start with, so I let it set in the house overnight to bring it up to room temperature.

I scrubbed and rinsed the skin, scrubbed it twice, and rinsed it four times. Then I spread a canvas on the floor, put the skin side down on it, and wiped the fur with a bath towel. I got all the water out I possibly could. I measured for the middle at both top and bottom and marked it with safety pins. I found the center of the door and nailed up the skin, fur side in: first a nail on one side, then a nail on the other side. I kept it straight and even and stretched it well. When I had it nailed up all around, I took chips, nice smooth ones, and scraped the skin side. I got all the water off, and some skin fibers. Then I rubbed it with a dry cloth. It looks very nice and white.

Am I glad I brought the can of nails from the boat! How did Indian squaws ever stretch their otter skins up to dry?

When I finished, I decided to do the tail and get that over with. It wasn't much of a job, after all. Of course, I had learned a lot about furs, and maybe that's why it didn't seem like a big job. I scraped and washed it, and now it's nailed to the bunk post.

Otter fat makes a hot fire. With all my skinning activities, the place was worse than a pig sty. When I was cleaning up the mess, I threw some of the fat into the stove. It roared. I looked in to see what was burning so well, and saw it was the scrapings from the tail. If such a little otter fat made the fire roar, I reasoned, a lot would get the stove red hot, so I went out and gathered up the last scrap of fat I had thrown on the snow. I also dragged in the carcass and trimmed all the fat from it. I'm so glad for that fat.

When I dragged the carcass away, I went way down the beach with it—far enough for an eagle to come eat it, yet near enough to be seen from my window. I want to watch what happens.

The wind still howls, swirls, and rages. It's awful cold, maybe ten below. All the peaks look like volcanoes with their great trailing plumes. Flying snow at that height and distance looks like smoke. I brought in some more wood today, but I didn't stay out long. It was too cold and windy.

And I saw a very interesting thing—that, for want of a better name, I'll call a rainbow cloud. The sun was up, not high, not yet over the hill. A snow cloud, thin and more like mist, went sailing off the mountain and out across the Arm. It caught the rays of the low sun and took on rainbow hues. The colors changed and twinkled as the snow tumbled through the air, disintegrated, then blew itself away.

While I was out in the cold, my breasts ached. They drew up and the nipples stuck out firm, and they ached. When I came in I examined them, and found they were swelling and have water in them, not milk, but clear water. Soon my child will be here, and I am not yet ready to receive her. So much to do and so little time.

36

I MADE A TABLE STOVE FROM THE THREE CARBIDE LAMPS AND A five-pound coffee can. I punched three holes near the bottom, at the right height to take the lamp flame. I made big ones so there'd be room for the entrance of air, then I punched small ones all around the top. I can set a cook pot on the can, light my lamps, place the flames in the holes, and boil water in short order. When my baby comes I'll need hot water, or maybe a cup of tea, and I might not be able to make fire in the stove.

This windy weather is hard on wood; the wind sucks the heat right out through the smokestack. I have an awful horror of running short of fuel. Today I chopped and sawed up all the limbs I had poked under my bunk. Now they are nicely stacked along my wood wall. I also split three blocks, and have them handy.

My wood reaches from the shelves in one end to the far corner, nearly the whole length of the cabin, and is stacked nearly as high as my head, even higher in some places. I have it nicely sorted: kindling, second wood, quick firewood, larger pieces to hold fire, then blocks and the soggy stuff.

I have decided to burn the floor. I'll cut the part I have already taken up, now, and save the rest for reserve. There are seven sills, all logs ten to twelve inches through, under the floor, which is nailed to them. If I can dig around them, saw them in two, pry them out, and cut them into blocks, they'll make a lot of fine wood. They are yellow cedar, and so is the puncheon. I cut a puncheon once, and I got two pieces of wood for kindling. It is

173

straight grain, and splits like a ribbon. It does seem a shame to burn the floor, destroy the work of Don and Sam so soon after they have done it. The cabin isn't two years old, and they worked hard to build it. But making firewood from the floor isn't really destroying the cabin. Don said we would get a board floor some day. To replace all the puncheon I take up, I bring in beach gravel and scatter it around.

The otter skin is a disappointment. It's as hard as a board, and I'm just sick about it. I might make it into a Robinson Crusoe umbrella, but it can never become an infant's robe in its present stiff state. I remember reading or hearing that the Eskimos chew skins to make them soft. It would take a lot of chewing to make this big skin soft. I just can't chew it, and I won't even try.

The fur is lovely, and it smells clean. I put my face in it, and it's the softest thing I have ever touched. I do wish the skin wasn't so stiff. There must be some way I can fix it. Baby must have one present.

If we were home she would have many gifts—a ring, a silver cup with her name on it, a necklace, a silver spoon, a baby book, dresses with lace and ribbons, fine soft knitted things. Even in this northland she would have gifts if anyone knew we were here. The old-timers love babies.

When Mrs. White's child was born, the prospectors came from miles around to see it. Like the Wise Men, they brought him their most precious things. Before little Jimmy White was a month old, he had all the sizable gold nuggets in the locality, sled dogs and pups, snowshoes, traps, and guns, mukluks and parkas, hand carved ivory and wooden toys, a tiny Yukon sled beautifully made and perfect in detail, and enough sourdough concoctions to ruin the digestive systems of all the gluttons in the land.

Friends and strangers came to see the little one. They stood around and looked at him and laughed and laughed. They said the oddest things.

"Is it a buck or a doe?" one man asked. Being informed it was a boy, he went on: "I'll be doggone. A buck fawn. Well, I'll just be doggone. The little son of a gun. Ha, ha, ha!" Then he fished around in his pockets, brought out a nugget weighing nearly six

ounces, poked it at the baby's mouth and said: "Here, you buck
fawn, you. Cut your teeth on that, you little son of a gun. Hey,
you like it, do you? you young bull moose, you."

They came again and again to see the child, watch him grow,
and commented extravagantly on his superior intelligence. But
they admired him from a distance; few of them were ever bold
enough to touch the infant. None ever asked to hold him. They
were too shy and awed. They especially liked to see him eat, and
strained their wits to make strange and odd foods for the baby.
Mrs. White told me a surprising lot of their culinary efforts pro-
duced good eats. A man cooking only for himself often becomes
a good cook; a woman has to have a man to cook for if she is
to do her best.

The wind blew harder than ever this morning, and it's a wonder the ice didn't break up. If that ice starts to break, it will go
with a bang. Down at the ocean I suppose it is breaking; still,
this is offshore wind, and there will be no big swells. So much
snow and rain fell just before the cold came, and fresh water
always floats on top of salt water—or at least it takes a while to
get thoroughly mixed up, and fresh water freezes faster and
harder than salt water—so this ice has had a chance to become
pretty thick and strong. It will hold against a hard wind. I think
it will take big swells to break it up. It might get a start from
grinding along the shore. I can see an open space at the point.
Out in front the shore ice is churned and piled about, and much
of it has disappeared. At high tide there is a wide space of open
between my shore and the solid sheet of ice. Wind keeps the
open space from freezing over again. As the wind and tide bang
the chunks of ice about, there is a grinding, crunching, and
groaning.

Don might walk home over the ice. I'm sure it's plenty strong
enough to hold the weight of a man. He could easily come home
over the ice if he could get onto it. It would be difficult to get
onto it here because the edges are so ragged. Down at the islands
the everlasting surge will make it even worse, and the currents—
oh, no, he mustn't try to come over the ice, for the currents
will cut it from beneath, leaving some ice paper-thin, and he

couldn't know which was which. The marine chart says the water in this Arm is four hundred fathoms deep. I do hope Don doesn't try to come home over the ice. Please, God, not that.

The water hole is getting deeper and deeper and the ice around it is getting thicker and thicker, yet the depth of the water remains the same. Every day, and sometimes twice a day, I chop out the ice and throw it on top. I always spill a little water, which quickly freezes, so the ice builds up around the hole, until now I have to reach far down to get water. I may have to go back to melting snow, but I won't do it until I am compelled to. I hate to melt snow.

I believe I have found a way to soften the otter skin. I doubled over a corner of it, and it didn't break as I thought it might, so I folded it some more. No breaks. I kept on folding and creasing it, and now it is no longer board-like; but it's still a very long way from being as soft as I want it to be.

I washed a few clothes today. I want clean things for the coming of my child. Surely she will be here soon. I am getting things ready to receive her, and I have done a lot of sewing. Tomorrow I will bathe and make myself presentable for a newborn child. I will have to keep right on wearing Sam's old work pants, or else go around in my shirttail, but this weather is a bit chilly for that costume. There isn't another garment in this place which will fit over my belly now. Lucky for me Sam left his old pants behind. I suppose I might have managed somehow without them, yet I am certainly thankful I didn't have to. Even though Sam didn't rescue me, I have had comfort from something that belongs to him. In the wilderness strange things attain value and bring comfort.

I still can't understand how Sam failed to see me in the dinghy. It seems impossible for him to have missed seeing me. And I don't understand how he failed to hear the powder blasts. They sounded to high heaven and echoed from the mountains. And the gun shots here should have been heard. Grand Fall Cove isn't very far away: I'm sure I have heard a rifle shot much farther away. How come he didn't see one of the bottle messages floating

or stranded on the beach? But then he wouldn't be interested in
a beer bottle that wasn't full of beer. I'll bet if I hadn't wanted
Sam to hear, if Lloyd and I had been trying to hide something
from him, he would have heard plenty quick.

"Somebody round here thinks he's the Pope of Rome," he
would have said, the way he always did when he'd found us
out.

Maybe he did see me and thought I was a ghost. Or more likely
he saw me and thought the dinghy was a floating snag with a
limb sticking up. I was fooled into believing a snag was Don in his
skiff, and Sam could just as well have believed the other way
round.

My time grows short. In a few more days, at most a week, my
child will come.

37

THE CHILD DOESN'T SEEM TO MOVE AS STRONGLY AS SHE DID. IT MAY be that since she dropped to the lower part of my abdomen she has more room to move around in and, there being less pressure, I don't feel the movements as much as I did before. She moves just as often and takes as much exercise, perhaps more. I am sure she is well and thriving. I feel fine. My side hasn't hurt since the weary journey; it's good to be rid of that pain.

I made a birth cloth today from one of Don's union suits. It is all wool and should serve nicely to wrap a newborn child in. It seems fitting and right for her first garment to be made from her father's clothes. I cut long spiral strips from the sleeves of underwear for belly binders. I'll wrap them round and round her, and tuck the ends in. I have only a few pins.

I plan to use string raveled from a flour sack to tie the cord. I boiled a piece to make sure it is clean. I'll use butter for baby oil, and it is all renovated now, with the salt out of it. I boiled about a quarter of a pound of butter in a pot of fresh water, strained it, set it outside to cool, lifted off the butter, and cooked it again. The result has a sweet taste, and is clear and oily. I believe it will serve the purpose better than anything else I have.

I've worked again on the fur, and I'm pleased with the result. I used a different system—pulled it back and forth around the bunk pole. I admire the fur more and more, and I want so much to get it soft enough to use for my baby. I believe I can make it soft.

178

There is not a sign of life around anywhere; even the mice have gone home. All wild creatures will find shelter from the biting wind and stay in their nests until warmer weather comes. The little deer will be down behind windfalls. The poor things will get so hungry.

I wonder where the ducks and geese have gone, and the loons that were always around here. Loons are very wise birds. The person who invented the saying "as crazy as a loon" simply did not know the first thing about them. Loons are wise, and even their children have more sense than some people.

I remember one summer day when Don and Lloyd and I were out in the skiff enjoying ourselves. We rowed into a little land-locked cove and came upon a mother loon with a young family. Lloyd wanted to catch one of the babies. Don managed the oars, and Lloyd and I stayed in the bow ready to grab a young loon as soon as we could get close enough.

The poor mother really carried on to distract our attention, but we kept right after the young ones. The babies can't dive, but there is nothing slow about the way they can swim, or change course. We got one little feller off by himself. He couldn't see his mother any more, though I am sure he understood the instructions she kept calling to him. After a while he got tired and flustered, or perhaps he only acted that way. He was near the beach and we were close behind. He went this way and that, flopping tiny wings, then headed straight for the land not a skiff length away.

We saw him hit the beach, and we got there only a few seconds later, but we couldn't see Master Loon. We looked everywhere. We knew he was there: he just had to be. He wasn't back in the water, and there was no place on the beach for him to hide, no rocks to crawl under, nothing but a scant scattering of old seaweed. Still, he couldn't be seen anywhere; nevertheless all three of us kept looking. We wouldn't give up. We knew he had to be there, and we were determined to find him.

Lloyd found him. Not a foot from the water's edge, lying on his back with his feet holding a piece of seaweed over him like an umbrella. He didn't seem frightened when Lloyd picked him up, but he held on tight to his seaweed. He was very small; Don said he was only about two weeks old. We all agreed he had a lot of knowing for so young a bird.

The weather has moderated. The wind shifted a few points and let up a little. The jays came back with their harsh calls, and I felt sorry enough to throw a few crumbs to the poor hungry things.

I keep most of my baby things in the empty milk case. I have lined the box well so no splinters can ever get into the clothing and prick my little one. I made four pockets along the sides of the lining to keep small things in. I sewed it with strong black patching thread. There is only a little of the fine white thread left, and I am saving it for one nice dress to be made from my good pettiskirt.

I dropped another needle. It is forever lost and gone, and I am most unhappy about it. Only two needles are left, and I dare not lose one of them. Anything as small as a needle dropped on this floor is hopelessly lost. Hereafter I will sit in the middle of my bed to sew, for I can't afford to take the chance of losing either my one big needle or my one little needle.

The milk case is pretty well filled with baby things. Don's shaving soap is in one of the pockets. Shaving soap should be good for baby. It seems right to bathe my child with her father's shaving soap, and especially so since I have nothing else except laundry soap, which wouldn't do at all. Don's face was so soft to touch after shaving, and it smelled nice, too.

I tore up a sheet blanket for diapers and made twelve good-sized ones, which I needed badly, as some of the few made from underwear were so small she would outgrow them in a month or two. Things are placed in the box in the order I expect to use them, with the birth cloth folded on top. The box is set beside my bed where I can reach it easily.

Only a few more days now until I will have my child in my arms. I can distinguish the different parts of her body with my hands. I identified a foot and really felt the heel and the little leg.

I remember reading about some Persian king—I think he was Persian—who was crowned before he was born. His mother was put on the throne, and the crown was placed on the correct part of her abdomen to be over the unborn king's head. I certainly would have no trouble placing a crown over my child's head.

I have been working and working at the otter skin, and I am making progress. It isn't hard work, but it does take time and means a lot of doing, yet I like it so much I can hardly keep my hands off it. A dozen times a day I pick it up, rub a part of it between my hands, brush it, hold it to my face, hold it at arm's length to admire it, and thrill over the possession of such a lovely piece of fur.

The wind has died away. It is very much warmer, and a haze covers the sky. I went wood gathering and was delighted with my outing. I saw twenty-six deer, and I brought some boughs for the ones who will pay me a friendly call. Many little kingbirds were in the woods, chirping and flitting about, picking at the alder buds, and showing the tiny red spot on the tops of their heads. Two ravens came to eat the otter. I wonder how they knew it was there; they haven't been flying over, so they didn't just happen to see it. Maybe they smelled it. My thrush never comes back, and I liked it so much. Those mean old jays—I really shouldn't feed them a crumb.

Today is warmer yet, hardly freezing. The breeze is southeast, and there isn't much of it. The sky is overcast and looks thick. I wouldn't be surprised if it started snowing soon.

Cloudy weather makes such a difference in the daylight. During the bright windy days I never lighted a lamp morning nor evening. I do love the twilight—the gloaming. Sam once said to me, "Your deeds are evil because you love darkness better than light." I wondered where he was when he heard that, but I didn't ask him.

On the dark and gloomy days I have to keep a light going all day long if I am doing sewing or anything I need to see well. Even so, the days are getting longer fast; winter is over the hump. Soon spring will come. I am glad. Glad!

I thought of my dinghy tied up down the beach, and wondered how it had made out with the ice. I decided to go get it at high tide. I took along the pike pole and led the dinghy home, using the pole to keep it from pulling onto the beach. It leaks so bad that I felt afraid just looking at it. I wish I could fix it so it wouldn't ever leak again.

I baked bread, lots of it, far more than I need for myself. The deer are fond of bread, and I thought I'd have an extra amount on hand. Five of them came today to bum a handout, and I didn't disappoint them. I think all of them have been here several times before, but I can be sure of only one—Sammy with the mark on his throat. He is the tamest of the lot, and knows me. He even eats out of my hand.

I'm having ptarmigan for dinner tonight. Now, as I write, I'm sipping hot broth. The whole flock was just above the water hole this morning. At first I only heard them calling their soft "*qu, qu, quc*" greeting to me, reminding me I need never be hungry while they are around, and I had to look and look before I saw them on the snow. I went back for the twenty-two, and killed two with two shots. I didn't miss. I could have got a dozen.

38

IT SNOWED NEARLY ALL LAST NIGHT, LET UP FOR A WHILE EARLY this morning, but now it is snowing again. This snow settles my wood gathering for the time being. I am not going out and flounder around the woods in soft snow. Anyway, I still have a nice supply of fuel, and the weather is warmer. I can cook a little on my carbide stove, and I have lots and lots of carbide.

This is a good little cabin, so friendly and helpful to me. I didn't like it at first because it seemed so empty and bare. The upper cabin seemed much better, but I love this place now, and I always will. In after years, when I'm far away, I'll sing, "There's a Little Old Cabin down by the Sea," and think lovingly of this place. I shall remember the treasures here, the warmth and comfort, the shelter from wind and cold, my wild friends, and the otter fur. I have never been in any place which brought me to a nearer kinship with God.

There is a wind today, gentle but deceptive, which reminds me of the time Lloyd and I were blown out into the open ocean. We were prospecting that summer near the outside of Baranof Island. Our camp was a pretty spot about ten miles from the Pacific. One day the men took packsacks and went away over the hills. Before they left they gave Lloyd and me a dozen small jobs to do—enough, they believed, to keep us in camp until they got back. They knew we were honorable and that we would obey. They also knew they could depend on us not to get any foolish ideas until we ran out of work, but what they had not

183

yet learned was how fast we could work when we really wanted
to work.

Back in those days we puttered around and took all day to do
a little bit of nothing. Don knew I worked fast around the house,
and got my cleaning and cooking done in record time, but he
probably reasoned camps were so different from houses that I
didn't know how to start or what to do next. Anyway, he and
Sam were accustomed to doing all the chores, and they were
always there to do whatever needed to be done. No doubt they
would rather do a chore themselves and get it over with than
to sit and watch us fumble around.

As I said, this time they left us with several chores to do, and
we finished the last tap of work in less than half a day. The men
were to be gone two days—possibly three days. What were we
to do with all that spare time? What does anybody do with spare
time? Why, go visiting, of course. We decided to go visiting.
There was a fox farm on some small islands about seven miles
away. We had never seen a fox farm. Repeatedly, we had asked
to be taken there, and were just as repeatedly promised we would
be, but it seemed the time was never right. Well, the time was
right for us then, and we planned to go without further delay.

Lloyd had a nice little round-bottom skiff which Don had had
built for his birthday. Lloyd named it the *Yankee Kid*, and
painted the name on both sides of the bow. Don had given him
many instructions on handling a skiff. I, too, had learned to row,
and thought I was pretty good at it. The men bragged about us,
and said we were nearly as good at the oars as a halibut fisherman.
We had no misgivings whatsoever. The wind was a fair wind,
and would blow us in the direction we wanted to go. It would
save a lot of rowing.

Away we went. How happy we were! We weren't doing anything the men had even hinted we shouldn't do. Certainly we
had never been told not to visit the fox farm. We were off with
never a care, and we traveled along fast, right down the middle
of the straits, precisely as if we were navigating an ocean liner.

The farther we went, the stronger the wind became and the
bigger the waves grew. When we tried to turn in to the fox

islands, we found we couldn't turn. Water slopped into the skiff when we got a little sideways to the wind. We had to bail whenever we deviated from a course square with the wind. We tried several times to turn around, but we didn't know enough about skiffs and waves to make a turn. We didn't even know how to hold the skiff to quarter with the wind. We could only be safe holding straight on. Straight with the wind was straight into open ocean, so straight into open ocean we went. Up, up we went onto one big swell, then down, down on the other side. And we did that time after time.

Ocean swells look very big when seen from a little skiff. I was at the oars, and all my energy and attention were required to keep the craft square with the wind. Lloyd did the bailing, which kept him pretty busy, but he did have a little breath left to speak.

"Mother," he said, "I don't like it." Soon he said again, "Mother, I tell you, I don't like it."

I didn't like it, either. I especially didn't like it since I knew Japan would be the first land we would come to if we kept on in the direction we were going.

I guess the Lord was watching over me even back in those days, for a fishing boat, coming into the harbor, saw us a long way off, and the fisherman knew very well no skiff had any business being there, going in that direction. He came and picked us up and was astonished to learn what we had done. He brought us straight back to camp, where we found the men waiting for us, and in a terrific stew.

Again Don had been uneasy, and could not endure the thought of leaving us alone overnight, so they had turned back from their trip. Before they got into camp, they could see the skiff was gone from its accustomed place. They really did some concentrated worrying for the half-hour they waited before the fisherman arrived with Lloyd and me.

Don was terribly distressed, and it shocked me to see him so worried.

Sam sputtered and grunted as usual, then he lit in on Lloyd. He didn't say a word to me, but talked about me as if I were a helpless infant. He talked right past me, as he always did, and spoke as if Lloyd were a man with forty years' experience in Alaskan waters.

"Who do you think you are? The Pope of Rome? A man been round this country as long as you have, taking his mother out and trying to drown her!"

Eventually Lloyd and I learned a lot, mostly, it seemed, what not to do, and right now I am making use of many things I learned out prospecting with the men. Poor Don, I know I distressed him a great deal before I learned enough to be trusted out of his sight. I'm sorry for all the worry I caused him. Yet in the end he was proud of me, proud of both Lloyd and me.

Snow again today, and lots of it. The bay looks like a level field.

My five bums came for their handout, and I fed them sparingly. One of them ate from my hand, but not Sammy. For some reason Sammy was stand-offish today. These deer lick their chops when they see food, just like a dog. The bucks have white spots on their heads where they have shed their horns. Deer fight over food. I have never seen them fight, but I have seen some lay their ears back and stamp.

A doe and fawn were near the cabin this afternoon. I hurried to offer them bread, but they wouldn't come and eat. Deer have to learn about bread. If I had some green brush, cedar or hemlock boughs, they'd come. I wish I had some; I would so like to get the little fawn to eat from my hand. He's tiny for a fawn this old, but he jumps around plenty lively. His face is much darker than his mother's. The mother looks scrawny and poor. It's an awful hard winter on the wild creatures.

I pounded up my cast and put it on the floor with the gravel. It was quite hard, much harder than I thought. If I had fallen, the cast would have given my arm good protection. Now that my arm is well, I haven't worn the cast for weeks. I don't use my crutch any more, either, but I'm not disposing of it yet. I might need it; in fact, I might need two crutches, for my ankles are swelling. The good ankle doesn't hurt a bit, and the right ankle and leg hurt no more than before.

My ankles look fat and pudgy, and when I squeeze them the print of my fingers is left on the flesh, somewhat like fingerprints made in stiff dough. The depression stays for several minutes. I don't know when they started to swell. I haven't noticed my ankles for some time.

I think it is time my baby came. I am all ready to receive her. Everything is ready except the robe. Maybe she is stubborn and refuses to come until she can have costly furs. I'll keep rubbing and twisting and pulling at the otter skin until it becomes soft enough to please a most fastidious little lady.

I always think of the child as a girl. What if it's a boy? Oh, it couldn't be. We have one boy. Lloyd wanted a little sister; I wanted a daughter; Don wanted a daughter. I know it will be a girl.

I do believe the ravens are playing a game. I know they are. They chase each other and do a lot of talking about who is the best flyer. I watched them for a long time. One of them had a stick in his claws, and he flew around and around with his stick, the other raven chasing after him. Then he dropped the stick, and the other raven dived for it and caught it in midair. I never thought of a raven as having a sense of fun. Poe's raven didn't.

It is getting colder, and a little wind has come up, but not the hard Taku. I went for a walk—not very far, only a step along the beach to get some fresh air. I enjoyed being out. The trees are so pretty in their snowy dress, but soon they will be green boughs and bare branches again, for the breeze is shaking them and bringing the snow down.

I'll bet the snow is fifteen or twenty feet deep at the upper cabin. It must be seven or eight feet deep right here at the beach. Much that was winter rain down here was snow up on the hill. The men couldn't have worked in the mine this winter. They would have been driven out by the snow two months ago. I've heard of this much snow in this section of Alaska, but not in late years. The first Christmas we spent up here we had none at all. We called it a green Christmas.

This awful deep snow and hard cold is going to kill off much of our wild life. Poor creatures, what a pity they can't all be like bears and sleep the winter through. But then, what would I do without my friendly bums to come around and ask for bread and lick their chops at me?

39

SINCE THE BABY CAME DOWN TO LIVE IN THE LOWER PART OF MY abdomen, I have been constipated, and I don't like it. I think it's the cause of my swollen ankles. I had absolutely nothing here to correct it, so I looked around to see what the wilderness might provide, and hit on the idea of eating seaweed. Certainly it can be called roughage. I know it's not poisonous because deer eat it. I went along the beach and gathered a mess. I took the light-colored plants, only those attached to rocks. I picked it over well, washed it thoroughly, and ate quite a lot—ate it raw. It wasn't too awful, but I certainly didn't like the stuff. It was very effective, almost more effective than I desired it to be. I was busy all day with the honey bucket. Once, I left the door open to air out the place while I emptied the bucket. As soon as my back was turned, a jay popped into the cabin.

I got even with him, all right. I fixed him properly. Such nerve. He dared to come into my house and invade the sanctity of my home. He even dobbed on my table. I caught him in the window, and he pecked me. I was going to kill him for his crimes, but decided that to disgrace him instead would be far greater punishment, so I took the scissors and cut his topknot off, trimmed his crest right down to his head, then let him go.

He joined his friends and relatives with a lot of bragging and jeering, but they soon let him know something was wrong with him. They all looked at him and carried on a noisy confab. Then they flew at him, pecked him, and drove him away. I watched his shame, and I wasn't one bit sorry for him. I hope he's the same jay that pecked my little thrush.

The otter skin is getting to be as soft as I want it to be. I have invented another way to soften it. I made a small mallet and gently pound the folded fur over a block of wood, on which I first tacked a bit of padding. The pounding goes fast, and produces the desired softness. With all the rough treatment the fur has taken, you'd think it would have a mangy appearance, but it doesn't. It has hardly lost a hair, and seems almost indestructible.

The flock of ptarmigan were here again, just in back of the cabin. Since they were so handy, I decided to lay in a supply of fresh meat. I killed eight, and only missed three shots. It was troublesome to find all of them in the deep snow, and I got worn out hunting. Never again will I shoot so many at one time. I knew I had shot eight, so I had to keep on looking until I found eight. The rest of the day was spent in dressing the birds. I have seven out in the snowbank, and one is in the pot right now, bubbling away fragrantly. I have dipped out a cup of broth, and as soon as it cools a little I'll drink it.

Don always poured my coffee into the Tom and Jerry cup Ben gave me. I brought it down off the hill, and I drink broth and everything out of it. It's lovely china. Ben was good to give me such a nice cup.

Ben was the kindest man, and so understanding. He came to visit our camp several years ago. He brought the cup as a gift for me. He also brought a chicken, fresh fruit, green stuff, and several other things. As soon as he arrived, he said to me, "You can go pick wild flowers and I'll do the cooking."

I don't know to this day what he did to the big old hen, but it was the best chicken I ever ate. Everything he cooked was good. He didn't do much baking, but he had a way with meats and sauces. He made good doughnuts, too.

He whistled at the birds, threw crumbs to them, and soon had dozens flitting around the door. He made us a clock shelf from some board he had picked up; cut curlicues in it, polished it, and fixed it firmly to the wall in just the right place. Ben was handy at doing all sorts of things, and so willing to do them, and was very pleased with our appreciation. He was a bachelor, and lived alone except for short visits now and then to friends, and the times he took in some stray soul to give comfort and good food to for a while. He came from the old country more than fifty years ago. We all liked Ben. I consider him the best visitor we ever had in the hills.

The fur is finished, and it's exactly as I wished it to be. I am very proud of it. So soft and warm—such a lovely thing. I shall wrap my baby in it when she goes for her outings, and we will walk pridefully along the beach. Not only will the fur keep her warm, but it will also serve as a fair warning to things who dare to bark at us.

The weather is bad again, and I had to dig my window out of the snow, which makes the third time. This cabin has only one window, two sashes side by side, and they are on the lower side and quite high. I have to stand up to look out. Digging the snow from my window helps to increase my light, and does give me a chance to look at the mountains across the Arm, and to see what weather the sky promises or threatens, but I can't see much else from it. It's like looking out a tunnel.

I do hope it stops snowing. Clearing a little snow from in front of my door and digging out the window was more of a task than I liked. As I come into my cabin, it seems like going downstairs into a basement. Snow seals every crack, so I only burn a little wood when there is no wind, and open the door for air.

I have bathed and washed my head. My hair has grown about three inches and is as curly as curly can be. I like short hair because it's so easy to wash and dry. I think I may keep it short and never again be bothered with hairpins. I think Don will like it short after he gets used to the idea and sees how little trouble it is. Don did like my hair. He said I had the nicest hair of anyone he had ever known.

At last the snow has stopped and the sky is clearing. I pray for a change in weather—pray that no more snow will fall for several days.

I took advantage of the lull and brought in cook water and fresh water—lots of it. All the receptacles are full. I had to clear the snow from my door and window again. I do hope this will be the last time I have to do it.

I resolved that today was the last time I will go to the water hole. I have to stretch too far down to dip up water, and I might slide in on my head. Then I *would* be in a mess.

My body is heavy, and my movements are slow and not too definite. I am becoming clumsy and awkward. I don't like it. Maybe I should sit down and just twiddle my thumbs until Baby comes. I do hope she comes before I use up all this water and burn all my wood. Darling child, do come soon. Come, little one, come to my arms.

I did rest yesterday after bringing in the water, but today I got busy again. I made fruitcake and put the last of my dried apples in it. I still have prunes and dried peaches and nearly half a box of raisins.

I believe my hands are swelling, not much, but just a little. I thought it proper to wear my wedding ring at the birth of my child, so I took it from the chain and put it on my finger. It fits too snugly; it always has been loose. I never wore it without the engagement ring, but now I must do so. How could I have been so foolish as to leave my beautiful diamond tied to a little old spruce tree! But then, it was my Christmas tree, and the ring did glisten and sparkle there at the top. It looked like a far-away star. I know in my heart that I will have my ring again.

Sunshine! And I aired out the cabin, spread a canvas over the snow, and put things on it to sun. Either some things around this place are smelly, or else I'm developing a sense of smell the equal of Sniffy Bill's.

Sniffy Bill is a man Don tells about. He was a miner and a logger, a wandering workman who could do many jobs. He had no home other than the bunkhouses he found in camps. Sniffy Bill was always the first man to get up in the morning, and instead of taking the best pair of socks, like any sensible miner or logger is expected to do, he sorted out the lot and threw each

sock to the owner in his bunk. By sniffing them he would un-
scramble the dozen or so pairs hanging around the stove. He'd
pick up a sock, bring it to his nose, sniff, sniff, then toss it to the
owner, saying, "Tom's sock." Sniff, sniff, the next sock, throw
it to another bunk, saying, "Here, Mike, your feet stink like a
bear's den," and so on through the whole bunch of socks. He was
never known to make a mistake.

Sometimes I seem to get a whiff of bilge from things off the
boat, and the deerskin rug still has a deer smell. It seems to me
that rug should have had all its smells rubbed off by the fast spin
down the hill. A deerskin makes a warm rug for bare feet, otherwise they aren't much good, for the hair breaks off all the time.
When I shook the rug today, hair flew all over.

I made a brush broom from cedar twigs, tied it in a tight
bundle, and used a sizable stick for a handle. It isn't a very satisfactory broom. Cedar twigs are too soft and pliable to make a
good broom, yet this one serves the purpose, and it's easier than
getting on hands and knees and brushing the floor with a cloth.
It will do for now, until I can find other brush to make a better
broom.

I cleaned out the stove and scattered the ashes over the beach-
gravel part of my floor. I rubbed a heavy stick back and forth
across it to work the ashes down into the gravel and smooth the
surface. Damp ashes have a clean, newly washed smell. I like them
on my gravel floor. I always put the slack carbide on the floor,
too.

I brought a few branches and put a bouquet of cedar and hemlock boughs on my windowsill and placed the finest of Don's ore
specimens on either side of it. The window has a nice look, as
though a man and a woman lived here.

The new snow sparkles in the sunlight and sends out myriads
of iridescent rays. The world has a clean look and a fresh sweet
smell. I didn't do much tramping around, just looked about, got
myself a sniff of the fresh wintery air, and poured forth my
thanksgiving for a day of no falling snow.

Again the woods are like fairyland. I do love to look at snowy
trees. There is no wind tonight, no sound save the everlasting

crunching and grinding and tinkling of the sea ice as the tides come and go.

There was a little show of blood, and when I saw it I remembered my mother saying it was a sure sign that the child would be born soon—certainly within forty-eight hours. I didn't remember about the show of blood until I saw it. I wish I could remember more things about the birth of my son. I only seem to remember all the people running around and making a fuss over me—a doctor, a nurse, my mother and my grandmother, one of my sisters, and the colored cook. Poor Don was worried to death with all the fuss and flutter. His lips were so tight they looked no wider than pencil lines. My father went fishing—sensible man. They told me I had a rather hard time with Lloyd, but the doctor fed me so much dope I didn't know much about it.

I have never seen a child born. I always felt inadequate to help and was too modest to want to be a spectator. I have never seen anything born—not even a cat. I do believe birth, as one of the processes of nature, cannot be a very fearful thing, yet I have been very afraid at times. I have prayed God to remove my fear. I am no longer afraid, yet I do wish someone were with me to help me take care of the child. I pray my mind will be clear, that I may keep my wits, and that my travail will not exhaust my strength or make me neglect my baby.

40

THIS IS A LOVELY EVENING. THE SHINY NEW MOON HAS SLIPPED behind the shadowy mountains. A calm and peaceful night: a good omen, a promise that all will be well.

Everything is in readiness. The best of my wood is at hand, with fine shavings nearby should the fire go out. My carbide lamps are filled and the flints are in order; they can serve for both light and heat.

I have food prepared, and I am fixing more. I am cooking ptarmigan. Good hot ptarmigan broth will strengthen me if the hours of my travail should be long. Strong tea is made, sweetened well, and put where I can easily reach it and heat it over the carbide lamps.

All that I can think of is done. I pray without ceasing. I call upon the Lord to watch over me, and to guide my hands. I feel at ease and at peace. The child sleeps.

I have made cookies, lots of them—good rich sugar cookies.

I took my bed apart, fluffed up the moss, beat and turned the mattresses, shook the blankets and the eiderdowns, and made it smooth and without a wrinkle. It is a fit couch for the little princess I am momentarily expecting.

I am eating lightly because I don't want myself to be stuffed. I sliced and toasted half my bread. Toast will keep better, and I like toast.

My own clothes are arranged near at hand, top clothes only. I shall still wear woolen underwear—it'll save so much wood, but

194

from now on it will be Don's union suit and not Sam's shirts and drawers. The first thing I'll do will be to burn these old pants of Sam's. They were dirty and mucky when I first put them on, and now they are positively filthy. When I do cooking or sewing, I have to cover myself with a hundred-pound sugar sack to keep from contaminating my work.

The hurt in my side has come back. I don't like it. I am waiting and hoping for labor pains. I don't want that torment in my side. I must put my rocks on the stove and heat them.

Another day, and still I wait for my child.

I went to bed last night with hot rocks held to my aching side. After a time the pain eased and I slept well, awakened only once, and saw the northern lights flashing in my window. I got up and stood for a few minutes at the open door, watching the heavenly beauty. Today is colder, but not windy, and there is a bright sun. The pain came again before dawn. It comes and goes. Nothing helps.

I have taken a halfway bath, and I am reasonably clean. I have eaten only a little solid food, but I drank broth and lots of tea. I had a bowel movement and carried the honey bucket to the beach and emptied it. Eight deer were there, smelling around the ice chunks for nibbles of seaweed. When they saw me they followed me to the cabin, begging for food. I fed them little bits of bread, and promised I would go in the woods and cut brush for them just as soon as I am able to do so. The poor creatures, I wish I could give them much more to eat. As it is, I may be giving them more than I should. It might turn out that I may need the food myself.

That side pain is bad. It does hurt badly. When it comes, there is no way to ease it. I have had no labor pains yet. I do wish labor would come quickly. Oh, I did hope my suffering might not be long.

I am restless. I must make myself be quiet, think of something and write about it.

This snow is just right for skiing. It would be such fun to be out on skis again with Don and Lloyd. The first winter we stayed

in Alaska, Don taught Lloyd and me to ski. He had some help
from an old man long out of Norway, and also from a little
black dog.

The dog was a female, and Lloyd named her Nellie, after the
schoolgirl he liked best. Don said she was half wolfhound and
half Chesapeake. She was long-ranged and high-geared. Lloyd got
her in the summertime, when she was a tiny pup. He made a little
harness for her and taught her to pull a stick of wood. She was a
friendly pup, and very smart. By the time snow came, she had
grown tall and learned to pull. Don helped Lloyd make a real
harness, and the two of them constructed a little sled, which
delighted the dog; she loved to pull.

About that time we started to learn to ski. Don took us to a
lake, and there on the snow-covered ice we got our first lesson
and made our first tries. The dog went along. She went everywhere Lloyd went; she even went to school with him, and lay
on the doormat between playtimes. It wasn't long before Lloyd
had Nellie pulling him on skis. Skiing was fun for everybody,
but I do think the dog had the most fun of all. She would positively laugh. Sounds silly to say a dog laughs, but I know this
dog laughed and wiggled all over when she was given the chance
to pull Lloyd on his skis.

After a while we got promoted to a road—a nice road well covered with the right kind of snow for skiing. There were gentle
ups and downs in the road, and a few long bends. It was a perfect
place for the second course of skiing lessons. The old man from
Norway said so, and Don agreed.

We made a few tries, did all right, and it was decided to go
on a short trip. We planned to ski to the cabin of a bachelor
friend and pay him a visit to show him how well we were doing.
Lloyd and the dog were in the lead, I came next, then Don, and
the man from Norway brought up the rear, shouting advice. The
first bit of the way was upgrade, just a wee bit upgrade, followed
by some level going, then a short downhill.

The happy dog pulled with all her might on the upgrade and
on the level bit, too. All went well. We were doing fine; the man
from Norway shouted so. The dog's idea of pulling was to pull

continuously. When the pulling ceased she felt something was wrong. Lloyd gained speed on the hill, the tug line went slack, and the dog stopped to see what was the matter. Lloyd couldn't stop, and neither could I. Both men *said* they could. Maybe so. Often people can do things they don't do. The fact remains the men did not stop. No one stopped until we were a scrambled pile. Nobody was hurt, but the dignity of the man long out of Norway was slightly damaged. I imagine he is still explaining how it happened. After that the dog, being a smart pup, always lit out when she came to a hill. She acted as if demons were pursuing her. We never had another mixup.

The pain in my side comes and goes more often; but it docs go, and then for a little while I have blessed relief. At times it is incredibly severe. I hold hot rocks to my side, change positions, do everything, but nothing seems to ease the pain. My child has taken her exercise, really violent exercise. I went to the bed and lay down. I relaxed all I could to make her movements easier for her. She turned clear around. I held my hands on her head and I know that she did turn a somersault, a complete flipflop. My side hurt much worse with her movements, and it was difficult for me to relax and give my little one a chance to play about.

When the pain is bad, the muscles constrict and make my abdomen feel hard and tight. Maybe I'm not doing right. I don't know what I can do. Oh, God, teach me what to do.

Let me order my thoughts, be calm, not bother my head about all I don't know. Write about something I do know. More about Nellie.

Lloyd's little black dog was smart about everything except deer. We just couldn't teach her about deer. We brought her out here when summer came, and the first day she started chasing them. Nobody can keep a dog that chases deer: no honorable person would want to keep a destructive dog. We all liked Nellie so much, and it was good for Lloyd to have a dog, so we tried every known way to teach her not to chase deer. She was unteachable.

Being smart, she learned how to catch deer. No dog could ever outrun a deer, and any dog who just followed along behind a deer all the time would soon learn it was no use. But deer never run straight; they run in circles. Nellie soon found that out, and she cut across the circle, met the deer coming, and grabbed it by the throat. We whipped her and tied her up, but a tied dog is no satisfaction to her boy master. As soon as she was untied, she was off after deer again. Lloyd begged for her life, believing he could teach her. Nobody could teach her, yet she did know she was doing wrong. She knew she would be whipped for chasing deer, because whenever she chased one, whether we knew it or not, she would come back crawling on her belly; but if she happened not to have chased one she would walk into camp with her head up: she gave herself away every time.

Her life was in Lloyd's hands, and a time limit was set. If he could not reform her, then he promised to be her executioner. One day he had her with him, on a leash, and they came upon a doe and fawn. Nellie jerked away from Lloyd and sank her fangs in the fawn's throat. Lloyd kicked her loose. She grabbed again. The fawn made a pitiful cry and threw its little head back as the dog mangled its throat.

Lloyd found a big rock at hand and killed his pet. For weeks we never talked about Nellie.

A day of suffering has passed and gone. A night of anguish and travail is before me. I'm awfully restless. I no longer want to write, but I will make a record.

I walk about. Keep my fire going. The cabin is hot. I opened the door for air, stood on my snowy steps and saw a two-day-old moon far over in the western sky. The tide is nearly low.

It is night now. A carbide lamp burns. Labor is upon me. I need to urinate and I cannot. I strain and strain, and I cannot.

The child moves violently. I must urinate.

My side has eased. I walk about.

All my abdomen is pain now—great waves of pain. I must urinate.

The water has broken. It broke when I was over the bucket. I didn't need to urinate; it was the birth water. That pain has eased.

More and more pain.

The cabin is hot. I stood in the open door. The Three Wise Men are overhead. Northern lights blaze across the sky.

I keep my fire and don't grudge the fuel. The cabin is hot. The second carbide lamp has burned down to a wee blue eye. I have lit the third lamp and refilled the other two.

The pain! Oh, God!

I am wet with sweat. I am nearly exhausted. Oh, Lord, how long?

Northern lights flash.

Help me, Lord. I am weak.

The fifth carbide lamp burns. The Three Wise Men are low in the sky.

Oh, Don. Oh, Don. Oh, Don!

Don, your child!

The child is born.

41

GLORY TO GOD IN THE HIGHEST.

Don, oh, Don, my beloved husband, this day a child is born unto you, in a lowly log cabin on the rugged coast of Alaska. A girl-child, perfect and beautiful, favored of God, blessed of the blessed, born under northern lights, born when all the heavens blazed in radiant glory, born with the coming of a new day. She shall be called Donnas, and she shall bring honor and rightness to your name, laughter to her brother, and be an everlasting joy to her mother.

I give thanks unto the Lord, who has heard my cry in the wilderness. Bless the Lord, O my soul, bless his holy name. Praise God, from whom all blessings flow.

My travail is over. My child is born. She is well and strong. I am well. Humbly and heartily I am thankful.

Baby cried before she was born. She put her little head out and cried; she really howled. She kicked and wiggled and yelled until she was worn out and exhausted. I held her head in my hand and helped her with my hands and my body, but she was so tight it took a long time to free all of her. After the shoulders came out, the rest was not so hard and I could help her more. I pulled the cord out as long as it would come, wrapped her in the birth cloth, and by that time she was asleep and all my strength was gone.

I was so tired I had not thought to learn the sex of my child. I did not even remember to cut the cord. I just lay back and went to sleep. When I woke up, I found her still fastened to me.

She awakened, made wee noises, and moved. I gathered her to me, found her little mouth, and urged her to nurse. She did, just a very little from both breasts. Then she was asleep again. I reached into the box for my string and the scissors, put the covers back, tied the cord quite well, and cut it off long. Then I looked at my baby and saw she was a girl-child. I was so glad.

I've made fire. I'm going back to bed. I'm tired—weak.

I rested in bed a long time, all the while trying to think of the things to be done, wishing for the strength to do all the needful things. Baby woke up again. I had let the fire almost burn out, so I hurried to make it up before giving her attention.

While the cabin was warming up, I lay beside Baby and urged her to nurse. She did, more this time, and she made wee small noises and wiggled a bit. When she finished her breakfast, I fixed her up. I greased her all over with butter, tied the cord again, quite short this time, and cut it close. I wrapped a binder around her, made it snug and tucked in the end. I wrapped her in the birth cloth again and put her under the eiderdown. She kept making little grunts and wiggling around. Then she went to sleep.

I'm dressed in my old clothes, put them on until I can have time to bathe and be fit for clean things. I was hungry, and I ate a good meal. I am still somewhat shaky, and I don't feel too good.

Oh, a bad pain is coming.

Those pains kept coming all afternoon, and lasted far into the night. I soon knew they were contractions to expel the afterbirth. I should have known that. I don't see how I could have failed to know it with the cord dangling out of me, but somehow I thought all my suffering was over, and I made no preparations for more— didn't even have a carbide lamp ready. The pain in my side was completely gone, and that was a mercy. The others weren't nearly so bad as the birth pains, yet they were bad enough, and I was so weak and tired. I resented the second labor that was upon me.

Baby was good. She woke once and cried. I snuggled her to me and tried to nurse her. I talked to her, and after a while she slept again. I didn't sleep until long after daylight. I was too exhausted —drained of all strength and energy—to sleep. I just lay there.

When the afterbirth came, I took it away and dropped it on the floor. I didn't even get up to wash my hands. I neglected my baby scandalously, and I suppose I would have neglected her more if she hadn't protested. When I came to my senses, I found her wet and dirty. She had had a bowel movement, and I hadn't even put a diaper on her. Even then she had to wait for attention until I made fire and warmed water. My movements are still slow and fumbly.

How glad I am for cooked food—good ptarmigan.

I'm going back to bed.

Today I feel pretty good, and almost rested. The birth mess is all cleaned up. I put the afterbirth in the stove and burned it, for I didn't want the ravens to eat a part of me.

I am bathed and I wear my own clothing. I have washed my baby well, dusted her with Don's after-shaving powder, and dressed her.

My little one is a beautiful baby. Her hair is nearly an inch long, and dark, like Don's hair. She is a small baby—not much more than six pounds, I guess, but she is well formed, plump and round, and her skin is only a little bit too big for her. Her fingers are long and she holds on tight. There is a tiny spot, not so big as a pinhead, on the inside of her left arm just below the elbow. I think it is a mole. She is a good child; all she wants to do is eat and sleep, mostly sleep. She nurses strong.

Donnas is such a pleasing child. I do wish Don could see her, and Lloyd, too. I will care for her most tenderly. She will have the best care any child ever had. She has a good color, not red like some babies, not blueish or yellowish, but pink all over— a nice healthy pink. She is going to be a tall woman, for she is quite long, and her arms and legs are long. I'm glad for that. I wouldn't want her to be dumpy.

My darling little girl-child, after such a long and troublesome waiting I now have you in my arms. I am alone no more. I have my baby.

42

I WENT OUTSIDE FOR A SHORT WALK ON THE BEACH TODAY. IT'S THE first time I've been out since the baby came. The tide was nearly low, and there were dozens of deer on the beach, maybe forty or fifty, maybe as many as a hundred. They were all over, from the point of the cove clear to the island, smelling about among the ice chunks for bits of seaweed. Poor things, they are starving. I wish I dared go cut brush for them. Soon I will, perhaps in a few days. I just can't let all the deer starve. I can cut a little brush, maybe enough to keep some of them alive.

I saw one lying down, and walked right up to it. It was a big old buck, all skin and bones; he paid no attention to me. I urged him to get up, told him the tide would catch him. He never moved.

Several of them followed me back to the cabin and begged for food. I fed them a little, and promised more. I promised to bake lots of bread and make a feast of rejoicing and thanksgiving. It will be the christening feast for the baptism of Donnas. I'll invite the deer to come share our joy and gladness and our food.

The weather is good, still cold and bright. Donnas and I are well. Thanks be to God that I had the time and strength, the will and the materials to put my house in order before my child came. Wood and water at hand, clean clothing and cooked food, all things for my needs were ready and waiting right where I could pick them up and use them. It's so nice, now, to do nothing but love my baby, my darling little one, my precious Donnas child.

I hold her in my arms all night and most of the day. I talk to her, sing to her, tend her needs, pet and love her.

I have great quantities of milk. It leaks out all over me, and I have to wear moss padding to protect my clothes.

I solved the diaper problem with moss, too. The water hole is deep and the way to it perilous; I am still weary and tired; diapers have taxed my puny strength. I prayed to be shown a wilderness way to keep my baby clean. My prayer was answered. I use the fine moss I saved from the old windfall. It is gentle to the child's little bottom, and so absorbent that scarcely ever does any moisture come through onto the diaper.

Donnas thrives and grows. She keeps moving all the time she's awake—stretching, turning, grasping with her dainty hands, kicking with her little feet. I've made tracings of her hands and feet. She didn't understand how important it is for me to have a true measure of her daintiness. She wouldn't hold still, but kept right on moving. It took several tries before I finished, but now I have the tracings. Don cannot see her while she is tiny, but from the tracings he can see how tiny she was. I know how glad he will be to see them; how he will look at them, smile, then hug me tight. I also clipped a lock of her hair—lovely dark hair softer than the otter fur. My baby smells good, a good baby smell.

I am busy sewing, making the christening dress from my petti-skirt, and it is going to be lovely. I have raveled the red top from a sock, and with that wool I'll embroider it—just a little—cross stitches. It simply has to have some trimmings.

Lloyd's christening dress was of fine batiste with many tucks, two rows of spiderweb insertion, and wide spiderweb lace on the bottom. It was so long it came to Don's knees when we carried him high. Lloyd was christened in Epiphany Church; Donnas will be christened by the side of the sea. All our friends and relatives came to see Lloyd baptized. Many friends will come to see Donnas baptized, but no relatives will be here, no godparents. Many deer will come, perhaps the ravens will fly over, the jays will be on hand, and a great eagle might look on from a far-off high perch.

I am busy cooking, too. I have baked two batches of sour-dough bread. It is good bread, well baked, soft, and it has a light brown crust. I always make good sourdough bread, and I have much better luck with it than I ever did with yeast.

I'll not forget the first sourdough bread I made. It was the third time I was out prospecting with the men, and the parka squirrels ate up all the yeast we had brought along. We had bis-cuits and bannocks until we were very tired of them. The men told me to make sourdough bread, but I was quite sure such stuff wouldn't be fit to eat. Don said it would, and urged me to try. He told me how to make it.

With many misgivings I made up a batch, and it came out the most wonderful bread I had ever made. It was so good, we ate it up fast and I was asked to bake some more. I was afraid to try because I hadn't paid very much attention to the way I had made the first lot; I was sure I could never make another batch like it, so for several days we continued to eat biscuits and bannocks. Because Don knew how I felt, and knew I didn't want to break my record, he told me sourdough bread always comes out fine no matter how careless the baker is. Well, I tried again, and again my bread was perfect.

The dress for Donnas is nearly finished, and it is nicer than I thought it would be. It really is nice. I made a pettislip, too. Now my child will be properly dressed for her christening. One more day of sewing and preparation and all will be ready. I also made two more batches of bread for the guests at our christening feast.

Tomorrow will be christening day. I have asked God to send us good weather for the ceremony and the feast. He has answered from the sky, and by the signs it looks as if tomorrow may be good.

I have been very busy with preparations. I like to be busy. The dress is finished and laid out where I can admire it as I do other things. I have opened cans of fruit and vegetables and the one can of olives. I dug under the puncheon and got the last of the carrots from our garden and all the marble-size potatoes, which I'll feed the deer. I got bigger spuds from off the boat for myself, scrubbed them thoroughly, and greased them ready to bake. I also peeled an onion. Only seven onions are left.

The dishpan is full of cut-up bread, just the size to throw to the deer. All the tiny potatoes and about half the carrots are in pails, ready for me to carry to the beach.

I cooked another ptarmigan; though I haven't eaten any of it yet, I did have my cup of hot broth. The feast is ready and waiting, and the guests know they are to come, because I've been giving them samples for a week. They hang around all the time, and they have told me they wouldn't think of missing the christening feast.

At high tide tomorrow we will have the ceremony. The sea shall be my little one's baptismal font. I will make the sign of the cross as I give her her name. Her dress is made from her mother's garments and her robe is of sea-otter fur. The deer from the hills and the forests will stand as her sponsors.

All day I have been prodding my memory, trying to gather from it the words of the christening service. I have been godmother three times and I have attended many christenings, so I think I can remember most of the service—enough for our needs, I feel sure. It will be a beautiful christening. The evening promises good weather.

43

Yesterday was lovely. A beautiful late winter day with a bright sun and a warm southerly breeze. It was a perfect christening day, and, I think, the last good day for some time; the sky is all overcast now. Our guests delayed the ceremony somewhat. They said they would rather not come at high tide since the moon is full and the tide extra high, so we put it off until midafternoon and half-tide. When the deer saw me go for a little walk and heard me call to them, they came, and all went well.

Donnas was dressed in all her finery and wrapped in the otter robe, only her little face showing deep down in the fur. She was so good, wiggling just a little, making small grunts, her little eyes open part of the time, peeping out now and then to see the vastness of the world where she has come to dwell. I carried her proudly to the water's edge, scattered food about, and waited for the deer to come.

"Dearly beloved," I told my baby and the assembled crowd, "we are gathered together here in the sight of God and in the face of this company to baptize this child, that she may be baptized with water and the Holy Spirit and be received into the spiritual fellowship of the kingdom of God and become a member of the same. Almighty and everlasting God, heavenly Father, Lord God of Hosts, we give thee thanks for all thy many blessings, the greatest and best of which is the placing of this child in our care. O God, grant that this child may be endowed with heavenly virtues and blessed through thy mercy. This I ask through Jesus

207

Christ our Lord, to Whom be all honor and glory, now and forever. Amen."

Then I knelt down at the edge of the sea and said:

"Donnas Martin, I baptize thee in the name of the Father, and of the Son, and of the Holy Ghost. Amen."

I dipped the tips of my fingers in the water and signed my child with the sign of the cross. Then I threw more bread morsels to our guests, whose attention had begun to wander. They ate my offerings and stood respectfully about waiting for more.

Donnas did not cry at the cold water, didn't even whimper. She is a well mannered little lady. I continued with the christening service.

"Defend, O Lord, this my child," I said, still kneeling, "with thy heavenly grace. Keep her in paths of righteousness for thy name's sake, and at last bring her into thy everlasting kingdom."

Then I said the Lord's Prayer, and Baby and I went back to the cabin.

Right quick, I looked to see if she had wet her diaper. She had not; and that was a sure sign, so the old folks say, that all the days of her life she will be upright and worthy, a person of honor and integrity, loved and respected by all who know her.

Since it was Baby's party, she got her feast first, and she went to sleep taking it. I let her sleep for a while, then wrapped her in the fur robe, took more food, and went out to our guests who were still hanging around, patiently waiting for more handouts. Earlier, I had spread a canvas, a gunny sack, and a blanket on the snow. Baby and I sat down and served the feast. The jays were there with all their relatives. I told my little one there would always be a rabble in the world, but the rabble, too, must be fed. I threw bread to the jays, and did not grudge it.

I tolled the deer nearer and nearer to me by letting the bites of food fall closer and closer. They came right to me, that is, some of them did. Some even ate from my hand. I held Donnas out, and two of them reached their noses close and smelled the furry robe. I told her not to be afraid. She wasn't, either. Her little eyes were open. She looked about and made little grunts and wiggles.

I held my baby close, wrapped well in her fur robe, loved her and talked to her. It's wondrous good to talk. It's been so long since I've talked to anyone. I'm learning to talk again, perhaps learning to talk too much. I told her all about us.

"I'm the queen," I told her, "and you are the little princess. The cabin is our palace. None are here to dare dispute our word."

I told her the deer are our helpers and our friends, our subjects and our comfort, and they will give us food and clothing according to our needs. I told her of the birds, the little ptarmigan, the geese, ducks, grouse, and the kindly owl; the prankish ravens and the lordly eagle. Told her of the fishes, the clams, and the mussels. Told her of the mink and the otter, and the great brown bear with his funny, furry cub. Told her of the forest and of the things it will give us; of roots, stems, leaves, and berries, and the fun of gathering them; of the majestic mountain uprising behind us with a vein of gold-bearing ore coming straight from its heart. Told her that all these things were ours to have and to rule over and care for.

And I told her how soon now we would go far away from here, go back East to all our relatives, to her fine big brother, who would make her days happy with his gentle, merry play; to her grandmother, who would bundle her in woolens against a possible draft; of her aunts and uncles and cousins, and even Jule, the colored cook, and how all of them would make much of my little Donnas, our golden nugget from out of the northland.

And I told her of her father; how a savage storm, a wicked wind, had come up out of the wild ocean and wrecked his skiff, left him far away on an island; that he could not be here now, but that soon he would come—when the ice is gone he will surely come, come to his babe in the nest. And I told her much, much more.

The deer stayed close by, some of them not too well mannered. Some were greedy, stamping their feet at one another, grunting, laying back their ears; all of them licking their chops. I kept throwing them food until there was no more. Then I sang, "Come, thou fount of every blessing, tune my heart to sing thy praise," and "Jesus, tender shepherd, hear me. Bless thy little lamb!"

The christening ceremony was ended, and we went back into the cabin. I ate my feast and gave Donnas her gift. It's the nicest specimen Don had, a beautiful piece of rock nearly as big as my fist, bright with shining gold on every face. It was part of the longish piece which fractured into three. Don gave one end to Sam, kept the middle part for himself, and gave the other end, the smallest piece, to Lloyd. It is white quartz blending into gray; ribbon quartz, Don calls our ore. Donnas can treasure it all the days of her life. With the gift, I promised to tell her the story of our mine; tell her over and over, again and again, how we came here, the things we have done here, all that has happened here; and of her noble father.

44

THE WEATHER HAS TURNED RAW AND DAMPISH, AND THE SUN IS NO
more than a far-away white spot in a gray hazy sky. I was outside only long enough to empty my slops and collect snow to melt
for a little wash water. I washed just a few baby things; other
clothing can wait until it rains.

Donnas was so good. She made no demands on my time, and
lay on the bunk folded in her furry robe, with just her head and
hands out; she kicked and grunted, spit and gurgled, and waved
her fists about. When I went near to see how she was doing, to
admire and love her, to coo and talk to her, she would turn her
little head to look at me, and make the beginning of baby smiles.
Soon her smiles will add to my already great happiness. She is
such a good baby, and hardly ever cries, only tells me of her
needs. My baby is thriving.

I have fixed her a bottle with a nipple made from my eagle
quill. She didn't take water very well from a spoon, and I wished
for a nipple so I could give her a bottle. While I was wishing, I
happened to see the eagle feather stuck up on the wall. The quill
was very like a long slender nipple. I cut it off, pulled out the
spongy fiber, fixed the hole, and tried it out myself. It was a
dandy nipple. I fitted it into a bottle stopper. Now Donnas
makes no objections to taking a drink of water.

The deer are a nuisance. They liked the christening feast so
much they request a repeat performance. They hang around
all the time. I woke up this morning hearing a noise at my door.

211

When I opened it to see what was there, I found a deer rubbing against the canvas storm door. I told him to go home, and threw a piece of snow at him. He turned round and hunted for bread, never thinking I would throw anything else at him. I couldn't feed him bread because I had none left, so I gave him a piece of fruitcake. I baked more bread for them this morning.

The weather is trying to be stormy. Big wet scattered snow-flakes are falling; it's half rain. The wind is swinging toward the southeast. Bad storms come from that direction.

I split some blocks today, and sawed a few puncheons for kindling. Having a baby took lots of wood, and keeping a baby warm and safe is going to take a lot more. I have to make the cabin quite warm before I can bathe her. I hate to see my fuel going, but then, this is the middle of March, and winter can't last forever. With spring Don will come, and he'll get us a world of fine firewood.

A most terrible thing almost happened. I'm still all excited. I must be calm, or my milk will sour and make baby sick.

Sammy got his nose stuck in a tin can. I ate some corn today and threw the can on the beach without first washing it. Poor hungry Sammy came along, smelled the good corn smell, stuck his nose in the can, and couldn't get it out. I saw him beating his nose up and down on the beach and went to see what was the matter. I saw my corn can was fast on his nose.

He kept pounding it on the beach, but instead of getting it off he just forced it on tighter. He ran round and round in small circles. I knew that he would never get the can off, and that he would die a terrible death, so I decided to shoot him and put him out of his misery.

I got my gun and was ready to shoot him a dozen times, but he wouldn't hold still, just kept jumping around, and I didn't have a chance to make a killing shot. I wouldn't pull the trigger unless I thought I could kill him. Don could have—he always shoots quick—so does Sam. Then Sammy started to jump. He jumped all over the place. Suddenly the can went flying twenty feet away. He must have hit it with his hoof.

Sammy lay down. I ran to the cabin and got the last of my fruitcake and fed it to him. He didn't get up, just ate the cake out of my hand. But he is up now. I saw him from the window, saw him go staggering toward the woods.

I'm going out and gather up all the tin cans, dig a hole in the snow, and bury them deep. I resolve never, never to throw a can on the beach again.

This afternoon I went out and cut brush for the deer. I left baby alone in the cabin, explaining that it was my duty as reigning queen to provide for my subjects. I told her famine was now on our land and I must go cut brush. I asked her to be a good girl and said I would bring her a surprise. Donnas just battered her eyes, yawned, and made no objections.

I worked fast, cut and hacked branches everywhere I could reach. I got quite a lot, too, enough to keep some of the hungry beggars from my door for a little while. I can't bear not to feed them, but I can't afford to have them eat me out of house and home. Even if they ate every bit of food I have, still many of them would starve to death. Poor things—I wish I had tons of hay to give them.

The flock of ptarmigan are still around, but I don't need fresh meat as I still have two birds in cold storage outside my door.

When I came home Donnas was asleep; she had never missed me. For her surprise I brought some blueberry brush and a piece of cedar to make a bouquet. The red blueberry stems with the green cedar are pretty now, but they will be lovely in a few days when the buds open and the twigs are covered with pearly white, bell-shaped blossoms.

Don often brought me wild flowers—flags, monkshood, columbine, alpine roses, lupine, and wild hyacinths. I love the fragrance of wild hyacinths. Sometimes he would bring me a single flower and put it in my hair. Oh, Don, how good is my memory of you!

I made Donnas a warm hood from a woolen sock and lined it with the pettiskirt scraps left over from her christening dress.

Then I put the hood on her, wrapped her in the fur robe and we went to the woods to cut brush for our poor hungry deer.

I put her on the snow while I cut brush as far as I could reach, and did this time after time and from place to place. We really cut lots of brush, Baby and I. The deer came to feed before we were finished.

When deer are hungry, they behave differently than when well fed. When a deer is feeling good, he will look up for his food, at least some of the time; but when he is weak with hunger he looks down all the time. There's lots of browse within reach if they would only stretch their necks to get it, but they act stupid, and don't seem to know anything about the food within their reach. Perhaps they are too weak to stretch up; maybe they get dizzy looking up.

We found another dead deer—a buck, and he was old. I looked in his mouth, and he had only one tooth left. That makes seven dead deer I have found.

We walked over to have a look at the boat. Ice is all around it, and it hasn't moved. The bight is a snug little anchorage, and I think the boat will not be damaged when the ice goes out. The entrance is too narrow for big sheets to go out in one piece, and the bight is not big enough for the ice to do a lot of churning; there's not much room for the wind to push the ice around, so I think the boat will be safe enough. I hope so. It's a good boat, and well built. It looked low enough to have a lot of water in it, which no doubt it has; but it can't be pumped now. Poor Don will be unhappy about the engine. No, Don will be so happy about Donnas and me that he'll not think of another thing in this whole wide world.

I made Donnas a bib, and to initiate it I fed her a taste of mush. She didn't like mush, and spit it out. From now on I shall give her a little solid food every day, just a taste. There is no shortage of mother's milk, but I think she should begin to have a variety of food. A little fruit juice will be good for her, and she should like the taste of it. I will open a can of fruit tomorrow and give her some of the juice. I'll give it to her from her bottle, through the eagle-quill nipple.

We went again to cut brush for our deer—went early in the

morning because the sky threatens bad weather soon. On our way back we had the nicest experience. A flock of little titmice were all over the brush and the lower tree branches, chirping and twitting. I stopped to watch them, and stood perfectly still, all the while talking to Baby and telling her of our nice friends. They came close all around, and lit on us. I could feel them on my head, and out of the corner of my eye I could see one on my shoulder; two were on my arm and four perched on the baby, hopping around on her fur robe. They were friendly and happy, twit-twitted all the time, and seemed to know we wouldn't harm them. They all have a fat look and are as round as balls; their feathers are mouse-gray, lax, soft, and fluffy. The beak is small and short and sharp, and seems to grow right out of feathers. Their eyes are black. They cocked their heads this way and that, looking at us.

I never thought a flock of birds would come to me. Perhaps they came to Donnas, and not to me. I think the little titmice are a good omen. I think our great hurts and troubles are now all over and done with. I think Don will come soon, and the whole of our future will be replete with gladness.

45

AN AWFUL STORM MUST BE COMING. THE BAROMETER IS DOWN TO twenty-seven point six. I never heard of it being so low. I am sure Don would say that the old Pacific Ocean was going to rear up on his hind legs and roar. This is the first time I have looked at the barometer since I brought it ashore. I had set it on a shelf behind other things and forgot all about having it. I just happened to come across it as I was looking for something else, and saw how low it is. Maybe I banged it when I brought it ashore and it isn't working correctly; still, the sky looks very stormy.

Half an hour before dark seven gray arctic geese came in and settled on the beach almost in front of the cabin. They are either sick or exhausted, or maybe they're tame geese. I went out to have a look at them, being careful not to frighten them away. I was ready to duck back into the cabin at the first sign of alarm. They didn't seem alarmed, and I went quite close to them. I then gave them food, and they paid no attention to me. Why should wild geese act so? Has something happened to me since my baby came?

The storm in all its violent fury is upon us. Strong puffs of wind came in the night, and soon after daybreak a full gale was blowing from the northwest, coming straight in all the way from the Aleutian Islands.

I have good reason now to be thankful for the point which
216

once caused me so much misery. Right now the point is the best friend I have, for it protects my home cove from the full force of the blast. The ice will go any minute, and the point will shear the drift away from my door. Good, kind, friendly point of solid rock which will stand against the fury of the storm, stand between me and great huge piles of tumbling, crunching, crushing ice. Good rock rib of old Mother Earth.

The ice is going. The swells are under it. It looks as if the whole bay is crawling, crawling like a snake. The sound of breaking ice is terrific. I can already see open water. I can see the ice heave up, twist and turn, pile on top of other ice. I like to watch a violent storm from a safe shelter.

The seven gray geese are huddled just outside my door, and they have eaten the food I gave them. Their feet and bills are orange, and they have a white line around the base of the bill. They are smaller than Canadian honkers.

This is the last piece of usable paper. But that doesn't matter, for I no longer have such need to write. I have no problems to ponder through, no pressing sorrow or suffering. I am not lonely any more; I have my baby for company, to give me comfort and joy.

Soon someone will come and find us here. With all my heart I hope it will be Don, but I know he can't come for a while yet, perhaps never.

Maybe the Indians will come to their fish camp at the head of the Arm. Every spring they go there to gather herring spawn. Herring are here now; I found a dead one on the beach this morning, and soon the bay will be alive with them. The Indians put brush in the water, and herring deposit their spawn all over it in clusters of small pearly eggs. I have seen Indian children eating herring eggs from a twig, relishing them just as if they were candy. I must sample them some day myself—might taste like caviar.

Sam might come any day now, or a prospector might stop by, or a wandering fisherman come to anchor for the night, or that nice bear hunter from Oklahoma might come back again this spring, hoping to get an even bigger trophy than he got on his last hunt.

Oh, it will be wonderful! That Great Day!

46

The Indians have come. Good, good Indians. Shy, fat, smelly, friendly, kindhearted Indians.

Early this morning Donnas and I were out on the beach, she getting the benefit of the warm spring sun, and I putting the finishing touches on the bottom of my overturned dinghy. I looked up from my work and saw two Indian canoes near the far side of the Arm.

I rushed to the cabin, grabbed my gun, and fired call shots. I shouted and waved. The canoes turned and started toward my shore.

Hurriedly I made up the fire and set coffee water to boil. I brought out my baby's best clothes and got her into them in a jiffy. I ran outside and waved, saw I had time, rushed back, and prettied myself up.

The cabin was already clean, and there were fresh blueberry blossoms on the windowsill and on the table. I shook out the otter skin to fluff the fur, wrapped Donnas in it, and went to the water's edge. There we awaited our guests.

Both canoes grounded at about the same time, and right in front of me. For a little while we just looked at each other. I was all trembly, and it was hard to behave with dignity. After what seemed a rather long time, I did manage to say, "Good morning."

"Hello." A breathing space, then another "Hello."

219

"I'm glad to see you." That came a little easier.

"You bet," was the reply, and following a pause, "By golly."

There was a consultation in Siwash.

"Not dead?"

"No. Not dead."

So the conversation went on until I had told my story. No one made a move to get out of the canoes, and it occurred to me they might be waiting politely for an invitation. I hastened to extend one, ending with, "And come see my baby." I held her out toward them.

They piled out, nineteen of them. They didn't seem to see the baby, or me either. All eyes were on the otter skin. There was much Siwash talk, then the spokesman fingered the fur. "Against law. You go jail."

They all laughed.

"Where you get otter?"

I pointed to the spot on the beach where I had killed the animal, then I acted out the part. That seemed to loosen my tongue, and I talked a streak. The Indians laughed and laughed. They came and fingered the fur, stroked it, looked at the underside.

Then an old squaw said, "Pret-ty good." Splendid words of praise.

I led the way to the cabin.

"Me Deckennaw," said the old spokesman, by way of introduction. "She Tukuee." He pointed to the oldest squaw, his wife.

Deckennaw and Tukuee came into the cabin with me, but the others, under his direction, came and went in relays. I made lots of coffee and brought out everything to eat I could lay my hands on. The Indians were hungry, yet they all ate slowly and with gentle manners. The children looked at me with round bright eyes; shy, nice children.

They had had a bad winter, Deckennaw told me. There was too much snow and ice for trapping, and spring found them without money or supplies. They were on their way to their fish camp to catch herring and gather the spawn. They had camped the night before at Grand Fall Cove.

I knew these poor people needed all the fish they could catch, and I hated to ask them to take time out to do anything for me, yet I thought I had been here long enough, so I asked to be taken to Big Sleeve.

"You bet," was the quick answer. But the west wind was blowing, and it would increase until sundown. It would be better to go in the morning, Deckennaw explained, to leave with the first light of dawn. A west wind was favorable for going to the fish camp, however, so he sent one canoe load on its way.

I was glad for a little more time in my cabin. I almost didn't want to leave at all, I was so mixed up.

Then old Tukuee came up, took hold of my foot, raised it gently and looked at it, saying a number of things I couldn't understand. She waddled off to the canoe. Soon she was back with a package, Deckennaw right behind her, and she began unwrapping the paper, white paper, lots of it. Oh, but I was paperhungry! With a broad snaggle-tooth smile and some Siwash words, she took out a pair of moccasins and held them out to me. I reached first for the paper, then for the moccasins.

"She say," Deckennaw translated, "she not see you Christmas. She say Merry Christmas."

Why couldn't I have hugged her? Why couldn't I have laid my head on her bosom and wept? Blessed Tukuee.

I picked up the Tom and Jerry mug that Ben had given me, and handed it to her. I gave her the dishpan and the cook pots, and filled them with all the little things off my shelves. I gave things away too quickly, almost throwing them at the Indians, but they kept their dignity, slowed me down. Gently they took the gifts, slowly they examined them.

I thought of my ring, and asked if someone could get it, and right away Deckennaw sent an Indian boy on his way to the upper cabin.

I gave the Indians more things. Gave Deckennaw the compass and the barometer. Gave the others food and clothing, the saws and the carbide lamps. Called them all, and filled their arms with what had once been my great treasures and would now be theirs. Told them to come take everything when I was gone. I gave with great joy and gladness, and only wished I could give them a piece of my heart; I loved them so.

Then my guests made ready to leave for the fish camp. The boy who had gone to fetch my ring would stay with Donnas and me until their return. They climbed into the other canoe and paddled out of my cove. In the Arm they raised a square sail, for it was a fair wind to the fishing camp. Soon they were beyond the island, out of sight.

When the boy came back from the upper cabin, he was wearing my diamond ring on his little finger. He had a shock of unkempt straight black hair hanging to his bright eyes and a big, big broad smile. I could have kissed him. Instead I handed him my gun, told him it was his.

To keep him from seeing the tears I could not hide, I turned to Donnas lying on the bunk. I showed her the ring, and she reached out for it. With a string I tied it to her wrist, and it is there yet. She is dangling it, trying to get it into her mouth, my beautiful diamond ring, my darling baby's first toy!

Now I have cleaned up the cabin, packed my luggage, and carried it down to the beach and stowed it in the dinghy. There will be no wait, not one minute lost.

By the time I have eaten, they will be back.

Goodbye, little cabin by the sea. Goodbye, goodbye. In my need you sheltered me. Goodbye, little cabin by the sea.

Don did come back . . .

He had caught the mailboat and put Lloyd's deer aboard, as planned, but on the return trip, the cranky Elto engine failed. Old Cal Darnell, loaded up with supplies and bound for a winter's trapping, came along in his gasboat and gave him a tow. The storm broke as they ran for harbor, and they were wrecked on the rocky shore of an island.

They made a beach camp and salvaged most of the supplies; built a skiff of driftwood and repaired the hull of the boat, and, taking advantage of favorable weather and tides, they moved the boat through the rocky labyrinth, gradually threading their way from bight to bight until they reached a protected anchorage.

There winter caught them. Old Cal burned Don's boots to keep him from trying to cross the treacherous ice to the mainland. In the spring, when the ice went out, the two men escaped with an improvised sail and a fair wind.

Don made his way back to Martha. The ordeals of that winter in the wilderness were forgotten in their rejoicing and thanksgiving.

The Author, Helen Bolyan

When we decided to reprint *O Rugged Land of Gold* we became curious to know more about the author. We were pleased to discover her son, Clyde Bolyan, in Anchorage, and it is through his contributions of information that we were able to piece together some of the history of Helen Bolyan's life.

Details of her early life are few. It is known, however, that she was born October 3, 1896 in Demotte, Indiana, the second of nine children. Her father was a carpenter as well as a farmer.

Presumably it was within this family that she developed some of the traits that served her so well in later life: courage, loyalty, steadfastness. Nevertheless, she left home at a young age, and after a short marriage and the birth of Clyde, she was out in the world, alone, with a child to support.

When the United States became involved in World War I, Helen took the unusual step of joining the military. She became a member of the Yeomanettes, the Navy's precursor to the WAVES. After the war Helen worked as a waitress and eventually attended the University of Maryland. She graduated in 1924 with a degree in home economics.

There were few ways for a single mother to support a child in the 1920s, but Helen was resourceful. She took another unusually bold step and accepted a teaching job in the Territory of Alaska, in Thane, a small town south of Juneau.

On her journey to Alaska she met her future husband, George Bolyan, in Seattle. They travelled to Fairbanks where George officially adopted Clyde, and Helen and George were married on April 9, 1928. The cover photo of Helen was taken in the same year, when she went to the National Education Association Convention in Cleveland, Ohio. Helen attended as the Alaska delegate to the conference. The photo shows her young, thoughtful and clear-eyed.

Soon after their marriage, Helen went to live with her husband at the Cobol Mine, located on a bay on the west coast of Chichagof Island, a large island in Southeast Alaska. The mine had originally been prospected and developed five years earlier by George Bolyan and his partner of many years, Frank Cox. Cox was a hardworking man of integrity, even if he was a little stubborn and a bit jealous of his partner's new wife. There was some tension between Helen and Frank, but also a real respect for each other and a willingness to work together.

Cox and Bolyan had prospected together in several locations before finding Cobol. Their method of working was to find promising ore, organize a mining company, sell stock and develop the mine. At one Chichagof site they actually put in six miles of railroad to haul ore. In 1923 they found ore on a beach and followed the creek to discover its origin. When they realized it was promising, they organized a company and named it Cobol, using the first syllable of both their names. It became their most successful venture.

Helen set her story during the earlier days of the Cobol operation, before it was developed and populated. Perhaps the excitement and energy of the early years stimulated her memory when she began to write. This is the time when many of the events in *O Rugged Land of Gold* occurred, such as the time she was injured, and the time she was stranded alone while her husband was marooned on another island. The birth of her child was based on an earlier incident in her life. Helen chose several experiences and wove them together into one complete story. This technique raises a few questions, but there is now no way to answer them accurately. It is important to remember that although some facts were changed by author or editor to create a smoothly flowing story, Helen wrote straight from her heart, just as she lived her life.

At its height Cobol had a post office, a weekly mail plane, and employed twenty people. It comprised several buildings, including a large house that Helen built herself. Clyde has many memories of these years, when he spent his summers at the mine and his winters attending school in Juneau. Helen also commuted between Juneau and Cobol.

Later, while Cobol was still profitable, Helen and George adopted two Yugoslavian children, a boy and a girl. Helen wrote a second book about these experiences, *Home on the Bear's Domain.*

Helen had always enjoyed traveling and decided in 1954 to visit London to attend the coronation of Elizabeth II, fulfilling one of her greatest dreams. She stayed in London, attended the ceremonies and visited all the famous sites. She then toured Europe with her husband; they went on to Africa where they spent several weeks in Ethiopia as the guests of a diplomat from that country.

They traveled on around the world to the Philippines. Then George went home to Cobol, the lure of mining stronger than the lure of travel. Helen continued on, visiting every place that interested her, including Japan and Australia. She returned home later that year.

Finally, in 1957, George and Helen left Cobol and retired to Corpus Christi, Texas, but they were not satisfied and returned to the Northwest in 1958. George died in Seattle in December of that year. Helen lived only a few months longer. She died of complications from pneumonia in July of 1959, at the Veterans Hospital in Seattle. They were buried together in the National Cemetery at Sitka, Alaska.

Mary Beth Michaels